DEAD IN THE WATER

Can we escape our past misdeeds? It seems not, as Eliza Hobbis' past catches up with her in a deadly way . . . When Eliza's body is fished out of Cotton Park gravel pits, the police believe it's suicide, but it quickly becomes apparent Eliza was murdered. If she had something to hide it was too well hidden for the police — there's no suspect or motive to assist them. As another body is found in the same gravel pits, the police are uncertain whether they are looking for one killer or two. DI Cobb faces his most baffling case . . .

VERONYCA BATES

DEAD IN THE WATER

Complete and Unabridged

ULVERSCROFT
Leicester

First published in Great Britain in 2010 by
Robert Hale Limited
London

First Large Print Edition
published 2011
by arrangement with
Robert Hale Limited
London

British Library CIP Data

Bates, Veronyca.
  Dead in the water.
  1. Murder- -Investigation- -Fiction.
  2. Detective and mystery stories.
  3. Large type books.
  I. Title
  823.9'2–dc22

  ISBN 978–1–4448–0704–2

'To Warwick, a great son
and inadvertent clue provider.'

Prologue

The water was very cold. So cold it robbed him of his voice and froze the muscles in his chest, squeezing the air out of his lungs. First he stopped weeping, then he stopped struggling. Finally he stopped breathing.

1

The water was very cold. So cold it froze her muscles. Panic took hold as she struggled to get air into her lungs and black water slopped into her mouth. She spluttered and thrashed clumsily around, the cold already making her limbs heavy and useless. The bank was only ten feet away but the bottom of the flooded gravel pit was thirty feet down.

'For God's sake,' she tried to call, but her voice was no more than a croak. Even so, the figure on the bank, hardly visible now in the gloaming, must have heard for it stirred, moved forward, then halted at the water's edge.

She tried again. 'For God's sake, isn't this enough?'

The reply, when it came, was bitter. Bitter words carried on the bitter wind. 'Oh, I don't think so. It wasn't enough before.'

★   ★   ★

Fred Westcote's wife, Joan, had long resigned herself to playing second fiddle to the one true love of his life — angling. She had hoped

2

that when he retired he might find a little more time to spend with her, but the day after he had finished work for good she realised her hopes were in vain. His weekends had always been given over to fishing, and perhaps she could understand that. A man needed some hobby after a hard week's work. What she hadn't expected was that not only would he still go fishing at the weekends, but every single, solitary weekday as well. More than once she wondered whether this gave her grounds for divorce — and had even tried threatening him with it to see if that brought him to his senses. It didn't. 'Honestly,' she'd once said to him, 'I think you care more about fishing than you do about me.' He hadn't disagreed and she'd never mentioned it again.

It made no difference what the weather was doing or whether it was light or dark, Fred could always summon up an enthusiasm for fishing that was sadly lacking whenever Joan suggested they do something together, like go to the cinema or visit some of the stately homes in the area, and now, as a cold sun struggled to rise above the horizon and the little village of Slipslade began to emerge from the long winter night, Fred was happily pressing chunks of thickly cut cheese between slices of white bread, filling a thermos with strong tea and sorting out his rods.

Joan heard him in the kitchen as she showered and dressed, but as she came down the stairs she was only just in time to see his backside disappearing out of the door.

'Fred, when will you be back?' she shouted.

His thin, sharp face turned briefly in her direction. 'No idea, love. So don't wait around for me if you've better things to do.' And with that he was gone.

A disappointed sigh escaped his wife's lips and she went to enjoy a lonely breakfast.

★　★　★

Cotton Country Park had once been a grand estate with a big house built in the Palladian style. Now all that was left of it were the footings and ice house. Early in the twentieth century the estate had briefly had a new life as gravel had been discovered under the western end of the parklands and three huge pits had scarred the landscape for several decades. Once the gravel had been exhausted the pits were abandoned, and as ground water began to seep in, slowly filling the pits, the area became a desolate scrub land where local lads used to hang out, drinking cider and fighting with each other. Wrecked cars would be tipped into the ever deepening water, along with the shopping trolleys the lads used to transport their cider in. Every now and then, in a hot summer and fuelled with cheap alcohol, some of the boys would go swimming, despite the warning notices, and every now and then one of them would drown.

The locals complained endlessly that something had to be done, and eventually the land was given to Gloucestershire County Council which had the pools cleared of their rusting wreckage, stocking them instead with coarse fish and landscaping the area, turning it into a country park. Now the edges of the pools were fringed with lush vegetation in summer, and the park had become a haven for wildlife. Swans, geese, ducks, moorhens and coots took up permanent residence on the ponds; reed warblers nested in the reed beds and water voles excavated homes in the soft banks. People came from miles around with their families in the spring and summer to picnic on the broad lawns surrounding the waters, or circumnavigated the pools by walking the many trails laid, and anglers fished all year round.

It was here that Fred Westcote came nearly every single day. He had a favourite peg on the furthest pool from the car park, where it was quietest, as the strollers didn't usually venture that far. As he approached that day, a heron, almost as grey as the dawn, rose from the shallows and flapped languidly away.

'Morning,' he nodded curtly to Alan Eames who was already installed at the next peg, hunched motionless over his rod; his hat pulled well down over his brow to keep the icy wind off his balding head.

Alan looked up and made the tiniest acknowledgement of the greeting by raising his hand. 'Cold one today,' he said.

Fred set up his stool, unpacked his rods and busied himself assembling the tackle. It was as he bent to drop his keep net into the weedy green shallows that he saw it. At first he thought the naked form bumping on the gravel bed was a manikin. After all, what else could it be — who would go swimming at this time of the year? He'd been here once in the summer when there had been a fatality and he'd never forget the scene as long as he lived, but in February the pit was only visited by fishermen and dog walkers well wrapped up against the weather. He was tempted to leave it where it was, but as it was hard up against the wooden jetty and likely to interfere with his catch he reluctantly decided something had to be done.

'Hey, Alan, come and give me a hand,' he

called to the silent and still figure nearby.

Eames looked up with a scowl. 'What's your problem?'

'Those pesky kids have been down here again, dumping rubbish. I bet they stole this an' all, but we gotta move it.'

Putting his rod down with an exaggerated sigh, as he hated being disturbed, Eames hauled himself to his feet and tramped over to the spot where Fred was staring into the pool.

'Got a gaff hook with you?' Fred asked.

'No I ain't. Be sensible, what would I want with a gaff 'ere? We'll have to lie down on the boards and use our hands. Any idea how cold that water is? Hope you've got plenty of hot tea in that flask of yours, 'cos I'm going to need it after this,' Eames grumbled as he took off his jacket and pushed the sleeves of his jumper up over his elbows.

Fred followed suit, and the pair of them got down on the jetty, and gritted their teeth as they plunged their forearms into the near frozen waters. It was easy enough to get hold of the dummy but there was something wrong about the colour and weight as they struggled to raise it and as it scraped against the wooden posts, the flesh scoured. Shock at realising what they had got hold of made them leave go again; both simultaneously reaching for their mobiles to call the police, and needlessly, an ambulance.

★ ★ ★

Only two Constables were sent to inspect the scene, as it seemed obvious from the fact the body was naked that this must be a suicide. Later that day a brief report fetched up on Detective Inspector Steven Cobb's desk, brought to him by his sergeant.

'So we've no idea who this is?' Cobb asked, having quickly scanned the report.

Sergeant Neil Bould shook his head. 'They've found her clothes but that's all. There's no handbag, no identification and no note. The clothes aren't going to help much either — trousers, sweater, shoes, socks, bra, underpants — are all chain store.'

'So, if she was a suicide she didn't want to be identified, and we've had no reports of a missing person?'

'None.'

Cobb sat back in his chair and blew his cheeks out. He really hated an unreported death. Even after twenty-five years in the Force he could never get used to the idea that a person could die and not be missed. He looked again at the report. White female, aged about 35-45, well nourished, newish clothes

— not a down and out then. Surely someone must be missing her? Work colleagues, friends, husband, lover, children? 'Get the press to run the story tonight. The usual stuff: description, artist's impression. With any luck, we'll get some results from that; and check with Social Services and the local psychiatric hospital. See if anyone with mental health problems has gone missing.'

Bould looked at his boss quizzically. With his blond hair, blue eyes and smooth, unblemished skin he looked like a rookie; a lad not long out of Hendon Training College, someone even a bit naive. Nothing could be further from the truth. He was not yet twenty-six, a fast-tracked graduate from Cambridge and no one's fool. 'You said 'if it was a suicide' sir. Surely it can't be anything else? No one in their right minds goes swimming in February, and she'd removed all her clothing so she couldn't have fallen in by accident.'

'Unless she was suffering from some illness that made her think she would come to no harm. You remember Charlie?'

The memory made Bould smile. 'Poor old Charlie — he probably did more to get drivers to slow down than all our speed cameras put together. I always rather liked Charlie.'

'So did I,' Cobb nodded his agreement. 'It was a tragedy, when you think how intelligent he was; I suppose it just proves the point: there's a fine line between genius and madness.' But it was madness that had got the upper hand with Charles Delany. Only twenty-three when schizophrenia was first diagnosed, his was a promising life ruined by a terrible illness. Having developed a belief that he was immortal, Charlie liked to put it to the test by performing handstands and cartwheels across the bypass. Cobb had lost count of the number of times Uniform had been called out by alarmed motorists. One occasion was legendary. It had been Boxing Day, snow was falling and Charlie was found standing in the outside lane showing off his newly learned juggling skills wearing nothing but a pair of boxer shorts. It was a miracle that he had never been hit by a car. He'd caused a few accidents, mind, but never been hurt himself.

After the Boxing Day incident, his parents took him away to a specialist clinic abroad, or so Cobb had heard. He hoped fervently that they had been able to help the poor boy.

He gave up pondering the past and turned his attention back to the current case, looking again at the scant details contained in the file. 'We need to see the pathologist's report.

Until then, we'll treat it as an unexplained death.'

★　★　★

'Looks like the newspaper reports did the business on the drowning at Cotton Country Park,' DS Bould said as he strolled into the inspector's office two days later.

'Meaning we've got a positive ID?' Cobb frowned at his computer, hit the save button and looked up.

'Woman who lives at . . . ' Bould consulted his notebook, '23 Meadow Rise, Slipslade . . . a Mrs Eleri Griffiths. Thinks it could be her next door neighbour whom she's not seen since Saturday morning.'

'Slipslade,' Cobb frowned, placing the village in his mind. 'Isn't that near where the body was found?'

'Not far. Meadow Rise is about a mile away from Cotton Country Park.'

'OK. Get yourself round there with a WPC. See if Eleri Griffiths has got any photographs of her neighbour. Let me know if you get results,' Cobb remarked to his departing back, and turned his attention back to the computer he felt almost permanently chained to these days. Time was when police work involved getting out there and solving

11

crime. He groaned inwardly and helped himself to coffee from the one luxury his office boasted, a coffeemaker that his next door neighbour had once given him in pity at his long hours.

★　★　★

Slipslade had once been a small Cotswold village but now it was a village of two halves. One half was still old mellow limestone mullion-windowed houses but, hidden away in a fold of the hills in the hope that out of sight would be out of mind, was a recently built estate of two hundred houses. The brickwork was yellow in the belief that this would be enough to make them blend in with the rest of the village, but sadly that hope had not been realised.

Meadow Rise was on this new estate, a long undulating street of modest detached houses with double garages and small, open-plan, front gardens.

Eleri Griffiths's front garden had no flower beds, but the lawn was neat and well kept. Much as she was. A small, plump woman with very obviously dyed black hair permed into rigid waves, she could have been any age between 50 and 70 with a rather smug air about her. She watched closely as Bould and

WPC Rose Cadoxton wiped their shoes on the doormat laid across the entrance to her neat house and then ushered them into a large through lounge that was dowdy, cluttered and, despite the picture windows front and back, somehow dark and depressing. It was a room without style or thought — full of old-fashioned unmatching furniture and a carpet the pattern of which was dull and lifeless from age and wear.

'Sit down, won't you,' Eleri said, with a smile. 'Now then, would you like some tea or coffee?'

'No thank you, Mrs Griffiths.' Bould declined the offer of drinks for both of them as he seated himself in the armchair by the big bay window at the front. He liked to have the light behind him when interviewing witnesses. Rose sat down on a hardbacked chair in the corner and took out her notebook.

Eleri settled herself primly on the edge of the settee and looked self-righteous. 'It's *Miss* Griffiths, Sergeant.'

'Very sorry, Miss Griffiths.' The apology was perfunctory. 'Perhaps you can tell us why you think the body found in the gravel pit on Monday is that of your neighbour?'

Eleri cleared her throat and began her tale, sitting bolt upright, hands folded one over the other in her lap. 'I recognised the drawing of her in the paper straight away. Usually I think those artists' impressions look completely unrealistic, but that one was Eliza Hobbis if ever I saw, and I haven't seen her since Saturday morning. Usually she's out in her garden all the time.'

'In February?'

'She's a very keen gardener and has a greenhouse too. She's always pottering around, doing something or other outside. We used to have long chats over the garden fence, the way you do.' She encompassed both Rose and Bould in her glance to see if they agreed with her, but they remained impassive and so she went on. 'It's not like Eliza. She hardly ever goes out apart from to do her shopping. I've been round to the house and rung the bell and knocked the windows several times but received no answer.'

'Could she have gone away somewhere on holiday or to visit friends?'

'Oh no. You see, she's a widow. She moved in only last December. She said this was where she was born and she wanted to come back here after living in Dorset for years. Although goodness knows what she came back here for — she didn't seem to know anyone. She never had visitors. I thought she was a bit stuck-up at first, but I think she was just one of those people who like to keep themselves to themselves, and we became such good friends in no time at all. We shared a love of gardening, you see; that's how we first got talking and then I used to invite her in for coffee and cake and she told me all about herself. I find I've a gift for that, Sergeant, I can always get on with everyone.' She ended her tale looking pleased with herself, as if she expected congratulations from the officers.

She didn't get it. If only we had a mirror to see ourselves as others see us, Bould thought, his feelings ambivalent. They met a lot of Eleri Griffiths in the course of their work — lonely people, usually retired, with a lot of time on their hands and nothing to do with it. Countless eyes watching silently behind twitching curtains, noting all the comings and goings in the neighbourhood because it was the only interest in their lives. These people could be very helpful to the police: or they could be nothing short of a nuisance. Standing up, he asked: 'I don't suppose you have a key to her house?'

Eleri looked piqued. 'Do you know, Sergeant, I did suggest she let me have a key. After all, I said, you never know you might lock yourself out by chance, and as I'm nearly always in, you could come round here

15

and save yourself the expense of a locksmith, but she said no; although she thanked me very kindly for being so thoughtful.' That last comment cheered her, and she looked around as if hoping the officers would murmur their appreciation. When none was forthcoming, she too stood up somewhat uncertainly.

'You say you hadn't seen her since Saturday morning. What was she doing then?' From the bay window with its mock-Georgian glazing bars he could see the tiny square of unkempt lawn to the left of number 23. If Eliza Hobbis really was a keen gardener no one would have ever guessed.

'She was getting into her car. I popped out to say good morning to her, and she said she was on her way into town to do some shopping.'

'Do you know what time she returned?'

'I'm afraid not. I was out myself from midday. I meet a friend — a gentleman friend — every Saturday for lunch.' Suddenly she was coy. 'He takes me to The Red Lion in Overingham. He never lets me pay, and it's not cheap there, you know.'

'Is that her car?' With a nod of his head Bould indicated a silver Renault parked on the driveway to his left.

'That's right. Of course, it's not new. She

said she couldn't afford to buy a brand new car.'

'Right. Thank you very much, Miss Griffiths. We'll go and take a look next door ourselves.'

'Wouldn't you like me to come with you?' It had proved impossible for Eleri to keep the dismay out of her voice, and Bould had to bite back a smile.

'That won't be necessary.'

'Oh.' She was almost comically crestfallen. 'What will you do if you don't get an answer?'

'We'll have to effect an entry, as it's technically called,' Bould replied, unnaturally grave. 'Now, if you'll excuse us. You've been very helpful Miss Griffiths. Goodbye.'

As they crossed to number 25 it didn't surprise him to see Eleri watching from her lounge window.

'What's the betting when we've finished she doesn't come out and engage us in some meaningless conversation 'just by chance' to see what we've discovered,' he remarked to Rose as they walked slowly round the front of the property. The only window at the front gave onto the lounge. From where they stood they could see the lounge contained only a three-piece suite in a regency stripe of burgundy and cream, a mahogany coffee table and a television. There were no books,

17

magazines, papers or anything to suggest the house was lived in.

Bould turned away and walked towards the side access. 'Let's see if we can get into the back.'

The side gate was unbolted and gave onto a narrow passage between a blank wall of the house and a larchlap fence. They had to go easy as they picked their way through a jumble of dustbins, a rusty barbeque set and a wheelbarrow without a wheel upended against the fence.

'Did she bring this stuff with her?' Bould wondered out loud, catching his foot on a rake missing half of its teeth, lying across the entrance. They rounded the corner and gazed in surprise at the garden.

'Do you think Miss Griffiths was having us on when she said Mrs Hobbis was a keen gardener?' Rose asked after a moment.

'I suppose it's possible to be a keen gardener but not a very good one. Of course, this isn't the right time of year to see a garden at its best.' After his unkind thoughts towards Eleri, Bould felt like being charitable. Still, there was no getting away from the fact that the back garden was simply a square of grass — lawn was too grand a word for it — with a very small greenhouse in the far right-hand corner and a few straggly shrubs ringing the boundary fence. 'Come on, never mind the garden; let's see if we can get into the house.'

The back door was locked and peering through the glass top half they could see it led straight into the kitchen. The room was as neat and impersonal as the lounge had been, except that a rack of dishes sat on the draining board with a tea towel thrown down beside them, as if Eliza had been interrupted whilst drying up.

The patio doors were locked as well. This didn't surprise Bould, as no doubt had a door been open Eleri Griffiths would have been in like a shot. There was nothing else for it. He effected an entry by smashing the glass in the kitchen door with the broken rake.

'It's your lucky day, Rose,' he said, finding that the key was in the lock and the door could be opened. 'You haven't got to scramble through broken glass after all.'

'Pity, sir. I was in the gymnastics team at school. I could have somersaulted through,' Rose replied tartly, and he didn't know if she was joking or not.

It was strange how empty houses had a silence all of their own. He always noticed it. They felt lonely, somehow.

They walked slowly through the downstairs rooms. 'What feeling do you get about this place, Rose?' Bould asked as they moved from the lounge into the dining room and saw a rosewood reproduction Georgian oval table with six upholstered chairs in satin stripe, and a glass-fronted rosewood cabinet.

'It reminds me of a show house but not a modern one. One from the eighties, say. The furniture isn't modern. It reminds me of my aunt's house. She's got stuff like this, but hers has a lived in feel. This doesn't.'

'Yes, that's what puzzles me. There are so few personal possessions. I wonder why she really came back to live in Slipslade if she didn't know anyone here? Let's look at what's upstairs. She's got to have some personal papers somewhere.'

And he was right. In the front bedroom, lit by flat slabs of weak sunlight, they found a metal filing box in the wardrobe. Whilst Bould lifted it onto the bed and started going through it, Rose wandered over to the bedside cabinet. Opening the drawer, she started rifling through and instantly came across a passport.

'Sir,' she called, and when Bould looked up she held it out to him.

He took it and turned to the back page. 'Well, well.'

The tone of his voice made Rose move to his side so that she could see what it was that had so astonished him.

He was looking at a photograph of the dead woman. There was no mistake about it, but according to the name printed alongside she wasn't called Eliza Hobbis but Susan Janice Davenport.

2

If there was one profession Steven Cobb was glad he had never thought of pursuing it was that of a pathologist. How anyone could spend their days cutting up dead bodies and remaining as cheerful as Jenny Sutherland did was beyond his ken. He could hear her whistling 'Happy Talk' as he entered her lab. A singularly inappropriate tune, if ever he'd heard.

'Hello, Steve, how's tricks?' she said, and straightened up from her dissection.

A small, grey-haired woman not far off retirement, she looked like everyone's favourite aunty, Cobb always thought, with her rosy cheeks and permanent smile and, in fact, she did appear to be some sort of informal agony aunt to the station's staff — and not just the female ones, from what he'd heard. 'Oh, you know, same as usual. How's life treating you?'

'Not bad, not bad at all. I really can't complain,' she replied, almost twinkling.

'I'm not surprised. You can't have long to go now, can you?'

'Two months, three weeks and two days.'

'Got any plans once your time is all your own?'

'First, I'm going backpacking round the world for a year then, when I come back, I'm going to learn belly dancing and join the local Am Dram.'

When he recovered from his surprise he said: 'Good for you,' and meant it. 'Have you had a chance to look at my body yet?'

Jenny laughed with glee. 'There's an offer I haven't had in a long time, but if you mean the lady found in the gravel pit, I've done the preliminary examination, and it appears to be a straightforward case of drowning. I'd say the time of death was somewhere around midnight, but it's hard to be certain as the water is so cold at this time of the year. It would have advanced rigor considerably, so I'll give you an accurate time once I've got the eyeball potassium levels back, but that won't be yet awhile. I'm also waiting on toxicology reports and I've sent samples of water from both the pond and her lungs for comparison, just to make sure she did actually drown there and not somewhere else.'

'You've got suspicions, then?'

She shrugged, 'Nothing factual but she obviously couldn't have come to be in the water by accident without her clothes on, and as you know suicides usually leave a note. Call it female intuition but I just feel a bit uneasy about things; and I guess you do too, or you wouldn't be here.'

He nodded in agreement. 'You're right — it doesn't add up. We might know more when my sergeant gets back. We think we've identified her.'

'That's good.' A warm smile of approval was bestowed on him. 'The anonymous bodies depress me. There's not much point in living if no one notices you've gone. I'll let you know when I've got toxicology and the water analysis back.'

'Cheers, Jenny. I'd be grateful if it was sooner rather than later.'

She grinned at him. 'I'll bet you would, but we're under-resourced these days, as I'm sure I don't need to tell you.'

The best was always saved for last. As he turned to go, Jenny said, almost casually, 'She was three months pregnant.'

To his irritation, Cobb found himself whistling 'Happy Talk' as he made his way back to his office. Jenny had that effect on people — she was irrepressibly cheerful. The thought of her belly dancing brought a smile to his face. Short and dumpy as she was, he could only imagine her swamped by the billowing costume and veil; it would be like watching a large plate of jelly gyrating, particularly as no doubt she would throw herself into it as enthusiastically as she tackled everything. Take her whole attitude to retirement — she was going at it full on and he admired her for it. The idea of backpacking around the world sounded marvellous. The freedom of waking up every morning and knowing the day was yours to do as you wanted, to go where ever the wind or whim took you.

The appeal of the fantasy he had conjured up engulfed him completely, but even as it did he acknowledged wryly it was probably simply because it was going to be somebody else's reality and never his. Jenny was long since divorced and childless and therefore free to take off to far-flung places without a second thought. He, on the other hand, was securely married to Sarah, whose elderly and increasingly frail mother lived with them, and as long as Dorothy was alive he knew Sarah would never be persuaded to take so much as a seven-day holiday, let alone a trip round the world, as it would mean leaving Dorothy to the care of others. Whilst he would not normally consider Sarah paranoid, as far as her mother went she was. You'd think care homes only employed specially trained assassins from the way she went on. He was as fond of his mother-in-law as any man could be, but they hadn't had a holiday in the last five years and what he wouldn't give for a week in the sun, but Sarah wouldn't hear of it.

Well, good luck to Jenny, he hoped she'd have the time of her life.

As he approached his office he saw Bould approaching from the other end of the corridor. 'That was well timed,' he said. 'What news have you got? As you look like a man who's lost a tenner and found a pound I take it things aren't going well.'

'They've certainly got more complicated, sir,' Bould answered gloomily, following his boss into the room. He waited until Cobb had sat down before taking a seat himself. 'Miss Eleri Griffiths was quite right; the dead woman is her neighbour. The problem is, she knew her as Eliza Hobbis, but her passport says she's Susan Davenport, aged forty-one.'

'Hmm,' Cobb pursed his lips and pondered this. Then he got to his feet. 'Coffee?' he said, going over to the machine on his filing cabinet. He didn't wait for an answer, but poured two cups out anyway. 'No milk, I'm afraid. You can have sugar if you want.'

'Thanks, sir; I'll take it straight, as it is.'

Cobb returned to his seat, took a sip of his coffee and then set the cup down on his desk where it remained untouched until the cleaners took it away in the evening. 'Did you learn anything else from this Miss Griffiths?'

'She says the dead woman claimed to have come from round here originally and had been living in Dorset for years. That's not true either.' He slid a sheet of headed paper across the desk. 'I found this in a file.'

It was a receipt for conveyancing from a firm of solicitors — Parry & Edwards based in Lampeter — and the address of the property they had sold for Mrs S Davenport was Brynteg, Lampeter, Ceredigion, Wales, for the sum of £250,000.

'This doesn't prove she was living there. It might not be the family home. It could be a property she or her husband inherited.'

'True,' Bould admitted reluctantly, 'but there was a metal box file in the bedroom with a lot of personal papers in it: not one made any reference to Dorset.'

The DI perked up at hearing this. 'Personal papers — anything of use to us?'

Bould shook his head. 'Nothing else, just utility bills, that sort of thing. Her car was still in the drive, so she didn't get to the gravel pits that way.'

'It's unlikely she would have walked there. It's got to be four miles, and Jenny thinks the time of death was around midnight.'

'But if it was suicide, she might not have been in a state of mind to care about that.'

'True,' Cobb conceded, 'but we're making an assumption here. Did the neighbour have anything to say about men friends visiting?'

After taking a tentative sip of the scalding coffee, Bould said: 'Apparently she had no visitors at all. Miss Griffiths said she seemed to know no one; but then Miss Griffiths also said the dead woman was a keen gardener, and that appears to be about as near the mark as saying I'm the new Pavarotti.'

Cobb grinned. Having heard his sergeant's attempts to sing in church at a colleague's wedding he knew just how bad a gardener the dead woman must have been. 'Nevertheless, Susan Davenport must have known someone quite well, for she was pregnant, according to Jenny. Three months gone. She's been living here since December, so it's most likely the father is someone she knew before she moved here. Maybe someone in Wales? You'd better get yourself over to Lampeter pronto. I want you to talk to these solicitors, see what you can find out. We're desperately in need of some background info.' Cobb shot a glance out of the small window to his left. He could see the bare branches of a spindly tree being helplessly tossed about by a cold, vicious wind. 'It's a nice day; you should have a pleasant drive. It won't take you more than a couple of hours to get there. We need to find out who this woman really is and why she changed her name. Was she hiding from someone? See if this solicitor knows anything useful.'

His sergeant rose, gathered up the letter and made for the door.

★   ★   ★

The road to Lampeter was long and winding, and cut through countryside that would be breathtakingly pretty come the spring but at this time of the year was dreary and bleak. Fields that were not quite green and not quite grey were edged by black strips of hedges. Endless hills serrated by tall conifer forests, either gave way to spectacular views or squeezed the road so tightly that only the sky directly above was visible.

Despite the freezing weather, Bould drove with the window down. Claustrophobia wasn't the right word for how he felt when shut off from the outdoors: cooped up was the better expression. When he was very young he had wanted to be an archaeologist, partly because it meant being outdoors most of the time, but there had been another reason as well.

That reason died a death one day when he was ten and his mother explained to him that archaeologists dug up the remains of people, not dinosaurs. The career switch hadn't been difficult. It had only taken as long as her explanation for him to decide that palaeontology would be his new career. Palaeontologists dug up dinosaurs. By the time he was twelve the original desire to become an archaeologist had reasserted itself. Not that he considered the professions to be dissimilar. They both involved dealing with incomplete stories, hunting for obscure clues to piece together a picture of what had gone on in the past. It wasn't until he was at university that it became more interesting — more *useful* — to bring his love of detective work into the here and now. It was academic to learn about how Stone Age people lived. Interesting, yes, but did it have any real relevance to modern people's lives?

At Cambridge he did start by studying Archaeology, before chucking it up for Psychology, something he stumbled into by serendipity. A fellow student he was going out with dragged him along to one of her lectures and, being in love, he had gone despite the fact that it sounded quite simply the most boring afternoon on offer, but it was his Eureka moment. Everything fell into place.

And suddenly all those obscure clues relating to where he was going with his life jigsawed together. It wasn't the past in people's lives that interested him, but the present. Criminal psychology was taking off and he was fascinated by the whole thing. It was easy from then on; fast-tracked into a police force he had quickly got into CID and now, at the age of twenty-five, he was a DS. It wouldn't be long before he would be an inspector either. Not that anyone would consider Bould to be overly ambitious. An early tragedy had changed his perspective of life and he knew what really mattered. Perhaps that was good. Whatever happened in life, he knew you had to look for some positive angle on it otherwise you became a victim, and then what use were you?

The hills fell away, the road opened out and the river Teifi lay ahead. He crossed by a long, narrow, ancient stone bridge and drove towards the town centre. It didn't look promising: rows of narrow terraced houses and a few shops with old-fashioned signage lined the way. At a 'T' junction he turned left, and suddenly the whole character of the place changed. A raft of expensive little shops crowded a narrow street winding away into the distance.

Built at a time when horses were the fastest

thing on the roads, the street was now choked with traffic going slower than the horses they had displaced, and although double yellow lines had been painted down each side, they seemed to be viewed as more of a challenge than a restriction.

Bould cursed his luck and sat waiting for the jam to clear, which it did when a young man came out of the newsagents, got into his illegally parked car and nonchalantly drove off. Seeing a sign to a car park, Bould was in no mood to waste any more time and turned down a slender opening between a pub and a New Age shop whose window was crammed with crystals in glittering display. His luck was in and he claimed the last remaining space.

Returning to the high street, but this time on foot, he turned left, past the pub and then, only three doors down, found Parry & Edwards. The solicitors had cannibalised what was once a pretty Georgian cottage and managed to thoroughly remove any vestige of character or charm.

In the front office a dark-haired, flinty-faced middle-aged woman sat morosely typing up an audio tape. Judging from the large, multibuttoned telephone by her side and the absence of any other person, she also doubled as the telephonist and receptionist as well, and she didn't seem pleased to be interrupted in her work, keeping Bould waiting a full minute before eventually setting her headphones down with a heavy sigh.

'Can I help you?' she asked in a voice that suggested she would rather not.

Bould produced his warrant card. 'Detective Sergeant Bould; I rang earlier and arranged to see Mr Parry.'

'Mr Parry didn't mention it to me,' she said, in a tone of voice that suggested he might be lying.

Bould gave her his best smile. 'Perhaps you'd just tell him I'm here.'

She shot him a look of pure malevolence, but nevertheless picked up the phone. 'Mr Parry, there's a policeman here to see you . . . yes, I'll tell him.' She replaced the receiver and turned to Bould. 'He'll be with you shortly; you can sit down if you want.' She vaguely indicated a very old bentwood chair behind him that looked extremely unsound.

Deciding it was safer not to put the chair to the test, he remained standing, taking the opportunity to look around. There were files strewn everywhere; not only was the secretary's desk littered with them, but two other desks, the tops of three filing cabinets and several chairs were covered, and when every available surface had been used, the rest had been dumped in uncertain piles, most of which had toppled over on the floor.

An inner door opened and a portly, red-faced man with scrubby grey hair appeared. 'Good afternoon, Sergeant Bould. Pleased to meet you; I trust you had a pleasant journey. I'm Ioan Parry.' From the small frame came a booming voice, and Ioan strode across the room, deftly negotiating the scattered files, to greet Bould with a strong handshake. 'Come upstairs to my room.'

He led the way up a narrow, steep flight of stairs to his office, and how different it was to his secretary's. A thick carpet, good solid old oak furniture and a temperature at least ten degrees warmer gave the room a mellow, clubby feel. Or it would have done if it hadn't been for the skull on an intricately carved mantelpiece.

'Take a seat,' Ioan said and settled himself into the captain's chair behind his desk then, seeing what Bould was looking at, laughed. 'A lot of people find my brother rather off-putting, but I like to have him near me. We were very close, you see.'

'I've come across people who keep a loved one's ashes on the mantelpiece before, but never a skull.'

'As I say, I was very close to my brother.'

The solicitor placed his hands flat on the table in an expansive gesture, gave Bould a candid look and changed the subject. 'How can I help you?'

'You acted for Mrs Davenport in the sale of this property. Can you tell me if it was her residence?' Bould pushed the receipt across the desk.

There was a silence whilst Parry scrutinised it carefully, before saying: 'Yes, that is correct. Mrs Susan Davenport and her late husband, Cecil, lived at Brynteg for twenty-two years. Where did you get this?'

Bould reached over, retrieved the paper and ignored the question. 'Did you handle all the Davenports' legal affairs?'

'Ever since they came here. They weren't local, before you ask.'

'Do you know why they came here and where they're from?'

'London, I believe. They retired here.' Then noting the look of surprise on Bould's face, he expounded. 'Cecil Davenport was a lot older than his wife — by nearly forty years. He'd been married before. His first died of cancer, so I believe.'

'Were they very well off?' That wretched skull on the mantelpiece kept claiming his attention. He wasn't sure it was legal but it certainly wasn't normal. He couldn't help speculating on where the rest of the body was.

'Comfortable, I'd say, rather than rich. Property in this part of the world was a lot cheaper than London twenty years ago. You could sell a very modest property there and buy a small mansion here and still have enough left to live reasonably well on.'

'And was Brynteg a small mansion?'

'Oh, no, most certainly not, nothing of the sort. It's a three-bedroom stone cottage dating from the nineteenth century.' Then he drew a deep breath, leant back in his chair and tapped an unopened file in front of him. 'I believe you told me Mrs Davenport had died in some kind of accident?'

'She drowned, yes.' Bould kept the explanation as brief as he felt he reasonably could. 'Obviously we are keen to trace the next of kin. Did the Davenports have any children?'

'There was a daughter from the first marriage — Diana — that was all.'

'What about other family — sisters, brothers — did Susan have any?'

'Not that I know of. Cecil made a new will shortly after they arrived here. He was keen for Susan to do likewise, but she resisted, on the basis that she had no extant relatives and consequently had no interest in what happened to her estate after her death.'

'Many people have no living relatives but still have a great interest in what happens to their estate. Did she not have any friends she wanted to remember?'

Parry made an expansive gesture as if to acknowledge that what Bould said was true. 'Apparently not. In the end she was persuaded to draw up a will and she left everything to charity.' Now he opened the file before him and extracted a two-page document on heavy yellow parchment sewn together on the left hand side with green ribbon, which he made a show of perusing. 'Mrs Susan Davenport has left everything to the Royal National Lifeboat Institute.'

Whether or not it was a case of reading too much into too little, Bould immediately felt that all too familiar jolt of anticipation when something significant came his way. 'Do you know why she chose the RNLI? Did she go sailing?'

'Not that I'm aware. Neither Mr nor Mrs Davenport ever went to the coast. In fact, they rarely left the confines of Lampeter.'

'Are you able to put a figure to the amount involved?'

Ioan Parry stroked his chin, glanced at the document again as if to reassure himself of its contents, and gave an oblique answer, 'This will was made twenty years ago and at that time she owned precious little. Since then, there will be what she inherited from her husband, which basically amounts to the proceeds from the sale of Brynteg, and incidentally I have no idea what she has done with that.'

So she hadn't asked Ioan to handle the purchase of her house in Slipslade. Interesting, now why would that be? More and more the impression Bould got was of a woman who wanted to distance herself from her past. 'What about her husband's will?'

'Cecil left Brynteg to his wife, as I just said. The daughter, Diana, got the rest of his estate. It came to just over £400,000.'

Bould sat up. 'But he can't have done that. By law a wife has to get half her husband's property.'

'Cecil and Susan were agreed upon it, so there wasn't a problem. Susan waived her rights.'

'Nevertheless, agreed or not, it's a strange thing to do. Why would he want to leave the bulk of his estate to his daughter and not his wife?'

If the solicitor knew, he wasn't saying, and went off at a tangent. 'Have you any children, Sergeant? If you have you'll appreciate how much love a father feels for his daughter, and

Susan herself was keen to make sure Diana got her inheritance. She was very fond of her stepdaughter, you know, and insisted upon the split being as it was.'

'Even though it left her very badly off?'

Ioan shrugged and took refuge in pomposity. 'It's not my role as a solicitor to tell my clients what they should or should not do. I am merely their paid servant.' The words were humble but they were said in a tone of voice that suggested Ioan Parry was nobody's servant. There was a pause, and then he added in a more conversational tone. 'Susan had worked for many years. She didn't need to but said she couldn't face sitting around the house doing nothing all day. As she was able to earn a living she had less call for money than you might suppose.' He ran a hand over the top of his head, gently patting his hair as if something had caused it to become ruffled.

Bould was conscious of a contradiction here. According to Eleri Griffiths, her neighbour didn't work in Slipslade, so what was she living off? Beside which, that house in Meadow Rise must have cost nearly £300,000, which was more than she'd got from the sale of Brynteg, so where had the extra £50,000 come from? There was no doubt in his mind that Ioan Parry was lying about something; it would be really helpful to know what it was. Still, he had been thrown another morsel. 'She worked here in Lampeter?'

'Yes. At Yr Gegin Cantref.'

'Sorry, you'll have to say that again.'

A look of amusement briefly flitted across Ioan's face. 'Of course, you don't speak Welsh, do you? Yr Gegin Cantref: it means the Homely Kitchen. It's a tea shop about five doors up.'

Somehow Bould had expected any work being done by this young second wife of a reasonably wealthy London businessman to have been something grander than waitressing, until he remembered how young she must have been when they arrived. She would have married Cecil virtually the minute she left school. She probably didn't have any qualifications to enable her to do a more skilled job.

But the whole situation just didn't stack up. Why retire to the wilds of Wales if you didn't want to lead a quiet life doing next to nothing? It must have been the husband's idea to move here as he must have been about sixty when they arrived. But then, what makes a girl of nineteen marry a man of sixty? The cynic inside him said it was money. Had to be, what else? Curiosity made him ask: 'How old is Diana Davenport?'

Ioan replied without hesitation, 'She's thirty-two.' He nodded to himself as if to confirm his statement.

'I'll need her address, as it would appear she's the next of kin.'

'Of course. It's Flat 25, Fitzroy Mansions, Maida Vale, London. I've only a mobile phone number for her: 07925 654125.' He rattled it off from heart.

'Thank you, Mr Parry, you've been very helpful.' Bould closed his notebook, having jotted down the details in writing, as well as having mentally jotted down the fact that the solicitor knew the daughter's address and phone number by memory. Now what did that mean? Most people had more than enough difficulty memorising their own mobile phone number. He rose to go, then said, as if this thought had only just struck him: 'What did Mr Davenport die of and when?'

'He had a stroke, last June it was.'

Back on the street, he walked along the narrow pavement to Yr Gegin Cantref, stepping twice into the road to let young women with baby buggies the size of small tractors past, and nearly getting hit by first a car and then a lorry. Both drivers, far from being contrite, sounded their horns furiously at him and the lorry driver shook his fist.

Yr Gegin Cantref was sandwiched between an ironmongers and a newsagent. It was also double fronted, and still retained the original bow windows. An old spring bell tinkled as Bould pushed the door open and stepped inside. An uneven flag floor, whitewashed walls, bare dark oak tables and wheelback chairs gave the place an authentic feel.

The room was tiny but it was popular, and every seat was occupied. The air was warm and the odours inviting.

On hearing the bell, a heavily made-up woman of indeterminate age emerged from a narrow passageway at the back, which Bould assumed led to the Gegin of the title — or was it the Cantref?

The waitress swerved between the tables holding high a plate in each hand. One contained a towering scone, oozing jam and cream; the other contained a chocolate eclair, twice as long as his hand and over half as wide, stuffed to twice its original height with thick cream.

'There's space upstairs,' she said in a heavy Brummie accent, indicating with her head a steep staircase that Bould hadn't spotted in the dim light.

He waited until she had served a middle-aged couple, and then approached her, his warrant card in his hand. 'I'd like to talk to the owner of this establishment about Susan Davenport, whom I believe used to work here.'

The woman looked harassed, and pushed a strand of unnaturally red hair from her eyes. 'This really is not a good time,' she sighed, 'can't you see how busy we are?'

'I'm sorry about that, but I'm investigating Mrs Davenport's death and I do need to talk to her employer. Would that be you?'

His words certainly had an effect, for her attitude changed immediately. 'Sue's dead? Good Lord, what happened?' She seemed genuinely shocked and upset. 'I'm Scheherazade Jones and I'm the owner of this place. I can't get over this. What happened? Has she had an accident?' She seemed to be thinking out loud, talking more to herself than Bould, her face puckered in a frown; the liberal dusting of powder emphasised the deep lines running from her nose to her mouth. 'Good Lord, what happened?' she asked again, staring at him with wide blue eyes that disconcerted Bould because the whites showed all the way round. But before he could reply, she placed a hand on his arm. 'We'll go into the back; we'll have some peace in there.'

She led the way down the passage, past the

open door to the kitchen where a young woman was busy washing up. Just beyond and on the opposite side another door opened into a little sittingroom.

It was like stepping back a couple of hundred years. Facing him was a tiny fireplace with a simple stone surround and mantelpiece. A round card table and two straight-backed chairs were placed before a sash window framed with chintz curtains. A bookcase filled with an assortment of books, some of which looked very old, stood against the other wall.

The character of the room was the complete antithesis of what Bould had expected, its quiet, elegant charm at odds with the Cleopatra-bobbed Scheherazade Jones. Scheherazade! What were her parents thinking of? There really ought to be a law governing what misguided people could call their children. The owner of Yr Gegin Cantref was no sloe-eyed, sultry Arabian princess but a lanky, middle-aged woman dressed in a lot of long, loose, garments that flapped around her as she moved. A plethora of bead necklaces hung down nearly to her waist and the whole effect was one of untidy and restless energy.

As soon as the door was shut she asked again without preamble: 'What happened?'

'I'm afraid she met with an accident and drowned,' he said and waited to see how she reacted.

'Oh no. How?' Her hand had flown to her breast. It was the hand of a woman much older than the face suggested, and was covered in impressive rings which, if they had been genuine diamonds, would have been worth tens of thousands of pounds.

'We think she slipped whilst walking by a lake and fell in.'

A look of complete bafflement came over Scheherazade Jones' face, and she chewed her lip. When she spoke again her front teeth were smudged with scarlet lipstick. What she said was so extraordinary that Bould wondered if the shock had been too much for her. 'No, I'm sorry, that's not possible.' She shook her head firmly to make the point.

'Why do you say that?'

'She never went anywhere near water if she could help it. She couldn't swim and was terrified of drowning. She had a real thing about it . . . you know . . . what do they call it. A phobia, yes that's it. She had a phobia about water. Oh, poor Sue.' She seemed completely dazed by the news, and groped for the back of a chair before collapsing onto it.

Bould, on the other hand, was thinking

hard. 'Did you know her stepdaughter Diana?'

Staring out of the window into the darkening day, Scheherazade smiled thinly. 'This is a very small town. Of course I knew Diana Davenport.'

There was something in her tone that made his senses quicken. 'Did Sue and Diana get on?'

Now she looked down at the table top, and folded her hands in front of her, resting them on the wood. When she spoke her words were quiet and deliberate. 'They hated each other. I know stepchildren can resent a new woman in their father's lives, taking the place of their own mother, but with Diana it was more than that, it was pure hatred. I've never known why, and Sue wouldn't talk about it. And her attitude to Diana was very strange. She appeared to dislike her just as much and she was always saying she couldn't wait for her to leave home, but at the same time she was always trying to please the child. She'd pander to her something rotten when she was little. I used to say to her, you'll spoil that child, you will. It's often a problem with stepchildren though, isn't it?'

For the second time in as many minutes Bould felt he was on to something here. 'Would you say Mrs Davenport might have given others the impression she was fond of her stepdaughter, intentionally or otherwise?'

'I wouldn't really know about that. I only knew her in work, but I wouldn't have thought so, Sue wasn't like that. She was quite open in her thoughts and opinions,' she said eventually. This was so much at odds with what Ioan Parry had told him. He'd known at the time the man was lying. But why, now that was the question he wanted an answer to. 'Is Ioan Parry married?'

The sudden and extraordinary change of conversation jolted Scheherazade. Her eyes flew to his face and dismay was in them. 'Yes, yes, of course he is. He's been married for twenty-five years to Megan — and very happy they are together too. Very happy, you ask anyone.'

It was interesting how defensive she had become. And to think he nearly hadn't bothered to seek her out; she really had been a little goldmine. And then, just as he was taking his leave, she said something that made him doubt her rationality.

'The sad thing is the situation between Sue and Diana could have been remedied if only they had had their chakras balanced. And there are crystals that could have helped too. They have enormous healing power if only people would open their minds. It saddens me, it really does, that so many people refuse to consider anything outside their experience. They don't realise it suits the vested interests of big business to prevent them becoming enlightened.' Scheherazade jumped to her feet, almost turning the chair over in her enthusiasm. Her hands made curious swooping movements and colour pinked her cheeks as she warmed to her theme. She clearly had a great deal more to say on the subject, and on a rising pitch continued, 'Tarquin Fox says — '

Not being interested in what Tarquin Fox, whoever the man was, had to say on any subject, Bould took a firm line and cut her off in mid flow. 'Did Sue have any friends that you know of?'

Brought back to the subject in hand, Scheherazade calmed down immediately. 'No, she and Cecil were devoted to each other. He was all she needed, that's what she used to tell me. They kept themselves very much to themselves.'

★ ★ ★

The station was nearly deserted when Bould arrived back. It had just turned seven, and he had a lot of paperwork to type up. The Desk Sergeant informed him that just about every

48

available man was over in Chipping Norton, dealing with what looked like some drugs-related vendetta. Two bodies found with gunshot wounds had led to a lot of public fearfulness and the police were maintaining a high-profile presence to reassure the town's residents as drugs, guns and Chipping Norton weren't words that usually went together in the same sentence.

At least it gave him some peace to get his various reports up to date, and at 9.45 he left the file on Susan Davenport on DI Cobb's desk and gratefully headed for home.

3

Steve Cobb was in a cheerful mood even though he'd only had three hours sleep the previous evening. The Chipping Norton gunman was under lock and key because he had unfortunately dropped his mobile phone at the scene of the crime and so led the police straight to his door. Even more stupidly, he'd hidden the gun, with his prints all over it, under his bed.

The paperwork would still be vast and would take more time to complete than the crime had to solve, but that was modern policing for you, and he just had to accept it.

The report that his sergeant had placed in a prominent position on his desk was soon buried beneath the Chipping Norton paperwork, and when Bould put his head round the door at eleven, he quickly discovered it hadn't even been noticed.

'Sorry, Neil, can you give me half an hour?' Cobb said, his cheerfulness evaporating by the minute as the paperwork got to him.

'Sure.' Bould began to retreat from the room, but then turned back as if a thought had just struck him. 'I think I'll grab something from the canteen . . . ' The unspoken question hung between the two men.

'Would you mind getting me a sandwich — it doesn't matter what sort — and a doughnut, one of the ones with chocolate icing. My blood sugar needs a boost.'

'Consider it done,' Bould replied, poker faced. It had become something of a joke between them. Cobb was notorious for his sweet tooth, which he would never admit to, always hiding behind a concern for his blood sugar levels. They went through this little charade most days of the working week.

When Bould returned half an hour later, duly laden with a ham salad sandwich and chocolate doughnut, Cobb had the report in front of him.

'This makes for very interesting reading,' he said, stabbing at the typed sheets. 'I can see several lines of enquiry opening up.'

'What do you think, sir? It sounds less and less likely to be suicide.'

The answer, when it came, was oblique. But first Bould had to wait for half the doughnut to be eaten. 'I've spoken to the Coroner. The inquest's tomorrow and she's agreed to open and adjourn it immediately 'pending further enquiries'. We're going to have to speak to this stepdaughter, if for no other reason than she appears to be the next of kin. It's a pity Susan left all her money to charity. Bang goes the best motive yet.'

'The solicitor said the victim was fond of her stepdaughter, but the tea shop woman said they hated each other, so someone's lying.'

What cuckoos in the nest stepchildren were, Cobb thought. Of course, he knew only too well about the perils of that, for Sarah already had a daughter when they met. It was a cross he had had to carry for many years, but one he carried lightly. And now, after all this time, the ropes that lashed the cross together had loosened and all but fallen away. He put it down to something called growing up — on both sides. Once Carly had gone away to university things had changed. It was as if they could understand what made the other tick once a hundred miles separated them. 'It must have been hard for the Davenport women — there was little more than a decade between them. It'd be like having your big sister for a mother.'

'It was also interesting that Parry knew Diana's address and phone number off by heart. Most people have enormous trouble recalling mobile numbers, and Miss Jones was just a tad too insistent that he had a happy marriage.'

'That wouldn't give us a motive for murder — it might if *Mrs* Parry had been killed.'

'So we are treating it as murder, sir?'

'It's either murder or suicide. We can rule out accident. She's taken her clothes off, and it looks like she went in at night. Jenny can't be sure of time of death, because with the water being so cold it's advanced the onset of rigor, but she thinks probably about midnight.' He finished off the doughnut and started unwrapping the sandwich. 'I can't see it as suicide, not if she was terrified of drowning. It's the last way she'd have chosen.'

'Maybe that's why she chose it, then, sir. She couldn't swim remember, so she'd be certain to die.'

Cobb considered the matter briefly. 'I suppose there is that possibility but I'm still not convinced. If it's suicide where's the note? And why the name change; why all the lies about who she was and where she'd been living? Someone's been up to something and we're going to find out who and what. The thing we need to consider is this: could it be that it was not just one person who didn't want to be discovered, but the whole family, because, if so, we need to look beyond the life of Susan Davenport alone.' He looked up to see if Bould was with him.

He was. 'You think that the Davenports, when they went to Lampeter, had secrets?'

'I think there's something very odd about the whole situation. Why would a girl of nineteen marry a man old enough to be her father, with a daughter not much younger than her?'

'Money?' Bould had a simple theory that if there was no other obvious explanation, money was inevitably involved.

'But why leave London to go and live in the wilds of Wales? And why didn't they have any friends? A young woman, hardly out of school and from London, decides to marry a man in his sixties, acquire a ten-year-old stepdaughter, move to a remote part of the country and then take work as a waitress because she couldn't stand being in the house all day doing nothing. Yet they didn't mix, didn't have friends. Does this strike you as normal?'

A frown lowered Bould's brow. 'But if they were in hiding why did Susan break cover and move here when her husband died. Does this mean whoever she was hiding from had found her?'

'That's what *we've* got to find out, and we also need to know if there was any particular reason why she picked Slipslade to settle in.' Sandwich finished, Cobb dusted his fingers together before taking a well-aimed throw with the empty wrappings at the waste paper bin. 'I can see no other reason for her to tell Eleri Griffiths that she'd lived in Dorset for years other than to muddy the waters, which has to suggest she was very frightened of someone tracing her.' He rocked back in his chair and looked pensive. 'We're going to have to do a lot of digging around. If she didn't have any friends here, as Miss Griffiths says, who's the father of her child? Where is he now? And we're going to have to find out a lot more about our Mr Cecil Davenport. Where did he get his money from, for a start? Half a mill in liquid assets, plus the house, is quite an impressive amount, even these days. See what you can dig out on him. And contact Diana Davenport — with a name like that she should have been a 1950s movie starlet — and arrange for us to see her.'

'Both of us?'

'I think so.'

★   ★   ★

Built in the 1930s with more than a nod to the Mars Groups, its white walls gleaming, Fitzroy Mansions epitomised the clean-lined, simple modernity of its period and resonated with the sophistication of the age. Nestled amongst solid sandstone Victorian buildings it looked like a young girl in her party dress surrounded by dowdy spinster aunts.

'I didn't think there were any lifts like this left,' Cobb remarked, pulling the iron lattice gates shut behind him. 'I'm surprised the Health and Safety boys haven't had something to say on the subject.'

Preferring not to get his boss started on the subject of H&S, as it seemed to be the one subject designed to make him lose his temper quicker than anything, Bould pressed the button for the third floor and the ancient cage started a sedate ascent.

Diana Devonport was expecting them, but didn't seem best pleased about it, all the same.

'I really don't know what help you think I can give you,' she complained, taking centre stage in a spacious, sunny lounge furnished in a very contemporary, very expensive style. The floors were sanded wood, of course, and the rugs, in shades of rich reds, yellows and blues, looked like genuine Persian. In one corner a tiered arrangement of tall, spiky plants reached for the ceiling. There was a large silver entertainment centre in another corner and a deep red sofa arranged opposite. Two matching, equally deep armchairs were ranged on either side, but far enough away to suggest a lack of intimacy. A very modern gas fire, burning over pebbles, stood flat against a wall, surrounded by a faux stone mantelpiece on which sat a stylised bronze sculpture of a horse. Several invitations were propped up randomly along its length. A bleached wood coffee table filled the space between the sofa and the entertainment centre, and against the far wall a matching bookcase stood. Behind their hostess, large glass doors opened onto a balcony containing three heavy stone urns filled with miniature daffodils, jonquils, crocus and muscari already in bloom. Cobb had a feeling he was in a photo shoot for *Ideal Homes* and the thought didn't make him happy.

'May we sit down?' he asked pleasantly when it became obvious no invitation would be forthcoming.

'By all means, if you wish,' Diana replied in a tone that suggested she'd rather they said what they had to and departed.

The two policemen exchanged glances, and took one of the armchairs each. Bould surreptitiously took out his notebook. Diana remained standing in front of the balcony doors and Cobb was reminded of an actress striking a pose in a melodrama, not least because she was one of the most striking women he had ever seen. With eyes as dark as coals, high cheekbones, sleek black hair that fell to her shoulders and olive skin, she looked exotic, like a Slavonic gypsy. She was taller than him, and Cobb was nearly six feet, and slender, dressed in tight black jeans and an open-necked white shirt. Maida Vale seemed completely the wrong place for her, and for a moment he had an image of her drinking absinthe and smoking a black Sobranie cigarette in some demi-monde café on the left bank of Paris.

Not usually given to such fantasies, Cobb cleared his throat and started routinely. 'I appreciate this may be a bad time — '

'Why? She wasn't my mother and if you want to know the truth, I couldn't stand her.' A challenging look accompanied the brutal words.

'May I enquire why?' Thinking 'softly, softly' was the only way to play this, Cobb's tone was mild.

'No you may not. It's a personal matter. My father should never have married her. He was three times her age. Frankly, it was obscene.'

'If you don't mind me saying, your father must have been not so young when you were born.' It was rather clumsy, but Cobb hoped it was the most inoffensive way to make his point.

She stared at him. 'Both my parents were not so young, as you put it. Some people have trouble conceiving. My mother was in her early forties and my father just fifty when I was born.' Talking about her parents had caused her face and tone to soften.

'It must have been very painful for you to lose your mother so young,' Bould ventured, hoping this might be a good pathway to gaining her confidence.

She looked at him as if she had only just realised he was there and nodded. 'It's just the most terrible thing. You can't imagine. When you're young your mother is your whole world. I kept thinking it must be something I had done, that I must be very wicked for God to punish me in this way by killing my mother.' She seemed lost in her personal reverie, then snapped out of it and, resuming her normal pitch, she continued: 'of course, when you grow up you realise it isn't so, but at the time . . . and then he married *her*.' The word resonated with contempt.

'How did they meet?'

Again she shrugged. 'I don't know. You have to remember I was only nine at the time. In those days parents treated children like children and not like little adults who should be consulted on everything.' Standing before the wide glass doors, with the winter sun directly behind her, it was impossible to read her expression, and her tone was now studiously impassive.

Cobb knew when he was being obstructed. 'So you wouldn't know why they moved to Lampeter.'

'No.' The answer was firm and very quick. Then, as if sensing this wouldn't do, she added in a more considered way, 'My father was nearly sixty. He wanted to retire to the countryside. He used to go to Wales for holidays as a boy and remembered how much he liked the area.'

'And your stepmother — did she like the area?'

'She did not. It wasn't to her taste at all. She missed London. I'm not surprised she sold up as soon as Dad died. I thought she'd come straight back here.'

'So you don't know why she moved to the Cotswolds under an assumed name?' When all he got was a shake of the head in reply, Cobb pursued the matter. 'You see, it seems very strange to me that if she hated the countryside so much and missed London that she would move to another small rural town.'

Now Diana showed signs of irritation. She marched over to the sofa and threw herself down, swivelled round to face Cobb, put her elbows on the armrest and leant forward intently. 'Inspector, I rarely spoke to my stepmother. In fact, the last occasion was at my father's funeral. She didn't discuss her plans with me and I didn't discuss mine with her. I can't shed any light on any aspect of her life since my father died or before they met: is that clear.'

'Why couldn't you stand her?' Cobb asked abruptly.

'Lots of reasons,' she answered readily enough this time, as if she had forgotten her previous reply. 'She wasn't my mother — obviously. We had nothing in common. In fact, our tastes and opinions were the complete opposite of each others.' Her eyes met his, but their dark gaze told him nothing. And then as if she knew this also wasn't enough, added: 'Being cooped up with someone in a small cottage in a small town where there was very little to do becomes extremely tedious. If you've nothing in common, tediousness eventually turns to something stronger, like total antipathy in my case.'

Cobb felt he was getting nowhere fast. Was it really possible she knew nothing about her stepmother's life? He changed tack again. 'What about friends, or other relatives? Her solicitor, Ioan Parry, said she had none. Is that really true?'

'She had no friends that I can ever recall during our life in Wales. We kept ourselves to ourselves. I might not have liked my stepmother, but she and my father were devoted to each other — they didn't need anyone else. Perhaps that's why I didn't like her very much. Perhaps I was jealous of the attention my father gave her and not me.' But she said it in a strange way, as if challenging Cobb to believe this as a plausible reason for her feelings. 'As to whether she had friends in London, from her life before she met my father, I couldn't tell you.' She got to her feet again, restless, and prowled the room. 'I left home when I was eighteen. I went to university in Bristol and then came to London, so I wouldn't, couldn't, know anything about her life for the past thirteen years.'

'Did you never go home to visit your father?'

Diana shook her head and addressed the balcony. 'He used to come to London to visit me. He loved this flat, he often said . . . ' The sentence was bitten off sharply. After a pause, she turned round to face the policemen and started again. 'I think I went home at the end of the first couple of terms at uni, but after that I developed a circle of friends and stuck with them.'

For reasons Cobb couldn't fathom at this time he felt she was deliberately stonewalling him. But one thing was for sure; he would find out what Diana Davenport was hiding from him. 'So you met again at your father's funeral last year for the first time in years.'

She conceded the point with the slightest movement of her head. 'We spoke very briefly at the reception afterwards.'

'Which was held where?'

'At Brynteg, the family home — which was possibly a mistake. It wasn't a big house, so we were lucky it was a fine day as we ended up spilling out into the garden.'

'I thought your parents didn't have any friends,' Cobb said, puzzled by the discrepancy.

Diana laughed and her face relaxed for a moment with amusement. 'Inspector, you have obviously never lived in the wilds of Wales. So little goes on that a death is a really big thing. Everyone — and I mean everyone — expects to attend both the funeral service and wake following. Did you know feuds between families can last for generations and all because someone was not invited to a funeral? Oh, the umbrage taken, you've no idea.' She rolled her eyes heavenwards in frustration at the memory of those times.

What Cobb wanted to know was why she

hated her stepmother so. He didn't buy the explanation that it was jealousy. In a small child, yes, it was perfectly believable, but this was a confident adult he was talking to, not some neurotic still upset by the thought of her father loving another woman. He took one last shot in the dark. 'Could your stepmother swim?'

'Do you know, Inspector, I really think I would like a drink. Would either of you like something?' Her glance encompassed both Cobb and Bould.

'A coffee would be very welcome. We had a long journey here,' Cobb answered for both of them and Bould looked up and nodded in agreement.

'Coffee . . . oh, right. I'm going to have some wine . . . sure you won't join me?' Diana didn't wait for a reply, obviously knowing they wouldn't drink on duty, and headed for the kitchen.

Both the policemen watched her stride out of the room before speaking. Then Cobb said thoughtfully, 'Now why is she playing for time over such an innocent question?' He stretched his legs and stood up, wandering over to the balcony. The view was disappointing. Below lay a street, lined with plane trees, stark in the winter light, and opposite another block of flats, but nondescript in a concrete

1960s style. He wandered over to the bookcase. Books always gave a very good indication of a person's character, in Cobb's opinion. A couple of the titles interested him greatly.

Diana returned carrying a tray containing a cafetière of coffee, a bowl of loaf sugar, a small jug of cream and two tiny cups, all of a matching service and a large glass of red wine. She set the tray down on the coffee table and poured out the coffee. 'How do you take it?' she enquired, every bit the gracious hostess.

'Just as it is,' Cobb said, and Bould murmured his agreement.

As she passed the cups round, Diana answered his earlier question. 'Of course Susan could swim. Can't everyone these days? They've taught it at school as part of the curriculum for decades now, I believe.'

'Did you ever go swimming together?' Cobb persisted, unsatisfied with her vague reply.

'No. Why would we? I learnt to swim at school — I'm a very good swimmer actually — and I'd go with my friends. That's what most children do. They do things with their friends, not their stepmother.' She looked up with a dazzling smile, and he knew she was mocking him.

'Did you never go swimming on holidays?'

'We never went on holidays. Honestly, Inspector, you haven't got to grips with the dynamics of our family yet, have you?'

He just couldn't shake her, but he was going to have one last shot all the same. 'Did you know she was pregnant when she died?'

'Really? God, no; I had no idea, but then I wouldn't, would I?' She picked up her glass and raised it in his direction. 'Cheers.'

Cobb and Bould sipped at their coffee and Diana tossed down half the glass in one.

'Do you live here alone, Miss Davenport?' Cobb asked casually.

'Whilst I can't see what that's got to do with you, yes, I do.' She took another good swig of her wine. As she didn't seem nervous, Cobb assumed she always drank like this.

'Can I ask what you do for a living?'

'I'm an accountant.'

He was speechless. Whatever occupation he might have imagined this exotic creature engaged in, such a mundane job as accountancy would never have made the list. Truth to tell, it was rather a disappointment to think of her spending her days seated at a desk poring over columns of figures. What on earth had he expected her to say, that she was a model, an actress? He must be getting senile — a pretty face didn't usually affect

66

him so. Downing the rest of his coffee in one — the cups were really very small — he got to his feet, and Bould took his cue and did the same. 'Thank you for your time, Miss Davenport. If you do think of anything that might help us, please get in contact.' He gave her his card but had no hopes in that direction at all. Here was a woman who, he felt, would not raise a finger to find her stepmother's murderer. The question was why.

The sunshine was gone, leaden grey skies wept icy rain on their heads as they left Fitzroy Mansions. Cobb turned his jacket collar up and said: 'Do you know any women who read *Jane's Fighting Ships* and *Jane's Defence Review?*' He thought if anyone should know what women read it would be Bould, who had something of a reputation with women. It wasn't that he was known as a womaniser — which perhaps was strange considering the number of girlfriends he'd had. Most of the female staff at the station hung onto his every word and wouldn't hear a word against him. Was it all a matter of perception? Did women have an image of a womaniser as someone a bit dodgy, a bit lecherous? Bould was none of those things and all his relationships ended with him still on very good terms with his ex-girlfriends.

God knows how he did it. Cobb couldn't help but feel slightly envious.

Now his sergeant was eying him in a slightly incredulous way. 'I'd be surprised to meet a woman who had heard of *Jane's Fighting Ships*, quite frankly, sir.'

'That's what I thought.' Satisfied with the answer, Cobb nodded to himself. Seeing Bould's inquisitive look he explained: 'There were copies of both publications in the bookcase in Diana Davenport's flat. Now what does that suggest to you?'

'They belong to a man.'

'But she said she lived alone. Do we think she's lying, Sergeant?'

'Undoubtedly.'

4

Diana woke suddenly, still tasting the foul water in her mouth, and feeling her lungs aching with the effort of trying to snatch at some air. She was tempted to look at the clock, but resisted, knowing she was going to be awake for hours now, but preferring not to know just how many.

Sitting up, she pummelled the pillows back into shape and threw herself back down with a sigh of annoyance. Why the hell she kept having this nightmare was beyond her. Drowning was the one thing she didn't fear. A qualified lifeguard, PADI dive master and one-time all-Britain university back stroke champion meant she was both confident and respectful of water, and the setting of this dream was bizarre. If she had dreamt she was diving and had run out of air — well that was something every diver dreaded and she'd have understood it — but why an icy pond that had no resonance with her?

On the positive side it made a change from the other recurring dream she had when she was being chased through an empty house of endless rooms by someone she never saw. The house was different every time she dreamt it, but she still knew it was the same house, in the way you did in dreams. And even though she'd dreamt of a dozen different houses, she could still recall the pattern of the paper in every single room, the colour of the curtains, the items in the kitchen. She would awaken then, just as the knife came down, and spend the rest of the night wide awake, as she knew she would now.

As soon as she shut her eyes, she was back in the water, feeling the weed feather her face, and the panic started to rise as her head was pulled down beneath the black water, her heart started to speed up in a frantic effort to get oxygen through her arteries. Oh sod it, sod it, sod it!

Furious at this inability to control her own mind, Diana leapt out of bed, switched the light on and looked at her bedside clock. It showed it was one in the morning. She'd had two hours of sleep. Oh, that was just great — she'd be good for nothing come the morning. What was it she'd read? If you couldn't get back to sleep within twenty minutes, go down and make a cup of tea, sit in a comfortable chair and read a little; or so some expert in the subject recommended. She'd give it a go, but it sounded to her as if it would make her more wakeful.

In the kitchen, waiting for the kettle to boil, she contemplated a large vodka before rejecting the idea. Her increasing dependency on alcohol to blot out the past was beginning to worry even her, and James was fast becoming a total bore on the subject.

So she had a cup of tea instead, smiling as she thought of the look of disbelief on James's face, were he here to see it.

In the lounge she dimmed the lights and put some music on, sitting back in the chair with her eyes shut, letting the sounds wash over her and breathing slowly, deeply, counting to ten on every inhalation and exhalation.

But when she returned to bed half an hour later it had made no difference. Lavender oil dropped on the pillows was supposed to encourage sleep, so she tried that, yet again, but without success.

Desperate now, and knowing that getting wound up would only make the situation worse, she tried a hot bath with some lavender bath oil, hoping that would do the trick. It didn't.

If only James was here; the nights were never so troubling then. But he wouldn't be back for another ten days. It wasn't during the day she missed him but during the nights. The presence of another living person chased

71

away the dead of her past.

She changed the bedding, laying out fresh, crisp sheets that smelt of lavender and finally fell into the arms of Morpheus as the clock's hands moved to ten to six.

★ ★ ★

The day was the best you could hope for in February. The light was so weak the sun might as well have been transported to the very edges of the solar system, and it struggled to break through the mist that blurred the land. A heavy rime frost coated each blade of grass, every breath the men took hung visible before them and the waters of the pond were stilled beneath a layer of ice.

Cobb had been drawn back here, as he always was in a murder investigation. So often, the scene of the crime held the answer, and he knew it did in this case.

Bould stood beside him, hands thrust deep into his pockets, and surveyed the lonely scene.

'We need to find out why and from whom she was hiding,' Cobb said eventually.

'I've been thinking about the name she chose. Eliza — makes me think of Eliza Doolittle. She became a different person. Do you think Susan chose the name deliberately?'

'A flower girl to a duchess. It's possible. As Susan was planning to become a new person, the reference might have seemed highly appropriate to her, or she might have just found it amusing, or she might not have even heard of George Bernard Shaw, and I don't see that it can have any relevance to her death.' Cobb watched two hazy figures carrying fishing tackle make their way along the bank to a little wooden jetty. 'There are an awful lot of contradictions in this case.'

'You mean, everyone's lying to us,' Bould said in a sardonic tone.

'It certainly seems that way at the moment.' Cobb walked forward to the water's edge. 'The thing with these gravel pits is that they shelve very steeply over a short distance. It looks to be only a few inches deep here, but less than a body's length out and it's over ten feet. If you weren't a good swimmer, or you were naked on a February night when the air temperature was below freezing, you'd be in trouble almost instantly.'

'We don't know it wasn't suicide,' Bould pointed out.

'We don't know it was.'

'But it wasn't an accident.'

'Right, and then that only leaves murder as

the alternative. But how do you get someone to go into freezing water in the middle of the night, particularly someone who's frightened of drowning in the first place? How did they lure her up here, and why?' Cobb seemed to be thinking out loud, his sight fixed on a series of dark smudges that would turn out to be a line of willows when the mist cleared. He was thinking, what a dreadful death. No one in her right mind would chose to kill herself this way, and so far they had come up with nothing to suggest Susan Davenport's balance of mind was disturbed. The GP records were sparse because she was rarely ill, and there was no mention of mental health problems. At least, not in Lampeter. She didn't seem to have registered with a new doctor since the move.

'Jenny said there was no sign of a struggle, no marks on the body of any sort. It's an outlandish way to kill someone, and sadistic too. You'd have to stand here to force her out into the deeper water. Stand here and watch her die,' Bould said, thrusting his hands deep into his jacket pockets and wishing he'd brought some gloves with him.

'I've just got the policeman's instinct on this one, Neil. All the facts point to something very fishy going on here — and that wasn't meant to be a pun, by the way.

Just look at it: her stepdaughter says her stepmother missed London, so why didn't she move back there?'

'She'd been away for more than twenty years,' Bould pointed out. 'The city's changed a bit in that time, and all her old friends would have grown up, got married, had families, moved away. She'd have lost contact with everyone.'

'True, but that doesn't explain the change of name. It doesn't explain why, in all those years in Wales, she never had any friends or visitors. They were running away from something, the whole family possibly, and after her husband's death she felt vulnerable. There was no one to protect her any more, that's why she changed her name and hid away in the Cotswolds. But what was she living on, and why did her husband leave most of his estate to his daughter?'

There was no arguing with the boss when he got one of his hunches, Bould had long since learnt that, and he respected those hunches, for they were usually right. He carried on with the same line of thinking. 'I've been thinking about that passport: Susan got it last July, almost immediately after her husband died. Both Parry and Diana said the Davenports never went away on holidays, so presumably she never had a passport before

75

and this is her first. Do you think she was planning on leaving the country? After all, if she really wanted to hide away from someone that's the best way to do it.'

'In that case what made her change her mind and why did she come here, a place to which she appears to have no connections whatsoever?' Cobb countered, staring moodily across the water.

'She must have already been pregnant when she left Lampeter. Do you think the father is to be found there?' Bould asked.

'I think so. Ioan Parry's going to organise the funeral, as her stepdaughter declined; we'll go and see who else turns up.'

'According to Diana, half the country will be there.'

'She also said life in the country was pretty static. You know what that means, Sergeant? It means everyone knows everyone else's business. If Susan Davenport was having an affair it's a racing cert that someone in the town would have got wind of it. What better place for the skeletons to come out of the cupboard than a funeral.'

5

Bould drove because — as Cobb had pointed out — he knew the way, but it was really because the boss wanted to think long and hard about the case and preferred not to have to concentrate on driving at such times.

The A40 was busy, but once they turned off just past Llandovery onto the A482 it was another world. There was little traffic, just mile after empty mile of road with an occasional grey stone cottage on the roadside — no front gardens and the backs overshadowed by high rock faces hung with icicles. At one point they passed a pub, standing alone, with its back pressed against the cliff, a tiny car park to one side.

'Where on earth would they get their trade from?' Bould wondered aloud. 'We haven't passed any houses in the last ten minutes.'

'All the traditional pubs are shutting fast,' Cobb replied, gloomily. It was a tragedy, another part of British life disappearing forever to be replaced with what? Vodka palaces where the youngsters drank themselves stupid and gave his colleagues work they didn't need. Instead of fighting crime, these days they were acting as nannies and peacekeepers for spoilt children. It was where they got the money from that constantly amazed him. When Cobb had been young a pint of bitter had to last all night. Sometimes a girl would catch his eye and they'd get chatting.

Then he'd offer to buy her a drink, praying she'd ask for a shandy and not a rum and coke, not because he was mean but because it made the difference between catching the bus home and walking.

The funeral was held in St David's Church in a little street round the back of the town. It wasn't at all what Cobb had been expecting. From the description of the isolated lifestyle the Davenports had led, some tiny ancient church tucked away from the mainstream of life would surely have been more appropriate, but here they were in an upright, ugly, Victorian edifice in an urban setting.

The officers settled themselves discretely into a pew at the very back and listened to a lengthy service conducted entirely in Welsh. That was the second surprise of the day.

The first had come when the coffin arrived, and there leading the mourners was Diana Davenport.

★　★　★

The wake was held in a local hotel, the Green Dragon, desperately in need of revamping, but solid and reassuring in its old-fashioned ways.

In a panelled function room across a narrow passageway from the public bar, Cobb and Bould pushed through the throng to seek out Diana. The atmosphere came as a further surprise to Cobb, who had expected a sombre mood from the mourners, and whilst it was true that they were subdued, they also seemed intent on having a good time. The drink was certainly flowing and the bar was doing a roaring trade.

That was where they found her, standing at the bar surveying the room with an amused air and knocking back red wine, whilst half-heartedly listening to whatever it was Ioan Parry was so keen to tell her. The difference between the two was interesting. Parry was dancing attendance on Diana, but she seemed scarcely aware of his presence.

The minute she saw the policemen she had all the excuse she needed. 'Sorry, Ioan, must go and play the gracious hostess.' She patted him lightly on the arm and moved swiftly away as he opened his mouth to protest. Cobb saw the look of dismay on his face. There was no fool like an old fool, as the saying went.

'Inspector, Sergeant, how good of you to come,' she said with a smile that showed her teeth and yet was entirely false. 'Have you got yourselves something to eat yet?'

When they had met in London, Cobb had felt that he was watching an accomplished actress; now he knew it. She was playing a part and relishing it. 'Not yet,' he said, wondering if she was aware of how much gossip she would be the centre of later, before realising that of course she did. That was the whole point.

Her dress, a simple sleeveless shift, accentuated her figure and ended several inches above the knee. Stiletto heels added another four inches to long, slim legs. Cobb could just imagine the overheated air in many houses tonight as the good wives of Lampeter vented their opinion of her dress, which, although it was black as became the occasion, still managed to make its wearer look as if she was destined for some glamorous First Night party in London, rather than the country funeral of her stepmother.

'Baby, there you are. It's impossible to get a decent beer here, so I've had to settle for Carling, would you believe.' A man, slim and dark, had pushed through. Everything about him shouted money, from the cuffs showing beneath the sleeves of his very expensive black suit, held together by lozenges of heavy gold that matched the signet ring on his little finger to the handmade black shoes. He had rather haughty features and lips that curled in what Cobb suspected — rightly as it turned out — was a permanent expression of disdain. Now he slipped his arm around Diana's waist in a way that clearly warned all other men off. He looked the policemen up and down in a faintly contemptuous way as if he had assessed their financial position and found it wanting. 'Aren't you going to introduce me, baby?' he asked blandly.

'Of course. James, these gentlemen are the not-so-local plod, come here no doubt in the hope of graveside confessions of a scandalous nature, where hideous family secrets will be revealed as I rent my clothes in guilt.' Her tone was both mocking and challenging as her glance darted between all three men surrounding her. Cobb could see she was in her element. 'Officers of the law, can I introduce James Grogan to you? Now please feel free to enjoy the buffet.' She gestured towards a small room leading off from the one they were in, and through the open double doors could be seen a large table covered with platters of sandwiches, cocktail sausages, pork pies and all the unimaginative finger buffet foods that Cobb loathed.

Diana had clearly intended her words to be dismissive, and she deserved a less crowded room in order to sweep majestically away at this point, but the crush prevented this so Cobb seized the opportunity to ask the question that had been gnawing away ever since he saw her in the church. 'I didn't expect to see you here, considering your relationship with your stepmother.'

'Didn't you?' She turned back, wide eyed and faux innocent. 'But I told you, everyone must attend funerals in this part of the world, even if they couldn't stand the dead.'

'Yet you weren't prepared to take the responsibility of organising it.'

'Why keep a dog and bark yourself?' Seeing his look of incomprehension, she laughed, tossing her hair back over her shoulders and he wondered if she was drunk already. 'Come on now, Inspector, all solicitors do little enough for their money as it is, and as this one bled his client dry I thought it only appropriate he should dispose of the body.' She gurgled with laughter at her own joke, stepping back at the same time and catching her heel on the leg of a bar stool. She almost lost her balance and would have slipped if James hadn't had hold of her.

'Baby,' James tightened his grip around Diana's waist steadying her. He didn't look

82

pleased, but she was too far gone to notice. 'You know we have to be back in London by eight. I think we should make tracks now.'

She glanced at her watch. 'Yes. I think I've done my bit: shown my face and all that. It should keep the old gossips quiet. Not that I ever intend coming back to this place again.'

'Then I don't understand why you felt it necessary to attend,' Cobb said, puzzled by her attitude. She may not have been saddened by her stepmother's death, but she did seem upset by something. She had been too bright, too determined to prove the events of the day weren't affecting her.

Now she gave him a crooked smile. 'Perhaps I just needed to see for myself that the bitch was dead and buried. Come on, James, let's get out of here. Goodbye one and all,' she called raising her voice as James hurried her out of the room.

Cobb watched her departing back thoughtfully. 'Bled her dry — what are we to make of that, Sergeant?'

'Sounds to me suspiciously like blackmail.'

'Possibly. After all, if anyone is well placed to know another's secrets, it's a solicitor. Or she could have just meant his fees were exorbitant.'

'What solicitor's fees aren't?' Bould said with feeling, having recently bought a new house. He was still smarting from the costs. No wonder lawyers were commonly referred to as sharks, although the comparison was probably grossly unfair to sharks.

'I wonder why she really came. Diana didn't strike me as a woman who would do something just because it was expected; neither do I think she cares a whit about what people think of her.'

'She was very different from how she was in London. She was so self-assured there, but she seemed on the verge of losing control just now.'

'Wasn't she just? The boyfriend was very quick to whisk her away. I wonder if he was afraid she might say something she shouldn't? Come on, let's get something to eat.' As his stomach felt as though his throat had been cut, Cobb reckoned any food was better than none, even the unappetising buffet on offer here.

Cobb was helping himself to some ham and pickle sandwiches on bread cut so thick, the term 'doorsteps' scarcely did them justice when someone said to him, 'Bore da.'

Looking up, he saw a young woman with inquisitive eyes staring at him. She had a professional air about her and her black trouser suit looked more like her normal business attire than a funeral outfit. 'I'm sorry, I've no idea what you just said,' he apologised.

She smiled thinly. 'It means good day in Welsh. I knew you weren't from round here. Two strangers at a funeral. Two *English* strangers; this will be the talk of the town for days. What are you doing here?'

Her directness impressed Cobb. 'We're police officers.'

'Investigating Susan's death, I suppose? There are all sorts of rumours flying around the town regarding what happened.' She paused expectantly and gave him a candid look.

Knowing he was disappointing her, Cobb refused to rise to the bait. He had questions of his own to ask. 'What's your connection with Susan, or are you just here because it's expected?'

'No, I knew Susan slightly. I'm Mair Evans, and I'm an estate agent; I acted for her in the sale of Brynteg.'

'Prices round here are a lot lower than in England,' Cobb observed, more to make conversation than anything else. '£250,000 wouldn't buy you a nice stone cottage of character where we come from.'

'It wouldn't round here either,' Mair said tartly. 'If you were hoping to buy something on the cheap I'm afraid you're in for a

85

disappointment because you're about ten years too late. That's when the English discovered Ceredigion and invaded. They couldn't believe their luck — the most beautiful countryside in the world and properties going for a song. What did it matter that they priced all the locals out of the market? It's just another injustice we Welsh have suffered at the hands of the English ever since Llywelyn ap Gruffudd died heroically defending this land against your wretched Edward I.' Having said her piece, she drew herself very erect and took an adversarial stand, as if she expected to re-enact the pitched battle at Cilmeri in December 1282 that had seen the last native-born prince of Wales defeated.

Oh good grief. He'd stirred up a hornets' nest now! Since they'd stopped burning down holiday homes some decades previously and opted for an Assembly Government in Cardiff instead, Cobb had assumed the Nationalists were reasonably happy these days, but it appeared not. He decided it might be better not to mention the fact that he'd never heard of Llywelyn ap Gruffudd in case that brought forth a further tirade and he didn't want to be distracted, because something she had said interested him greatly. 'I was under the impression that

£250,000 was the price Brynteg sold for.'

'Who told you that?' she demanded, still angry. 'For your information, it fetched £320,000.'

Cobb felt his pulse quicken. 'Are you sure?'

She gave him a withering look and replied stiffly, 'I do know my job if nothing else.'

'Of course, I didn't mean to imply anything to the contrary; it's just that we have it on good authority that it went for a quarter of a million.'

Mair shook her closely cropped head. 'Well, you've been told wrong, then. That's the trouble with this town; it's nothing but rumours and speculation. If people don't know the facts they won't admit it, so they make something up instead.' Her anger now seemed directed towards her fellow citizens and Cobb decided she was just too wearisome to cope with. Besides which, he wanted to find Ioan Parry.

'Please excuse me; I've just seen someone I need to speak to. It was most interesting talking to you,' and he meant it. Apart from the history lesson he'd found out something pertinent to his investigation.

'Where is he, can you see any sign of the man?' Cobb didn't need to tell Bould who it was he was seeking as they moved back into the main room.

Bould nudged his boss, 'He's over there,' and he jerked his head in the direction of the bar.

'Sergeant Bould, fancy seeing you here! Who's your friend?' The thick Brummie accent was a dead giveaway; he didn't need to turn round to be faced with that overly red hair to guess who had accosted him. Bould felt obliged to stop and introduce Cobb to Scheherazade Jones.

'I'm very pleased to meet you, Miss Jones,' Cobb said gravely. 'I wonder if you could tell me something.'

'Anything. Just ask.'

'Did Susan Davenport have a new man in her life after her husband died?' It was a long shot but every woman needed a friend to confide in and the tea shop owner seemed to be the only person, apart from her husband, that the dead woman had had any contact with.

Scheherazade looked at him as if he was out of his mind, which wasn't encouraging. 'Are you kidding? Sue with a new man! No.'

'What makes you say that?'

'She was devoted to Cecil. She didn't want anyone else.' Having got that out of the way, Scheherazade turned to Bould and laid her heavily beringed hand on his arm. 'You need your chakras balanced, you do. I thought that when you were here last. Would you like me to sort them out for you?'

Out of the corner of his eye, Bould could see the amused look on Cobb's face. 'Thank you very much, Miss Jones. Some other time maybe. Now if you'll excuse me.' He shook his arm free and felt almost guilty at the crestfallen look on Scheherazade's face.

'Come and have some tea at the shop when you're done here,' she called at his retreating back.

He raised a hand in acknowledgement.

★ ★ ★

'What's this, I'm not under arrest, am I?' Parry joked uneasily, as Cobb and Bould bore down on him. He trickled water from a jug bearing the name of a brand of lager into his Scotch, 'Your very good health, gentlemen,' he said, raising his glass in salutation. His tone was one of bonhomie but his eyes ping-ponged from Cobb to Bould and back again, and Cobb wondered if he had seen them talking to Mair.

'Why do you ask, have you committed a crime?' Cobb said.

'Good Lord, no, the very idea.' He sounded genuinely put out at the suggestion.

'I do hope for your sake that's true,

because we've just been given some information that makes us think otherwise.'

'If this is your idea of a joke, Inspector, I don't find it funny.' He pushed away from the bar, suddenly a picture of outraged indignation.

'Just a minute, sir, we haven't finished yet,' Bould had his hand on the solicitor's arm; his grip wasn't tight, but it stopped Parry in his tracks. 'It's just that we've learnt Brynteg was sold for £320,000 yet your bill of conveyancing to Mrs Davenport stated the selling price was only £250,000. How do you account for the discrepancy?'

'There is an authentic reason for this, I promise you gentlemen. Oh, Lord, here's my wife. Please don't say anything in front of her.' Beads of sweat shone on his forehead, and he mopped them up with a large handkerchief.

A stick-thin woman, with short bleached hair, who had clearly had a face lift but still managed to have a grim air about her, approached. She ignored the policemen and proceeded to address her husband in Welsh in a high-pitched voice that quickly grated on her audience. Whatever it was she said elicited a series of dumb nods of agreement from Parry. Eventually, when she had had her say, Parry responded with something that didn't seem to be well received, as she gave Cobb and Bould a frankly disgusted look and then turned on her heel and stalked off.

Parry mopped his brow again, his bluff bonhomie vanished. 'Can we go to my office?' he appealed. 'I wouldn't want anyone to hear what I have to say to you.'

'By all means,' Cobb replied. 'I look forward to hearing your explanation.'

The Green Dragon was the hotel Bould had passed on his previous visit to Parry & Edwards and was all but next door to the solicitor's office.

As they passed through the reception area, the stony-eyed secretary was typing at high speed, a set of headphones attached to her ears, a stack of manila files covering most of her desk. She barely bothered to glance at her employer as he led the officers through, but he stopped to ask her something in Welsh, to which she gave a brief reply without looking up or interrupting her typing.

When they reached the stairs, Parry hesitated before asking, 'Would you like some coffee, gentlemen? I could get Eleri to bring some up if you — '

'Eleri?' Cobb said sharply, 'is that a Welsh name?'

Flummoxed as to why the origin of his secretary's name should be of interest, but happy to be able to oblige so easily, Parry replied: 'Yes, it's very popular in this part of the world. You'll hear it a lot around here.' He looked from one to the other as if waiting for an explanation, and then, when none was forthcoming, he headed up the stairs, the policemen following.

Once he'd shut the door to his office, Parry beetled round to his captain's chair and, once settled behind his desk, seemed to be trying to regain some air of authority. It was short lived.

Cobb settled himself down opposite and Bould took up a station by the window, there being no other chair in the room. He kept one eye on the street scene below.

'I should probably caution you at this point,' Cobb said, happy to pile the pressure on in order to get the solicitor's cooperation.

The ploy was successful. Parry paled in alarm and crumpled instantly. 'There's no need, Inspector, I'll tell you the whole story. It is true that Brynteg sold for £320,000 but the reason the sale bill showed only £250,000 is because Mrs Davenport owed me £70,000.'

'I hope you can prove this, and don't expect us to simply take your word for it.'

'There's nothing in writing, if that's what you mean, but it was like this: she came to me

92

a couple of years ago and said she needed £50,000 in a hurry. She said she couldn't ask her husband for it.'

'So you agreed to lend it to her just like that, did you, with nothing in writing at all? That's extremely trusting of you. How could you be sure you'd ever get your money back?' Cobb was disbelieving. Then he leant forward in his seat and fixed Parry with a searching look. 'What did she want the money for?'

'I've no idea. She wouldn't say, but she was desperate. She said she had to have it or she'd go to prison. She practically got on her knees and begged me.'

Cobb stared at the space above the solicitor's head, apparently lost in thought. When he judged he'd let Parry sweat enough, he said: 'But now, here's my problem. I can't see why you were prepared to lend her this money. How was she supposed to repay you?'

'Her husband was forty years older than her. He'd got heart trouble. I didn't need to be a genius to work out he'd die long before she did, and as I'd made out Cecil Davenport's will I knew she'd get the house. We agreed when he died, she'd sell up and pay me back out of the proceeds.'

'And you agreed to do this out of the kindness of your heart?' Cobb sounded as sceptical as he looked. 'How much interest did you charge her?'

'Now look here, Inspector, it was all above board I can assure you,' Parry had started to bluster, which told the policemen it most certainly wasn't all above board.

'How much?'

'It was what she'd have had to pay a commercial bank, if they'd have given her a loan, which of course they wouldn't,' he gabbled.

Cobb sighed, his patience was running out. 'How much, for the third time?'

The solicitor gave in. 'We didn't set an exact figure, we just agreed she would pay me £70,000 when the house was sold,' he muttered and had the grace to look shamefaced.

'So you lent her £50,000 for a couple of years and took £20,000 as interest! That's 20% a year. I wonder what the Law Society will have to say when they hear about this.'

'Don't bring the Law Society into this, I beg of you. I'll be struck off.'

'Yes, you will, won't you?' Cobb agreed pleasantly. It would give him great pleasure to see this unscrupulous fellow get his comeuppance. He was still angry at the way a vulnerable woman had been exploited, and decided to make the solicitor suffer some more. 'Mark you, the Law Society is possibly the least of your problems. Illegal money lending is a serious crime, particularly when the rates are usury.'

Out came the pocket handkerchief again as a rivulet of sweat trickled down Parry's cheek. A tic started in his right eye. 'I was only trying to help the woman — '

Cobb held up his hand. 'Oh please, don't give me any of that, Mr Parry. You knew all Mrs Davenport was going to get from her husband was the house, yet you had no compunction about robbing her of part of the proceeds. Didn't it occur to you that she was going to need every penny she could get? You were her solicitor; you held a position of trust, and you've abused your position shamefully.'

'Look, I'll give you all the help I can, if you only — '

'Only what? Keep this to ourselves. Forget it, Mr Parry. Mark you; you can still do your best to help us. You told my sergeant that Susan Davenport and her stepdaughter got on very well, but we've heard from another source that they hated each other. Now, perhaps you could shed some light on this little discrepancy.'

'You've been talking to that lunatic woman who owns the teashop. You know, she's into every so called New Age mumbo-jumbo going?'

'That doesn't mean we can't trust what she tells us. Do you know, I'm getting tired of having to repeat myself endlessly to you. Just answer the question, will you?'

Parry sighed heavily, and appeared to have decided to throw in the towel completely. 'It's true, they hated each other. They were like that when they arrived and things only got worse as they got older. Diana couldn't bear to be in the same room as Susan.'

'Speaking of Diana,' Cobb gave each word weight. There were some people he liked to see squirm, those he viewed as beneath contempt, and Parry came right at the top of his list at the moment. 'I understand that you know her address and mobile phone number off by heart. That's quite impressive. I have terrible trouble remembering my own mobile number; other people's are right out of the question. We'd be interested to know just what your relationship with her is.'

Parry seemed shocked and immediately became indignant. 'Our relationship is strictly professional, Mr Cobb. I've known Diana since she was ten.'

'What's that got to do with it?'

There was no reply. The silence grew and under the DI's icy glare Parry became disconcerted again. He studied his hands. When he eventually spoke his voice was low and hesitant. 'There was nothing between us; I give you my word on that. If you must, you can ask Diana herself but I'd be happier if you didn't.

'You've seen her — what a beautiful woman she is. I just sometimes find a reason to telephone her and we talk a little; I pretend it's to do with her father's estate or some such. I've no doubt she's guessed at the real reason. But there's no harm in hoping now, is there?' He looked up, pleading mutely for some sign that the policemen knew and understood what he was going through, but was met with impassive faces and silence. His gaze fell back to his hands. 'Well, I thought if Cecil could get a wife forty years younger — and he was no matinee idol — then maybe — '

'You fancied your chances with Diana.' Bould couldn't keep the incredulity out of his voice.

'Mun, you've seen Mrs Parry! It's the only thing that keeps me going. Yes, I know it was foolish. I can see what you think of me, but where was the harm in it?' Appealing once more to them, in a sort of man-to-man way, Parry looked up and spread his hands out in supplication.

'That depends,' Cobb said. 'Harassment is a serous offence. Perhaps we should have a word with Diana to see how she feels about your unsolicited phone calls.'

'Why don't you just divorce your wife if that's how you feel?' Bould asked.

Parry looked at him as if he was mad. 'Have you any idea how much that would cost me? She'd take me for every last penny. And round here people don't get divorced, certainly not professional people. I'd be ruined.'

'You're ruined anyway,' Cobb said caustically. 'Right, let's get back to the subject in hand. Why did Susan and Diana hate each other?'

Beads of sweat broke out on Parry's forehead again, but by now his handkerchief was a sodden mass. He gave up trying to mop his brow. 'I don't know. That's the truth; you have to believe me.'

'I still don't understand why you lied to us. What was the point of saying they got on when they didn't?' Bould asked, forsaking his window vigil and walking round to stand over their already intimidated quarry.

Embarrassed, the solicitor stared at some faraway spot. 'I didn't want you to think badly of Diana. You might have thought she was the cause of the problem.'

Oh, the vagaries of human nature! The man was vain on someone else's behalf. When he spoke, Cobb was stern. 'You do realise this is a potential murder enquiry and you're just wasting our time. As a solicitor, you should know better than that. So, you've no idea why they didn't get on but you do know the situation was established by the time they arrived here.'

'Yes.'

'Right. Having got that out of the way, let's go back to the money you lent Mrs Davenport: do you have any idea why she needed £50,000?'

'No. I've told you, she wouldn't say.'

Leaning on the desk, Bould said, 'But she told you she'd go to prison otherwise. Did that not make you think of anything?'

'If you mean she was being blackmailed because she'd done something criminal, yes, that's the only thing that made any sense to me, but before you ask, I don't know who it was she wanted the money for or why; I don't know anything above what I've already told you.'

'Then you can't actually give us any help, can you, Mr Parry?' Cobb pushed back his chair and got to his feet. 'You will be hearing further from us on this matter, of that you can be assured.' A brusque nod of his head was all he could manage as farewell.

Halfway across the room, Cobb stopped

dead in his stride. 'Good God, is that a real human skull?' He stabbed the air in the direction of the mantelpiece.

'It's my brother,' Parry spoke wearily, as if he was fed up of having to give this explanation.

'What's it doing here?' There was a note of outrage in the DI's voice.

'There's no law against it, I can assure you. Ask the vicar; he'll still be in the Green Dragon, and for the rest of the evening too, if his past form's anything to go by.' Even with all his own troubles, Parry was still able to summon up a certain amount of malicious glee when talking about another's character.

'I wasn't asking if it was against the law or not — I was asking why you've got it on your mantelpiece.'

'I was very fond of my brother. I like to have a part of him near me.'

Cobb eyed him in a way that suggested he found the explanation lacking. 'If I'd come here to make a will I think I'd find it a little off-putting.'

A spark of defiance. 'I can only say, then, that the Welsh are made of sterner stuff. No one's ever said anything about it to me. Besides, everyone round here knew my brother and he was very highly thought of indeed, I can tell you.'

They left him there, standing proud in the room, one hand lovingly caressing his brother's skull, and descended the stairs in silence.

Once outside, Cobb exploded. 'I'll make sure that smug bastard is struck off if it's the last thing I do. What's the betting Susan Davenport wasn't the only person in this town who's been ripped off by our Mr Parry?'

'You think he's made a habit of this?' Bould asked as they made their way through the now-empty car park behind the Green Dragon as the last of the light dwindled away.

'He'd be ideally placed for it. Most solicitors who get struck off do so because they've got sticky fingers. Still, that's not our concern. The Law Society can send in forensic auditors to find out just how badly behaved he's been. More to the point, why did Susan want £50,000 so desperately?'

Bould unlocked the car and swung the driver's door open. 'As Parry said, she must have committed some sort of crime if she was worried about prison.'

'But where — here or in her past life in London?' Cobb climbed into the passenger seat. 'By the way, why didn't you tell me Eleri Griffiths was Welsh?'

'Because I didn't know; she doesn't sound Welsh and I'd never heard the name before.'

'Parry says it's a common name round here. You said she was lying about Susan being a keen gardener — could she be involved in this?'

'Why would she identify the body? Wouldn't she keep quiet if she'd killed her?'

'Murderer's vanity — she wants to affirm her belief that the police are not half as clever as she is. Pretends to help us and all the time is laughing up her sleeve at our inability to catch her out.'

'You haven't met her, sir. I don't see Miss Griffiths as being capable of murder — at least, not that way. Poison perhaps; something cosy and remote, but not marching her victim down to a frozen pond in the middle of a winter's night, and somehow forcing her into the water. She couldn't force a cat to drink a saucer of milk if you ask me.'

'Still, I think we ought to pay her another call tomorrow, and perhaps we'll take a nice big bottle of milk with us.'

6

She woke with a start, lungs empty, terror filling her stomach, and blood pounding in her ears as she gasped for air.

Beside her, James stirred and opened one eye. 'What is it, baby?' he mumbled, still half asleep.

Panic subsiding, Diana said: 'It's all right; I just had a swine of a dream, that's all. Go back to sleep.'

And he did, instantly, when what she really wanted was for him to wrap his arms around her and say everything was going to be all right, even if it wasn't.

The strange thing is the funeral should have made her feel better, but it hadn't. Having been convinced the dreams would end once her stepmother was buried just made the night's terror worse because it was so unexpected, and it began to dawn on her that perhaps these hauntings would never end. She had thought, watching the earth as it cloaked the coffin, that the past was also well and truly buried. That was why she had dragged the pair of them all the way to that godforsaken one-horse town of Lampeter;

even knowing she would have to speak to that reptile, Ioan Parry, hadn't stopped her going. Now it all seemed to have been utterly pointless. Nothing had been achieved.

Her skin was damp; her hair sticky. Creeping out of bed so as not to disturb James, she padded into the bathroom and took a warm shower. Perhaps if she sold up and moved abroad. A fresh start somewhere where no one knew her and she knew no one; perhaps peace would come with anonymity. Maybe she could take a leaf out of Susan's book and change her name; the thought of becoming a new person appealed so much, as long as you could shed your memories and emotions as easily as you could your old name. Deep down she knew that wasn't possible. New name, same old Diana Davenport. Same old memories and same old nightmares.

Maybe if she went somewhere hot, like Australia, where there would be no icy Februarys to remind her of that terrible day. It was probably time to move on from James anyway. They'd had a good innings but he wasn't to be trusted, and she could never forgive him for that.

As she watched soapy foam cascade down her arms she wondered why they were still together. How was it he had this hold over her. Is this what they called love? Magazines were always full of stories of women who stood by their men regardless of the terrible things they had done. It was something that was beyond her comprehension. How could you stay with a man who beat you regularly, gave you injuries that required hospital treatment? Yet in a way that was what he had done to her and she was putting up with it.

'Baby, what are you doing?' James was in the doorway, looking annoyed.

She stepped out, contrite that she had woken him. 'I couldn't sleep. I thought a warm shower would help.'

'You need to see someone; get this sorted out.'

'What good would talking to someone do? It's my problem, and I'll deal with it my way. I always come out on top.' She started briskly towelling herself down and spoke with some force.

He came over to her. 'You don't even know what the problem is, so how can you sort it out?'

'I do know what the problem is — I can't sleep at night for unpleasant dreams.'

'So you need to find out what is causing these dreams, for my sake if nothing else. You're not as strong as you think you are. Why else do you drink so much? You're losing control; look at the way you carried on today.'

She stopped drying herself. 'What's that supposed to mean?'

'You were drunk at the reception.'

'Don't be ridiculous. I only had two glasses.'

'At the reception. What about the bottle you put away before we left London?'

'It wasn't a bottle; don't exaggerate. I had a glass or two, that was all, and can you blame me after everything I've been through?' She couldn't look at him, focusing instead on a spot on the wall above his shoulder.

He was instantly defensive. 'And what's that supposed to mean?'

'You know what that means. My childhood with that woman in Wales and everything I went through before and after we went there.'

'Well, that's just it, baby. I don't know what you have been through. Oh sure, you're always hinting at your traumatic childhood but I can't see what was so terrible about it.'

'No, you wouldn't. You weren't there.'

'Sounds pretty idyllic to me, growing up in the countryside; a rich father . . . ' he let his words trail away.

'Here we go again. I might have guessed we'd get round to your family background before long.' She heard her words, and hated herself for saying them. She was picking a fight quite deliberately and didn't know why. On reflection, she did know why. There had been a time when he had always been there for her; now he had to be punished for transgressing.

'I'm going back to bed. I need to get some sleep before it's time to get up and go to work. Try to be quieter.' There was disgust in his voice, and the look he shot her dared her to disturb him again.

He didn't know what she knew. He'd have looked more disgusted if he did.

After he'd gone she sank down on the edge of the bath and towelled her hair.

Idyllic childhood in the countryside!

If David hadn't died perhaps she wouldn't have been so lonely. Only children were always lonely. How she'd envied her school mates who had brothers and sisters. She hadn't often been allowed to have a friend round to play. Susan had hated children and made no pretence about it. It was strange how some women completely lacked any form of maternal feeling. She didn't have it either, but that was hardly surprising, all things considered.

★   ★   ★

'You know what puzzles me?' Cobb asked, somewhat rhetorically as he chewed on a jam

doughnut. 'The Davenports have been living
— hiding — quietly away in Lampeter for
nearly twenty years before Susan is threatened. Why — what happened then? Did some
figure from her past appear suddenly, by
chance maybe, and recognise her?'

'Perhaps it took them that long to trace
her,' Bould replied. He had stuck to black
coffee without sugar, as his girlfriend had
suggested to him the previous evening that he
was getting a little flabby around the waist,
teasingly patted his stomach to make the
point, and as he found himself thinking of
Cathy Treharris rather more than he had
thought of any woman before, he had taken
her remark very seriously indeed.

Cobb sighed, a long and regretful noise. 'I
think we're going to have to do a lot of
digging around in the distant past. We'll start
by going through the records, see if either of
the Davenports' names crop up.'

'How far back do we go?'

'I suppose that depends on which one of
them has the guilty secret. If it was Diana
then thirty years should do it. If it was Cecil,
then we might be going back even further. If
there's nothing in the records we'll have to go
through the newspapers of the day, see what
they can throw up. Thank god we live in the
age of modern technology.'

'But it appears to be Susan who was being blackmailed. Parry said she told him she couldn't ask her husband for money because she faced a prison sentence.'

'Assuming Parry's told us the truth; there's something about that man I neither like nor trust.' Cobb brushed the sugar off his fingers, gulped down the last of his coffee and stood up. 'Right then, let's go and beard the redoubtable Miss Griffiths.'

★ ★ ★

Eleri seemed pleased to see the policemen and ushered them into her lounge and then went, unbidden, to make tea, eventually returning with a tray containing not only an old-fashioned china tea service with dainty cups and saucers but a plate of chocolate biscuits as well. Cobb was more than pleased to help her eat them, but Bould politely turned them down.

'Now then, Miss Griffiths, I expect you've seen in the local papers that your neighbour's name wasn't Eliza Hobbis but Susan Davenport and the reason we've come to see you is because we need to clarify your story,' Cobb said, and gazed sternly at her.

Shifting uncomfortably on the sofa, Eleri averted her eyes and then occupied herself by nibbling on a biscuit.

He let the silence grow before continuing. 'You see, you told my sergeant here that Mrs Davenport was a keen gardener but we can't see anything to suggest that is the case. In fact, her garden's a bit of a mess.'

'It is winter, Inspector.' She answered primly, trying to regain her composure, but colouring slightly all the same.

'True, but then I've just had a look at her tools. Now, keen gardeners look after their tools; they have a comprehensive set and keep them clean and well oiled, and broken tools get thrown out. The state of Mrs Davenport's few tools tell me she was no gardener, so we would just like to know why you told us this story. For it is a story, isn't it?'

He could almost hear the pop as she deflated, and as her cloak of smugness fell away he could see Eleri Griffiths for what she really was: a lonely and unhappy woman. He wondered how many people she got to speak to in a day.

Staring into her teacup she said in a small voice, 'I don't know why I said that. The words just came out, I couldn't help myself. I do it a lot, I don't know why I say some of the things I do.'

But Cobb did. It made her feel important. 'Do you come from round here?' He asked, and surprised her with the change of subject.

'No, I don't,' she perked up, appearing pleased to have been spared a ticking off. 'I come from Ty'n-y-Groes,' adding helpfully, 'it's in Wales.'

'Whereabouts in Wales?'

'Gwynedd.'

'Could you be more specific?' Bould enquired.

'It's not far from Llandudno.'

'What made you leave . . . ' Cobb briefly considered trying to pronounce her home village and thought better of it, settling for a simpler: 'Wales.'

Eleri folded her hands into her lap, straightened her shoulders and, looking directly at Cobb, started her tale. 'After my father died my mother sold the farm — there was no son, see — and she didn't want to stay in Wales. She'd been a Land Girl in the war, that's what she was doing in Wales; she wasn't a local girl at all. She didn't ever really settle; the winters were too cold and the hills too bleak. She liked the Cotswolds better; she knew it from her childhood, so we moved here. We got a good price for the farm because some incomers from Birmingham bought it. They didn't know a thing about farming; they just wanted to play at it. And then there was the history of the place

— morbid it was, their interest, if you ask me.

'The history . . . can you explain?' This couldn't have anything to do with their investigation, but Bould was intrigued all the same.

She was more than happy to oblige. 'There was supposed to have been a murder done there in the past, see. Some milk maid done in by the farmer because she resisted him, if you know what I mean.' A pause here and a meaningful look, as if she wasn't certain they would know what she meant.

'Go on,' Bould encouraged.

'It was a long time ago but the farm was ever after known as Yr Ty Coch.'

'Meaning?' Unlike his sergeant, Cobb hadn't got time for irrelevancies.

She turned to him, eyes huge and dark, and in a theatrical voice said: 'It means the Red House, Inspector. Red as in blood. The house of blood.'

Saints preserve him if this wasn't turning into a Victorian penny dreadful. 'And you moved here with your mother, when?'

'Nine years ago, it was, almost to the day.'

'Forgive me for pointing this out, but you don't have a Welsh accent,' Bould said.

'No, my mother was English, as I have already told you. She preferred me to speak as she did.'

There was no explanation as to why this should be and Bould assumed it was due to snobbery. Perhaps her mother had thought she'd married below herself.

Cobb asked: 'You didn't work?'

'I was a PE teacher in Wales, but I'm retired now.'

Would the occupation of everyone concerned with this case never cease to amaze him? He knew it was often the case that when fit people gave up sport they quickly ran to fat, and she was no spring chicken, but even so not in a month of Sundays would Cobb ever have guessed at this plump, prim little woman's former profession.

'Did you specialise in any particular sport?' Bould asked.

She turned towards him, pleased to be able to genuinely impress. 'Yes, as a matter of fact, swimming was my forte. I could have swum for Great Britain if I'd wanted.'

7

Sergeant Bould smiled as he turned the corner and saw the sleek blonde head of a certain WPC emerging from an office.

'Hello, Cathy, how are you doing?'

He was rewarded by a great smile that deepened the laughter lines round her mouth. 'I'm doing just fine, Neil. How's tricks with you?'

'Things are going OK at the moment.' He smiled back and asked: 'How do you fancy dinner on Saturday?'

Her mouth turned briefly down in disappointment. 'I'd love to but I'm on duty . . . I'm free Friday evening, though.'

'That's good with me. Friday it is.'

'Great. There's a new Thai restaurant opened in town; shall we try it?'

'Why not? I'm always up for something new.' Thai food wasn't his favourite, but if she wanted to go there, it was all right with him.

He entered the CID room in fine form. It was half empty, which was DC Constable's bad luck. His worst luck, of course, was choosing to become a policeman with that surname. It was just as well he had a good

114

sense of humour because it had certainly been put to the test ever since he'd joined the Force.

At the moment he was engaged in sipping at a mug of strong tea whilst intently studying his computer screen.

'Good — just the man I need: I've got some research for you,' Bould said, slapping the case notes down on the desk.

'Fire away,' Constable replied, never taking his eyes off the screen. He seemed to be scrolling through columns of figures.

'What's that all about?' Bould nodded towards the screen.

'Just tracking how some of the money from the Post Office robbery last November has been laundered, sir. These crims are getting smarter every day. Look here; see how they're moving it around.' He leant forward and tapped the screen with his pen, indicating a particular set of figures.

It was horses for courses. Like his boss, Bould preferred to be out there on the streets, but the modern police force needed staff like Constable who thought heaven was contained in a computer screen. He even looked the stereotypic computer geek. In his mid twenties, tall and gangly with thin brown hair, already showing signs of receding, he had that pale look of someone who rarely sees natural light, and he was a godsend to their team.

'Can you put that on hold for the moment? I want you to see what you can find on a Cecil and Susan Davenport. They were living in London up to around twenty years ago. Neither has a criminal record — I've checked that out already — so local or national papers might be a starting point. If necessary, widen the search, but see if they might have been involved in something they shouldn't have.'

'You only want me to check around twenty years ago, not more recently?'

'They've been living in Lampeter in Wales since then. It's a very small, close-knit place; the sort of place where everyone expects by right to know another's business, so we'd have found out any scandal from there by now.'

'An address in London would be a help.'

'Sorry, we don't have one. In fact, the only reason we think they came from London is because that's what they told people. But as they seem to have told people a lot of things that weren't true we might be heading down a blind alley here. All the information we have — such as it is — is in the file. Still, I have every confidence in you turning something up, Ian.'

Constable grinned. 'It's amazing what you

can find out these days without leaving the room. Do we have any deadlines?'

'Just the usual; we wanted it yesterday, but there's no rush.'

'Great. I only joined the police because I wanted a job with no pressure.'

★　★　★

'You know what I like best about a late start? It's not having to rush to get ready for work in the mornings. It makes me feel really decadent.' Cathy said as she padded barefoot into Bould's kitchen.

He laughed and poured out two cups of coffee. 'I doubt you'll be feeling very decadent by the end of your shift tonight. Fancy a cooked breakfast? I could do us scrambled eggs.'

'Do you know something? You're the most domesticated police officer I've ever come across, and I'm talking both male and female. Just look at how neat and clean your kitchen is.' She sounded bemused as she looked around. It was not just neat and clean but ultramodern too; it looked more like the sort of professional kitchen you'd find in a restaurant — stark in its simplicity. A kitchen created to produce good meals, rather than one for living in, for sharing wine and meals and laughter with family and friends.

'My mother died when I was fourteen. As the eldest of three by some way I decided I'd better learn to cook, as there was probably a slightly lesser chance of everyone dying from the effects of my cooking than there was from the heart disease we'd all end up with from our only other culinary option — a endless diet of takeways.'

'What about your father?'

'He handled his grief by working all the hours he could. Beside which, he was ambitious for his children. He had plans for us to go to university.' Bould had broken six eggs into a glass bowl and set about whisking them up with some milk and butter.

Cathy leant against the black granite work surface and sipped her coffee. 'And did you?'

'Yes, we all did. My youngest sister's a doctor and my other one became a merchant banker.'

'There's variety for you. Two ended up serving the community and the third wrecking it.'

Her sardonic tone brought a smile to Bould's lips. 'Actually, it's all three of us now. Janine was working for Lehman Brothers when everything went so badly wrong. She lost her job and decided that money wasn't everything after all. She's now retrained as a teacher.'

'Good for her! Look, is there anything I can do to help? I feel even more decadent standing here doing nothing whilst a man cooks me breakfast.'

'No, nothing. Just enjoy the peace and quiet whilst you can — it won't last.' He poured the eggs into a pan, adjusted the gas flame on the hob and carried on whisking the mixture as the heat did its work. Cooking, like gardening, came under a therapeutic heading, despite his lighthearted remark. His father had thrown himself into work and he had thrown himself into cooking and had found the ability to create something out of nothing extremely satisfying. Now, if there had been some way to combine haute cuisine with an outdoor life that would probably have been what he'd have ended up doing. A sort of Indiana Jones meets Jamie Oliver.

As it was, he'd never had the chance to put his cooking skills to any sort of useful purpose in the workplace. The part-time job he'd had when a student flipping burgers in a fast food restaurant didn't count, obviously. Absolutely no culinary talent required there whatsoever. Alan Palmer, the owner, had been sufficiently impressed to offer him a permanent full-time job on graduating, thereby demonstrating the utter contempt in which he held Cambridge University degrees. Bould could still recall the look of incomprehension on Palmer's face when he'd turned him down. It made him smile now, just recalling it.

'Come on, share the joke,' Cathy teased.

But he shook his head, 'It was nothing, I was just reflecting on a possible career I might have had long ago.'

'You'd have liked to have been a chef?' she guessed and, having finished her coffee, peeked into the cafetière, hoping there was enough for refills. As there wasn't she tipped the grounds into the bin, filled the kettle and added new coffee to the pot before getting to what was really on her mind. 'Neil, you know I want to join the CID? Well — '

His mobile phone started to ring and the display told him he had to answer it. He cut her short. 'Damn. I'll have to take this.'

'Neil, sorry to spoil your free morning. I hope you're dressed. I'm down at the gravel pits. Get yourself here right away,' his boss instructed. 'We've got ourselves another body.'

★   ★   ★

The weather was still making its mind up whether to snow or not as Bould left his

120

house. It tried blowing a few thin flakes in on a gusty north wind and then stopped, thought about it and started again. In the gutter, dust and what was left of last year's leaves were swirled up into mini-tornados.

He'd left Cathy soaking in a hot bath, seeing no reason for her morning of planned decadence being ruined just because his was. All he'd had time for was a shower taken so quickly the water barely had time to run hot.

By the time he reached the gravel pits the weather had settled for hail; hard and stinging in the teeth of the biting wind, it drove into Bould's face as he hurried over to the little knot of people gathered around something lying on the ground by the water's edge, at almost exactly the same spot another body had been hauled out only a fortnight ago. The branches of the trees lining the bank were being whipped helplessly from side to side in the gale.

Cobb saw him coming and moved aside so the body was visible. It was Diana Davenport, naked and looking like the statue of some exotic goddess carved from the whitest marble.

Cobb said, 'Local dog walker spotted the body just over an hour ago.'

Bould took a good look at the corpse. 'Do we have a cause of death, sir?'

'Jenny thinks she may have been strangled.'

At the mention of her name, the pathologist looked up. She was squatting on the far side of the body, and despite the terrible weather was still smiling. With hair plastered to the side of her head and a network of rivers coursing down her face, she blinked several times in an effort to clear her vision, and wiped her brow, which cleared it of the rain for all of a split second. 'There's some bruising around the neck and the pattern looks about right, but whether that was the cause of death or not I can't say at present.'

'Bearing in mind she's naked, is there anything to suggest a sexual assault?'

Jenny pursed her lips and frowned. 'Hard to say, but it doesn't look like it. There's no other bruising, no sign of a struggle, nothing under her finger nails, but I'll have more to say once I've done the PM.'

'I'd like the results as soon as possible,' Cobb said. 'I want to know if she was dead before she went into the water, or whether she drowned.'

'What's she doing here?' Bould wondered. 'Does this place have some significance?'

'I'd say so, seeing as how we're the best part of a hundred miles from London; and bearing in mind that as she didn't exactly

122

strike me as grief struck, I'd doubt she came here out of sentimentality. So, let's get back to the office. We need to do some serious brainstorming. There looks to be precious little forensic evidence here. We don't even have her clothing, and someone is going to have to tell the boyfriend. He appears to be the nearest she's got to a next of kin.' Turning his back on the wind, Cobb started to walk towards his car and his sergeant fell in step. They each pondered their thoughts until they reached the Audi; then Cobb said: 'I've called the whole team in; the CS isn't going to be best pleased. This will all have to go down as overtime.'

★ ★ ★

'What have we got? A woman and her stepdaughter found dead in the same location. The first drowned, the second probably didn't, but there must be some significance in the fact they were found in the same place; particularly if Diana Davenport didn't drown. Putting her body in the water is the killer's way of making a statement.' Cobb stood before a whiteboard displaying what precious little information they had so far gleaned about the case scrawled in red pen underneath the photographs of two dead women, and addressed the half-dozen members of his team seated in a semi-circle.

'Is water, rather than the gravel pits themselves, the salient point?' Bould asked. 'I remember Ioan Parry telling me Susan Davenport had left all her money to the RNLI. She was supposed to be frightened of water and never went near it, according to her employer, so why would she leave her money to the Lifeboat people?'

'Good point,' his boss acknowledged. 'Usually, people make such a bequest out of gratitude. It's possible the reason Susan was frightened of water was because she had nearly drowned at some point in the past, so it may or may not be of any relevance. Ian, have you come up with anything useful yet?' He had to call DC Constable by his first name because if he said 'Constable' half a dozen people would answer.

He got his answer in a shake of a head. 'Nope. Give me some more time on it. There's a hell of a lot of stuff to go through and it's a shame she couldn't have had a more unusual name — something like Tijuanna Inkwell would be good.'

'No one has a name like that,' Cobb snorted. 'Keep at it. The more I think about it the more I think the key to all this is in the past; way back before they left London. If we can find that out, I think we'll have cracked the case. Has anyone managed to locate the boyfriend yet?'

Rose Cadoxton stirred in her seat. 'We've had no joy. He's not answering the telephone at the property and we don't have any other contact details.'

'Right.' Cobb had made up his mind. They needed to search the flat anyway. 'Sergeant Bould, get your jacket — it's your lucky day. Aren't you always saying you'd like to spend more time in London?'

★ ★ ★

It wasn't hard to gain access to the block of flats. The 'trade' bell let them in.

'Look at the time, it's after midday and that button is still operating,' Bould spoke in a tone of weary exasperation. 'Don't any of these people realise the risk — anyone can gain access. There's just no point in having a security system unless they use it intelligently.' It was a favourite theme of his.

They took the lift to the second floor and when there was no answer to Diana's bell, they knocked on the door and when that achieved no result they rang the bell of the neighbouring flat.

'Yes, can I help you?' A woman, old with

grey hair swept up in a chignon and flawlessly made up, held the door open about three inches and addressed them with suspicion. 'If you're selling anything at all, I might as well tell you now I never buy from door-to-door salesmen.'

They waved their warrant cards at her through the gap and suspicion gave way to curiosity, but the door remained unyielding. 'Is something wrong? I don't suppose you've finally decided to come and do something about those wretched children at last.'

Cobb ignored that last part, and not wishing to conduct his interview from the landing asked, 'May we come in?'

In response, she opened the door wide and they entered a hallway of old-fashioned elegance. Following her into the lounge, Cobb wondered if she had been a dancer in her youth. Despite appearing to be about eighty she was ramrod straight, slim and walked as if she was cutting daisies with her feet.

'Please sit down gentlemen. I am Honoria Lucas. Can I get you some refreshments?' Her words were formal; 'old school' Cobb thought and revised his opinion from ballet dancer to minor aristocracy.

He looked around a room filled with the possessions of a long life. There was a lot of furniture, all of it antique and top quality. The walls and ceiling were painted in duck egg blue, and an impressive chandelier hung from an exuberantly moulded ceiling rose. A few ornaments graced the mantelpiece and the top of a beautiful walnut escritoire. There were several paintings on the walls, all of them with their own brass viewing light above. The place reeked of money, and plenty of it.

'No thank you, madam.'

'Then how may I help you?'

'It's actually your neighbour, Diana Davenport we're interested in. I wonder if you know if she lives alone.'

'Good gracious, I've never known Diana live alone! She's always got some young man or other in tow.'

'We met her recently at her stepmother's funeral in the company of a James Grogan.'

'Oh, him.' She was both dismissive and contemptuous at once.

'You don't like him?' Bould asked. He was admiring a small painting on the wall which appeared to be an original Augustus John.

'I suppose compared to some of her young men he was passable. I'm afraid I'm going to have to sit down, gentlemen, even if you won't. It's my knees, you know. It's only one of the terrible perils of getting old.' She smiled briefly as if this was a joke and lowered herself carefully into a dusky pink velvet wing chair, set to face the balcony windows.

Cobb moved round and pulled up an easy chair so that he was on eye level with her. 'Is there some reason why you disapprove of James?'

'He works in the City — so vulgar, don't you think? He's a hedge fund manager.' If she had said he was Harold Shipman there couldn't have been more scorn and revulsion in her voice. 'Obsessed with money and liked to talk about how much he earned. In my day, one never did that: ostentatious therefore vulgar, as my father always used to say.'

'Do you know where he is now?'

'He's been in Leeds most of the past week; something to do with work, he said. Then tonight he is motoring down to Oxford to visit some old college friend. I'm expecting him back tomorrow evening.'

'What about Diana? You said you were expecting him back. Do I take it that she has also gone away?'

With a gentle inclination of her elegant head to show he had assumed correctly, Honoria replied: 'She's gone to Wales to clear out her stepmother's house and sort out some personal possessions.'

'When did she leave?'

'Yesterday around lunchtime.'

'And is that what she told you herself, that she was going to Wales?' Bould asked, relinquishing his scrutiny of the paintings.

'It is. She asked me to keep an eye on the apartment whilst it was empty. You can't be too careful these days, as I'm sure you will know, being a police officer.'

'Did she, by any chance, leave a key to the flat with you?' Cobb said. He was hoping she had, otherwise they'd have to get a locksmith out. The doors of these flats weren't made to be broken down by a hefty kick or a muscular shoulder, and even if it could be done, he could just picture CS Black's face when presented with the repair bill.

'Indeed she did. She wanted me to go and water her plants.'

Cobb got to his feet. 'If you could fetch the key for me, Mrs Lucas. We need to take a look round the flat.'

'I cannot let you have the key, Inspector. Even I know you need a warrant before you can search a property.' She spoke calmly but firmly and gave him the sort of look she probably used on 'those wretched children'.

Cobb had been hoping not to have to tell her before he had spoken to James, but could see there was nothing else for it. 'I'm afraid I have some very distressing news for you. Diana Davenport was found dead this morning.'

Honoria took the news completely in her stride. He had expected some protestation, some cry of dismay, but she remained silent and regal in her chair. Eventually she spoke: 'Poor Diana. I suppose it was drugs.'

'What makes you think that?'

'I just assumed . . . ' surprisingly flustered, her composure broken, Honoria made a strange, swift motion with her hands as if physically pushing the idea away. 'I'm sorry. Am I wrong?'

Bould crossed the room, an expression on his face like that of a hound who had just picked up the fox's scent. 'But why did you assume that it was drugs? Did you know Diana was taking drugs?'

'All young people take drugs these days. We even did it in my day, you know.' Her blue eyes, faded almost into transparency with old age, danced with amusement. 'Now I've surprised you. Why do young people assume all the sublime pleasures in life were invented by them? Vice has been in the world for at least the past two thousand years, and probably a lot longer. Hedonism didn't start in 1960, you know.'

'I'm sorry to labour the point, Mrs Lucas,

but do you know for a fact that Diana was taking drugs?' Cobb asked, even though he couldn't see that it had any relevance at the moment.

Their hostess hesitated, obviously deciding how to frame her words and started delicately: 'Young people speak so casually about their drug habits. At first, I think it might have been to see if she could shock me, and later on it was just in a very matter of fact way.'

'Did she specify which drugs she used?' Bould said.

'She mentioned smack.' It sounded totally incongruous, almost surreal, hearing the street slang from such a refined mouth. In the small silence that followed, Honoria struggled to raise herself from the chair, impatiently waving away the officers' attempts to help her. Cobb was glad she didn't have a walking stick; she was the sort of grande dame who would have used it to give them a good whack, had they had the nerve to try to help her.

Once upright, she said: 'I'll go and get the key to her apartment,' and walked out of the room without any trace of difficulty.

'Have you seen these paintings, sir?' Bould spoke in a low voice, anxious for Mrs Lucas not to hear him. 'They must be worth a

131

fortune. There's a John here and a Matisse, and a Van Gogh.'

Cobb looked sceptical. There was money here, right enough, but surely not that much. 'They're probably just very good reproductions,' he said, having taken a good look at all three. The Van Gogh was studied particularly closely. 'If this one is genuine it would be worth millions.'

'I hope her security is good. I think I'll contact the local Crime Prevention Officer when we get back and get him round here to advise her. An old lady like this, on her own, with seriously expensive art on the walls. It's asking for trouble. She thought we were door-to-door salesmen, and when you think about that entrance system downstairs.'

'This is the key to Diana's apartment, Inspector.' Honoria had returned soundlessly and quickly. In her outstretched hand was the key attached to a solid silver key ring with a large 'D' encrusted with diamonds.

'Thank you,' said Cobb, taking the key. 'Would this be her own or a spare one?'

'It's the one she always leaves with me, but she has her own.'

'It's a very expensive key ring just for the spare key.' Cobb turned it in his hand, feeling the weight. 'I would have thought she'd have used this for her personal keys.'

'I believe it was a birthday present from a previous beaux; James didn't like it because of the connotations and preferred her not to use it. May I ask, if I'm not being presumptuous, how Diana died, for you haven't told me.'

Cobb gave her his most diplomatic smile. 'I'm afraid we are not at liberty to say just yet, Mrs Lucas. You wouldn't have any contact details for Mr Grogan would you?'

'I'm sorry to say I don't.'

'Ah well, thank you for all your help. You've been most kind.'

On the way out, Cobb turned to the old lady and said, 'Your knees don't seem to give you any pain walking.'

She laughed thinly. 'No, Inspector. It's a peculiar thing, but it's only sitting down and getting up that gives me problems. Once I'm on my feet I have no trouble at all.'

★   ★   ★

They let themselves into a hallway the same size and shape as the one they had just left; but that was where the similarity ended. Mrs Lucas's property spoke of old money and old times, but Diana's flat was contemporary with a vengeance.

'It's not going to take us long to search this

place,' Bould observed wryly.

'There's something to be said for the current trend towards minimalism,' Cobb agreed, and walked through to the master bedroom.

Fitted wardrobes in oak with brushed steel handles ran along one wall, a matching chest of drawers and dressing table stood opposite and in between was a steel-framed king-sized bed. The wardrobe contained both male and female clothing and a great deal of scuba diving equipment.

'Water. We always come back to water.' Cobb said, holding up a drysuit. 'This has to be hers; it's too small for a man.'

'She was strangled and dumped in the water,' Bould carried on the thought process. 'There was no need to do that if she was already dead.'

'We need to know where she died and why her killer made a special journey to dump the body in the gravel pits.' His fingers touched something hard at the back of the wardrobe. Drawing it out Cobb saw it was a book, a Clive Cussler novel. He read aloud the inscription on the fly page: ''Here's to a very Happy Christmas and lots more of them. D',' then he asked Bould: 'Why would he hide away Diana's Christmas present?'

'He could have been intending to take it to

Leeds. If he was working up there for the week he'd have had a lot of hours in a hotel bedroom to kill. He might have put it there, meaning to pack it and then left it behind accidentally. You don't think it could have any significance, sir?'

'No, how could it.' The book was dropped where Cobb found it, at the back of the wardrobe.

Bould started rifling through the chest of drawers. 'Could Diana's death be revenge for Susan's? Might she have been put in the same pond as some sort of closing of the circle?'

'The other alternative is that the killer's seeking revenge against the whole of the Davenport family for some past wrong, but whatever the significance of the gravel pits is I've no idea.'

'Sir.' In his open hands Bould showed his boss the packets of white powder. 'They were in the top drawer.'

'We'll get them analysed when we get back, but no prizes for guessing what they are. As Mrs Lucas said, they're all at it these days. What we need to find is her handbag, the one she was using when she died, and see if you can find a mobile number for James anywhere. We need to contact him.'

'Why would Diana have told Mrs Lucas she was going to Lampeter to sort out

Susan's belongings?' Bould flicked through the contents of Diana's underwear. It was a hateful task and made him feel vaguely voyeuristic, particularly when he saw the type of underwear Diana went in for: mostly red or black satin and lace and very sexy. He was glad to be finished with it and move on to the second drawer, which contained thin jumpers, all neatly folded and fitted in together like jigsaw pieces.

'Because she didn't want to tell her where she was really going and we need to know where that was . . . unless Ioan Parry somehow fits into the picture. I don't like that man, and trust him even less. You said he knew her address and phone number by heart.' Cobb had been going through the hanging clothes in the wardrobe, taking each one down and going through any pockets, but receiving no response to his remarks, he turned round.

The jumper drawer sat on the bed, half empty, an assortment of tops in an artist's palette of colours strewn around it. Bould held a sheet of paper in his hand and was reading it intently, a frown on his face. 'Check this out, sir,' he said quietly and handed the paper over.

It was a certified copy of a death certificate, dated 12 February 1987, for a David William

Davenport, and whose date of birth was 14 June 1979. The cause of death was shown as heart failure, but what really caught both policemen's attention were the names of the boy's parents: Cecil and Marion Davenport, and their address.

'This boy was eight when he died. Is heart failure common in eight-year-olds?' Cobb wondered aloud but didn't expect an answer. 'How interesting that Diana never mentioned she had had a brother.'

'It was hidden at the back of the drawer, folded up in one of these jumpers, so she didn't want anyone else to see it.'

'I don't suppose she would, if she's been telling everyone she's an only child. Some people can't cope with the death of a loved one — they blank it out — it's possible she could have been in denial, or maybe she couldn't bear the sympathy of strangers when she told them.' Cobb found himself jumping to her defence; all deaths were tragic, but that of a child the most. Plato, or was it Aristotle, said you never got over the death of a child and he knew that to be true. Julia had only been six hours old when she had died in her parents' arms. Some people had been astonished at his and Sarah's grief, even going so far as to ask them how they could feel such attachment to a child who had scarcely been: such a brief life had left no time for a personality to grow, nor even any time for a name to be given until the last hectic few minutes of a life that had existed only between one sunset and one sunrise, but in that time she had danced across their hearts and left footprints that could never be washed away, no matter how many tears they wept.

Sarah had found it impossible to conceive again, and Cobb knew in his heart of hearts that was why he had found it difficult to bond with Carly for so long. In an insane way, he resented the fact that she — the product of Sarah's union with another man — lived whilst their own daughter had died, and even when he was able to acknowledge his attitude was irrational and unfair it was still a long time before anything positive came of it.

The anger he had felt on this pointless waste of a life not given the chance to be spilled over into his working life. Murder had always saddened and repulsed him, but now it took on an almost personal aspect. The callous contempt some people had; the arrogance with which they snuffed out another's life for reasons that were often so petty as to be beyond comprehension, for several years drove him forward in a way that first impressed, but later worried, his superiors. Latterly, the anger had dimmed. He still couldn't make sense of his loss but he had learned to accept it.

'There's this as well,' Bould held out a colour photograph, old now, with curling edges.

It had been taken in a sunny garden one summer. The boy was squinting into the camera but there was no mistaking the colouring and the high Slavonic cheekbones. He had a heart-shaped face and anyone could see he would have been mischievous.

Cobb turned the photograph over. There was a date on the back: 2 June '86. 'This was taken six months or so before he died, yet he looks the picture of good health to me.'

'Could it be this Sudden Death Syndrome? It's not just babies that are affected; I've read of adolescents, otherwise fit and healthy, who've dropped dead for no reason.'

'Often after playing an energetic sport like football, yes, I know. We'll need to find the doctors who treated him. In the meantime, as we're here, I think we'll pay a visit to 62 Goldhurst Terrace. It's a long shot after all this time, but we may find a neighbour who remembers them.' Cobb tucked the paper away. He looked round the room, noting the mundane things of everyday life. A hairbrush on the dressing table, perfume and make-up, nail scissors and an emery board, all anonymous, inexpensive, even trivial items — thousands like them were sold every day — yet each one a deeply personal possession that together made up some part of Diana Davenport.

In the bathroom they found two types of shampoo, shaving foam and aftershave.

'Why did she make out she lived here alone? What was the point? It doesn't appear she kept him a secret from the neighbours.' Puzzled, Bould picked up the bottle of CK for men and turned it over in his hands as if half expecting to find the information he wanted printed on the back.

'More to the point, why did she take him to the funeral? He couldn't have known Susan.'

'She was pretty tanked up by the end. Maybe she wanted a chauffeur.'

'Everyone in this case seems to be a compulsive liar — either that or they've got more secrets than all the Borgias put together; and that's no mean feat.' Dispirited, Cobb walked through to the kitchen and began to methodically work his way through the cupboards and drawers. There was nothing of interest; in fact, there was virtually nothing there at all. He concluded that the pair must have eaten out most of the time, because of the lack of cooking utensils and a fridge that only contained two large bottles of vodka, a dozen cans of Red Bull and three bottles of white wine.

Returning to the lounge, he met Bould coming out of the bedroom. 'Any joy with a contact number for the boyfriend?'

'Nothing, sir.'

The bookcase was the only item of furniture that could possibly hold any surprises, so they removed all the books, upending them to see what fell out. Nothing did.

'Right. Let's go to Goldhurst Terrace and see what might be — ' Cobb stopped abruptly, for out on the landing he could hear a key turning in the lock. It couldn't be Mrs Lucas and she had said James wasn't returning until the following evening. Did this mean someone else also had a key to the property?

Both policemen turned to face the lounge entrance and waited. The front door opened and closed and the sound of a couple of cases being dropped down reached their ears. Then they heard footsteps coming smartly down the hallway and finally James Grogan walked into the room, immaculately dressed as ever, even though he was only wearing a white open-necked shirt and chinos. His thick black hair was swept back off a face that was already beginning to show the effects of too much rich food and drink. In a very short time he would become fleshy and portly, but with his luck it would probably just give him a certain air of authority, of gravitas.

There was something about him that exuded privilege, money and good living. He was the sort of man Cobb automatically disliked on sight and not entirely without good reason. Too many Grogans had sat before him in countless interview rooms up and down the country, refusing to speak until their solicitor arrived, arrogantly confident that they were too superior to the rest of the human race to be charged with anything, even when the evidence was stacked against them. Should a solicitor be foolish enough to point out that it would be more sensible to plead guilty, they sacked the hapless lawyer. Astonishingly, even when confronted with irrefutable proof they invariably refused to acknowledge they had done anything wrong. They accepted that the crime in itself might have been bad had it been committed by a lesser member of the public, but not by them. Oh no, they always found it easy to justify their behaviour.

Grogan stopped in his tracks, discomposed. His head swivelled from Cobb to

Bould as if he was following a tennis match and his lips turned up in an open sneer. 'What the hell are you doing here?' Without waiting for an answer he continued, his words an insolent drawl, 'and how the hell did you get in?'

'Your neighbour, Mrs Lucas, lent us the spare key.'

'*Lady* Honoria Lucas.'

Cobb ignored the correction. 'The reason we are here is because we have some bad news for you. Diana Davenport was found dead this morning.'

As if he hadn't heard, Grogan stared long and hard at Cobb but his lips lost their disdainful curve. 'I'm sorry. I don't understand. What do you mean?'

Grief struck people strangely; the newly bereaved often went into denial. Cobb had seen it many times. Once a woman had physically attacked him, clawing at his face and leaving deep scratch marks, when he had to tell her that her husband was dead. They had had to call out the police doctor to sedate her heavily that night.

'Miss Davenport's body was found in the same flooded gravel pit as that of her stepmother,' Bould said.

'You're saying she drowned. Impossible — she was an excellent swimmer.' The uncertain tone had left his voice; he was on sure ground here.

'I'm saying she was found dead in the gravel pits at Cotton Country Park. The exact cause of death has yet to be determined,' Cobb explained formally.

It began to sink in. Like a blind man, Grogan felt his way to the sofa, and collapsed in it, burying his head in his hands. 'Oh God, not Diana, oh God, no, not her as well.' A sob escaped from behind his fingers. Then he seemed to pull himself together; clasping his hands tightly before him as if physically holding himself in one piece. 'Was it an accident?' A look of wonder replaced the grief on his face. 'What was she doing in Gloucestershire?'

'That's what we would very much like to know,' Cobb answered. 'You can't shed any light on the matter?' When he got a shake of a head in response, he continued: 'She told Lady Honoria that she was going to Wales to sort out her stepmother's house. Do you know why she would have lied like that?' When all he got was another shake of the head, Cobb got tougher: 'Lady Honoria also told us you would be away until Sunday night. Can you tell us why you returned today?'

'Umm,' Grogan looked around as if for

inspiration. He seemed too dazed to think straight, and spread his hands wide. 'My friend's father was hospitalised with a stroke this morning so he had to drive up to Manchester as a matter of urgency. Obviously, there was no point me staying on as he wouldn't be back until at least tomorrow night, so I came home.'

Bould got his notebook out. 'Can we have the name and address of this friend?'

A malevolent look was cast his way. 'For God's sake, do you doubt my word? And anyway, what are you implying — that I've got something to do with Diana's death?'

'Please be reasonable, sir,' Cobb intervened. 'These are routine questions we have to ask. As I said, the cause of death is undetermined at present, but we have reason to believe it was not an accident.'

'You don't think I had anything to do with it? I loved her!'

'Then why did she tell us, when we visited her ten days ago, that she lived here alone?'

When he answered, Grogan spoke incredibly slowly, as if he was constructing an entirely new vocabulary, or talking to an idiot. 'I have no idea, perhaps she thought it was none of your business, as — I have to say — I would agree.'

Now if there was one thing Cobb did not

like, it was members of the public telling him how to do his job — even if they were apparently grief stricken. 'It is most definitely our business, I'm afraid, Mr Grogan. I've had two unexplained deaths on my patch in little more than two weeks, and that these two deaths are connected is beyond question. Two women, related by marriage, found dead in the same spot . . . so we need to know the name and address of your friend in Oxford.'

Looking slightly chastened, Grogan said surprisingly meekly, 'It's Patrick Belfield, 32 St Bernards Road.'

'But he isn't there at the moment, from what you've said. Can we take it he's staying at his parent's address in Manchester?'

'He's staying at his father's house; his mother died some years ago. Do you want that address as well?'

'Please.'

'64 Manton Street, Handforth. It's near Wilmslow in Cheshire.'

'Thank you, sir. We'd like the phone number too. Will he be able to confirm you were together last night?'

Anger filled Grogan's eyes, he clenched his fists, and Cobb got the impression the man wasn't used to taking orders or having his word questioned.

But when Grogan answered, he sounded

calm and reasonable. 'Yes, he will. We went to the cinema and afterwards we had a late supper at an Italian Restaurant in Oxford. We returned to his house at around midnight.'

'And then?'

'Then I went to bed — by myself.'

'So no one can actually account for your movements after midnight?'

Grogan exploded. 'For God's sake, are you suggesting I got up, drove to Gloucestershire and, having lured her there, killed her? Why, why would I do that?' He had leapt to his feet and was shouting as he strode towards Cobb.

Bould stepped smartly between the two. Nothing was said, but looks were exchanged and Grogan swung away breathing heavily.

'You must understand that we have to explore every possibility, otherwise we'd be accused of not doing our job properly,' Cobb said blandly. 'There is one other thing I would like you to do when you feel up to it. Please have a careful look around the flat and let me know if any of Miss Davenport's clothes are missing. We also would like to find her handbag, that is, the one she was using at the time of her death. We can't find any sign of it. I'd also like to know if her car is here. If it's not, we need to know the make, colour and registration number as soon as possible.' He fished in his pocket for

147

a card. 'You can reach me on this number any time.'

It was taken with barely a glance, so Cobb pressed the point. 'It's very important we find her clothes and handbag.'

Now his words hit home. Grogan reacted strongly. 'You mean she wasn't wearing anything. Oh my God, was she . . . you know . . . had she been assaulted?'

'We won't know until we get the results of the post-mortem but, if it helps, we have no reason to suppose that was the case. What we do think is that Diana's death is connected to that of her stepmother. When you feel up to it we would like to speak to you about their relationship.'

'I can tell you all you need to know right now because I know nothing about their relationship. I've never met Susan, and Diana simply refused to talk about her. Will you excuse me, Mr Cobb? I feel in need of a drink. I won't ask you to join me because you're on duty. In fact, if you've finished, I'd rather like to be alone.' Grogan began walking towards the front door, without looking back at the officers and seemed to be in complete control of his emotions once more.

★   ★   ★

Darkness had fallen by the time they reached Goldhurst Terrace, which was a long street of solid red-brick Victorian semi-detached villas built for the burgeoning middle classes. With nice solid brick walls surrounding the houses and mature gardens, full of shrubs and small trees that competed to fill the space, it was a pleasant street, shady in summer. Most of the houses had been turned into flats and number 62 was no different.

They chose to ring the ground-floor bell, and a harassed looking young woman with lank blonde hair pulled back into an untidy ponytail answered, juggling a baby on her hip. In the background they could hear the excited commentary of an American football match.

When she saw their warrant cards she went and fetched her husband, who clearly wasn't pleased at being dragged away from the television.

'No, I've never heard of any Davenports,' he shook his head to emphasis the point. 'But then, we've only been here for five years and this house was converted to flats getting on for twenty years ago. It's possible some of the other people in the street might remember them but I doubt it. We don't know any of the people next door, and that house was converted to flats back in the seventies from what I've heard.'

They tried a few more doors around about and drew a blank every time. Even when they found people in, none of them remembered the Davenports.

'That was a waste of time,' Cobb said, as they walked back to their car. Not that he'd expected anything else. It was only curiosity that had taken him round there. He wanted to see what sort of house Cecil Davenport, businessman, had lived in. And it didn't appear that he had been particularly successful. Goldhurst Terrace, behind the Finchley Road, in Swiss Cottage was a very expensive and desirable area today — but then that went for all of inner London — and Cecil had been sixty when he left at the end of the eighties, which meant he could have bought the house as far back as the 1950s — a time when Swiss Cottage was far from upmarket. It was one of thousands of equally undistinguished semis in what, in the fifties, would have been the suburbs.

'At least we've got the address to go on. Ian Constable might be able to do something with that,' Bould said, determined to get something out of what appeared to have been a completely wasted visit to Swiss Cottage.

'That child — David — we need to contact the GP who treated him and find out what was wrong with the boy.' They had reached

150

the car. Cobb stopped, one hand on the door, and turned to Bould. 'Do we think the child's death has anything to do with the murder of his stepmother and sister?' He didn't really expect an answer, he was just thinking out loud, throwing ideas around.

'It might at least explain why they left London and hid away in Wales. Where they went to live — it's very remote and lonely. You haven't seen the house, sir, but I drove out to it after I saw Scheherazade Jones. There was no other property for at least a half a mile in any direction.'

'Licking their wounds, you mean? Yes, and it would also explain why Susan Davenport wanted a job to take her out of the house. It wasn't her child who died, so would she have been grief struck? Probably not: maybe she didn't even care. Did she marry Cecil thinking that she was set up for life? If so, it must have been a terrible shock when the boy died and they decamped to Wales to turn in on themselves. All this time, we've been thinking they were running away from *someone*, but perhaps it was *something*.'

8

It was amazing what a difference a good night's sleep made. The world seemed a brighter, more hopeful place. It helped that the sun was shining, even holding a little warmth that led the more optimistic folk to affirm that spring really was just round the corner.

Heading towards his office, Cobb's mood became even more cheerful when he saw Bould approaching from the direction of the canteen, bearing gifts in the shape of chocolate doughnuts.

'Good man,' he shut the door and poured some coffee, noticing that his sergeant had already helped himself. 'Now sit you down, I want to do some thinking: but first things first. Let's concentrate our thoughts on the Davenport case. The first thing that puzzles me is why did Diana Davenport go to her stepmother's funeral? If you dislike someone, you keep away; it's as simple as that. Instead of which, she travels a considerable distance, takes the day off work — boyfriend as well — for what?' He took a bite of the doughnut and washed it down with scalding black coffee.

'She seemed quite upset about something, judging from the state of her.'

'Yes, and that was odd too. She struck me as a very confident and self-contained young woman when we met her in London, yet a week later she's a wreck. Why — what happened in between times? Perhaps we should look into her movements, see if she was in contact with anyone significant.'

'Could she have gone to the funeral specifically to see Ioan Parry? She said he had bled Susan dry, so maybe she knew about the money he'd lent her and the interest he'd charged?'

'Susan and Diana hadn't spoken to one another for years, so how could she have known? Parry himself wasn't likely to tell Diana, so unless . . . '

Taking up where his boss had stopped, Bould finished the thought, 'Unless it was Diana Susan gave the money to.'

'But why? Why would Susan give her stepdaughter money? Diana got most of her father's estate, she's got a good job; she shouldn't be short of money.'

'Maybe she did it just because she could. Scheherazade Jones said Susan always seemed to be trying to make amends for something to do with Diana, and Parry said she told him she could go to prison for what she'd done.'

'So Diana might have been blackmailing her stepmother, but over what? Does her brother's death come into it? The death certificate stated heart failure — natural causes. There doesn't seem to be anything suspicious there, but then I'm not a doctor.' He descended into silence as he finally took a bite from a doughnut. 'Get the team together in half an hour and I'll come down to talk to them.'

The pair left the office at the same time, Bould turning left to the CID room and the DI heading down to the morgue.

'Hello, Jenny, what have you got for me?' It was amazing how the sight of the pathologist always lifted Cobb's mood, even when she was, as now, bent over a corpse.

Straightening up from her examination of Diana Davenport, Jenny replied: 'She was manually strangled by someone standing in front of her and was dead when she went in the water.' A bloodied scalpel was dropped into a metal dish. The ting it made seemed to fill the tiled room.

Cobb glanced away from the lifeless form on the slab. 'What about time of death?'

'Sometime between 8 p.m. and midnight. I'll know more when I get the eyeball potassium levels back. What I can say is that the blood pooling in the body indicates that she was sitting down, either at the time of death or immediately afterwards and remained in a sitting position for some time.'

'Would you say that suggests after she died she was transported in a car to the gravel pits?'

Jenny peeled off her latex gloves and pushed some errant strands of grey hair from her eyes, beaming at him as a teacher might reward her pet pupil. 'Yes, that would certainly fit the bill.'

'Anything else to tell me?' he asked hopefully.

'No, nothing. I'll see what toxicology has to say, but there's no sign of a struggle; there are no scratches, bruises or marks on her hands to suggest she tried to fight off her attacker, which is unusual.'

'We know she used drugs, and I've seen for myself how much alcohol she can put away. If she was under the influence of one or the other, might that explain the lack of a struggle?'

'Yes, indeed it could. Have you found her clothes yet?' Jenny asked over her shoulder as, her work finished, she went to the sink and started sluicing her hands and forearms down.

'No clothes, no handbag and no indication as to where she died.'

'That's a shame.'

'That's one way of putting it. If you could let me have the toxicology report ASAP I'd be very grateful.'

'I'll do what I can, but every department is understaffed at the moment.'

'Don't I know it! Still, it won't be your problem for much longer. You don't know how lucky you are.'

The whiteboard was beginning to look like a demented spider had spun a web over it. Red lines linked various photographs of victims and places to questions that awaited answers.

Cobb studied the board and tried to see if there was anything that jumped out. The significance of the gravel pits worried him. They weren't well known or easy to find. A stranger to the area would be unlikely to know of their existence. He looked at the picture of Susan Davenport. It was her passport photograph. They could find no other, so it wasn't the best. There was no clue to personality in the face that stared directly into the camera.

But the manner of her death had been premeditated, so someone had a grudge against her, and a particularly strongly held grudge because the retribution they had chosen to mete out was particularly nasty.

Drowning was not a kind way to kill someone. It wasn't quick and it wasn't easy. She had been frightened of water — that had to be relevant.

'Right, let's brainstorm this one,' he turned to the assembled team sitting or standing attentively in a semi-circle in front of him. 'Ian, I want you to find out all you can about the brother. We particularly need to trace his GP and any other doctor who treated him. Rose, I want you to check up on James Grogan's movements. Check with his friend and the restaurant in Oxford to see if he was really there when he says he was.'

'Oxford to Slipslade is less than an hour's drive. It would have been tight, but he could have done it in the time available,' Bould said.

'What's his motive?' Cobb looked round, inviting a response.

'Most murders are domestic, sir,' Rose pointed out.

'Yes, they are, but how does Susan Davenport fit into this? She'd never met James Grogan and it's unlikely, therefore, that he could have known where she was living, even if he did have a motive for killing his girlfriend's stepmother. Now Diana was strangled, probably somewhere else, her body stripped and it would seem deliberately dumped in Cotton Country Park gravel pits.

Why? What's the significance of that place?

'Susan Davenport's husband was a businessman. Before the gravel ran out, those pits were a flourishing business. Did Cecil Davenport have some financial connection with them? The answer to these murders lies in the past — I'm convinced of that. The fact that Susan changed her name, and came to live in a place where she had no connections whatsoever encourages me to think she was frightened of someone. She'd come to Slipslade to hide away, but someone found her. Could it be someone who felt swindled by her husband? Someone bitter that the Davenport family had money that the murderer felt was his or hers by right? Is that why he killed the two remaining family members?'

'But why wait twenty years? If Cecil had been involved in a dodgy business deal, why not kill him at the time?' Ian Constable asked.

'Perhaps it's taken twenty years for our murderer to trace the family,' Bould contributed. 'His business dealings would have been in London. Once he'd upped sticks to Wales it might have taken someone a long time to trace him, by which time he was dead of natural causes. So if you're looking for revenge you'd have to settle for the widow.'

'If they were hiding away, why didn't they change the family name? Davenport is not a particularly common name, so would it have taken that long to trace them? Remember, the killings only started after Cecil died. Was his death the catalyst for all that has happened since, as DS Bould has suggested?' Cobb was throwing ideas into the air. Thinking aloud was his favoured method of getting the whole team involved and he was pleased that everyone chipped in with their own thoughts.

'I've already done a search for Cecil Davenport and his business connections,' Constable said. He was sitting at his desk as if he couldn't bear to be separated from his beloved computer, which was pretty much the case. 'He seems to be as clean as a whistle. He owned a small factory in the East End making women's clothing. He expanded the company in the sixties and then sold out about the time he married Susan. It all seems quite legit and above board.'

'Keep on digging; there might be something,' Cobb said. 'The other way to approach this is to ask ourselves what the two victims had in common, other than Cecil Davenport.'

'If what we've been told is true, Diana had nothing to do with her stepmother once she reached eighteen, so there isn't likely to be anything that connects them, is there?' Rose has started off confidently enough, but faltered as she went on, rethinking what she was saying, before coming to the logical conclusion. 'Unless it goes right back to her childhood.'

'Exactly. We keep coming back to the past.' The trouble with that was everyone from the past was dead. Cobb didn't find that thought encouraging. You couldn't interview the dead. 'So . . . to recap. What have we got? A clothing factory owner who sold out and moved his daughter and second wife to Wales after his son died, and where they kept themselves to themselves. Twenty years on, he dies. His widow promptly moves away, changes her name, gets herself pregnant by a mystery man and is murdered. Less than two weeks later, her stepdaughter is also murdered and her body placed in the same pool.

'What might be useful is if we could find out whether Cecil Davenport was always reclusive, whether he had ever expressed the desire to retire to the country, and whether they moved in a hurry — surprised their friends. They must have had some, so let's see if we can trace any. Is it Cecil who had the guilty secret, or his widow?'

'It's not going to be easy finding their old

friends from twenty years back,' Constable pointed out.

'No it isn't. Especially when we haven't got anything to go on,' Cobb agreed. 'DS Bould and I had a scout round their London address on Friday and couldn't find anyone who remembered them.

'We might have better luck trying to find out why Susan needed £50,000 so desperately. The solicitor, Parry, claims she told him she could go to prison so it's likely she was being blackmailed.'

'Then could she have been killed by whomever was blackmailing her?' The question came from PC Aaron Walker, a tall, thin man with a mop of curly black hair and an enormous amount of restless energy that seemed to make it physically impossible for all of him to remain completely still at any time. So if he was standing, as now, he constantly jingled the coins in his pocket and when he was sat at a desk, unless both his hands were occupied on the keyboard, he would drum out some endless tune with his fingers, much to the rest of the team's irritation. Once or twice tempers had flared as someone or other complained they couldn't concentrate because of the unceasing noise of his fiddling, and he would swear to stop it — which he managed to do for no longer than it took him to say it.

In the brief silence that now followed his question all that could be heard was chink, chink, chink, as the coins knocked together in Walker's pocket.

It was beginning to get on Cobb's nerves, so he answered rather testily, 'It's usually the other way round. Blackmailers don't kill the goose that's laying their golden eggs.'

'Could she have threatened to expose whoever it was by going to the police? If she was being hassled for more money and she was unable to pay, she might have said she'd go to the police even if she didn't mean it, just to get them off her back, and maybe they believed her and decided to kill her to protect themselves,' Rose suggested.

'It's certainly a possibility we must consider, along with everything else. We also need to know who the father of her child is. The neighbour — Miss Griffiths — says she didn't have any visitors. Those that knew her in Lampeter say the family kept themselves to themselves. So where and who is the father. I was hoping not to have to plump for something along the lines of an immaculate conception.'

'But perhaps it was something along the lines of an immaculate conception,' Bould said thoughtfully. 'She was forty-two, time running out if she was getting maternal and no man in her life. What about IVF? Perhaps not in Britain, because of her age, but abroad there are plenty of clinics that don't have the same regulations we have here.'

'Good point,' Cobb nodded his approval, 'but there's nothing in her medical records about this, and I'm assuming she would have consulted a doctor first.'

'I wouldn't be too sure,' Constable said. 'You can find anything you want via a computer these days. She could have got details of a clinic online.'

'There wasn't a computer in the house,' Cobb said, 'and bearing in mind the family lifestyle in Wales, I'd be very surprised to discover she knew how to use one. Their lifestyle seems to have more in common with the Amish than Microsoft. However, if she was pregnant through IVF then it's not likely to have any bearing on her death. If her child was conceived in the more usual way then we do need to find the father.

'And finally, we need to find Diana's car. Her boyfriend's told us it's missing. We've got an all-Forces trace out and hopefully when it's found we'll know where she went to the night she died.

'Right, that's all for now. You've all got your tasks. Ian, you're going to trace the GP and see what other business dealings you can uncover, particularly regarding the company that operated the gravel extraction. It's a long shot but there must be some significance in both the bodies being found there, especially as Diana certainly didn't drown and possibly died elsewhere. Rose, you've got the boyfriend's movements to check out, and Aaron, I want you to look into the personal life of the Davenports in London. Find their friends and any family members on either side we could speak to. There must be someone out there with the information we need.'

9

The address was ocean view, Anstey's Cove Road, Torquay.

'Nice to be able to retire here,' Bould observed, driving slowly along the road high above the English Channel. On his left, wide grassy banks gave an interrupted view over water the colour of the sky, which on that February day was the brilliant pale blue of late winter. Sunlight hitting the sea splintered into thousands of diamonds, temporarily blinding Bould.

'It's this one,' Cobb said, indicating a large early twentieth-century villa on the right.

Spring had reached Devon earlier than it had in Gloucestershire. The air was heady with the scent of Winter Sweet, softening the hard edge of winter.

A white wall surrounded Ocean View. Its principle aim seemed to be to contain the jungle of shrubs and plants spilling over the top and brushing the heads of passers-by. The path to the front door was lined with daffodils, Kaufmania tulips and muscari in full bloom. It looked as if an artist's palette had been thrown into the garden.

A large middle-aged woman answered the door. She was wearing a pinafore and holding a duster in one hand and a can of polish in the other.

'We're looking for Dr Mathers; he is expecting us,' Cobb explained by way of introduction.

'Oh yes, that's right. He did tell me. Do come in. He's in the lounge — it's upstairs where the view is — I'll take you up. I expect you'd like some coffee and cake; you must be famished after your journey. I'm Dora Adams, I come in every day and look after doctor. His wife died three years ago and I think the poor man's lonely. I cook all his meals for him.' All this was delivered in a breathless monologue as she led the way up the stairs.

As soon as they entered the lounge they could see why the living arrangements were upside down. The whole length of the front wall was given over to windows that faced south over the sea, allowing the sun to pour into the room all the daylight hours.

With the help of a stick, an elderly man struggled from a wing chair pulled up close to the window. If he hadn't been so stooped he would have been at least six feet tall. The skin on his face was as yellowed and papery as parchment and his hands shook but his voice

166

was firm and clear. 'In the summer the sea is full of vessels. I never tire of watching them, you know. I guess it's the little boy in me but there's something magical about a boat. It's the sense of escape and adventure they engender. I look at the yachts and think 'you could be going anywhere in the world' — but they're probably only going round the coast to Dawlish.' An impish grin lit up his face and he held out his hand. 'Gordon Mathers, pleased to meet you. Come and sit down; I've no doubt Dora's gone to bring the three of us enough refreshments to feed a battalion.'

'It certainly is a wonderful view you have, Dr Mathers,' Bould observed, looking around the large room. It was light and sunny and yet had the feeling of being a temporary refuge, like a summer house. It didn't really feel lived in. Perhaps it was because there seemed an odd jumble of furniture in the room, as if the owner hadn't been able to decide what he wanted to use it for.

There was a sofa and several unmatching chairs arranged in a semi-circle around the window and behind there were an old drop-leaf dining table with barley twist legs and four chairs with shabby upholstery dating from the pre-war period — basic but sound in construction and created with no intention of being objects of beauty. The carpet was a pale green, and well worn to the point of being threadbare in places. The walls were haphazardly hung with an assortment of pictures that were mostly seascapes of the quality found in the many little art galleries around Torquay selling paintings as holiday souvenirs, but there was a rather fine series of nineteenth-century aquatints of various Devon landmarks. The room smelt of the sea and exuded a peace and calm Bould had rarely come across.

'I always wanted to live by the sea, probably because I was born in Birmingham and that's about as far from the coast as it's possible to get in Britain,' the old man said. He noticed the other two looking at a briar pipe lying in an ashtray on the windowsill. He grinned again. 'I know, don't say anything, and me a doctor to boot. You'd think I'd have better sense. Well, it's too late now; I've got to the age where something is going to carry me off sooner rather than later, so it might as well be the tobacco and it's one of the very few pleasures left to me — apart from naval gazing.' He looked up, his eyes glittering with pleasure at his own joke.

Cobb got the impression that the old man was nobody's fool and how they reacted would colour the whole tone of the interview. 'And you must see some fine naval sights from your window,' he replied, rising to the occasion.

The doctor chuckled, nodded in approval and then, hearing the clatter of crockery as his housekeeper entered carrying a heavily laden tray, said in some amusement. 'Ah, here's Dora now. What did I say?'

And indeed Dora did seem to have overestimated the number of visitors she was catering for. Apart from an old-fashioned china tea service and a collection of knives and cake forks, balanced somewhere in the middle of everything was a large Victoria sponge.

'Here, let me help you,' Bould sprang forward, lifted the tray from Dora's hands and set it down on the old table.

'Thank you, sir. Now, would you gentlemen prefer tea or coffee to drink? I prefer tea myself but I know what you young ones are like. It's all latte and cappo-whatever it's called. We used to have coffee bars when I was young back in the fifties and we drank what they called frothy coffee. There was even a pop song about it; what was it called now? Oh yes, 'Fings ain't wot they used to be'. It was 'fings' not 'things'. It's the way they talk in London. It was ever so popular.' Dora came to a halt only because she had run out of air.

Cobb wondered how Dr Mathers coped, but he had paused too long to let her know that he would prefer coffee, and black at that, because she had refilled her lungs and now, to everyone's astonishment except perhaps the doctor's, burst into song.

Her audience was treated to a fine version of the song in question and its coffee related theme, warbled in a surprisingly fine alto. Then she beamed at the speechless police officers.

Cobb didn't take any chances this time and leapt into the pause. 'I'd like a black coffee, please.'

'And I'll have the same,' Bould hurriedly followed suit.

'And I don't need to ask doctor what he'll have,' Dora said archly. 'Rain or shine, doctor only drinks tea. He likes it ever so strong and with three sugars. I wouldn't dream of telling him that amount of sugar is no good for anybody, what with him being a doctor and all, but it isn't,' she said in her matter of fact way as she bustled out of the room with all the frenetic energy of some demented mechanical toy.

'Dora's a good woman, I don't know what I'd do without her, but she does take some getting used to. I think she's lonely and comes here as much for company as anything,' Mathers explained, unconsciously parroting the same claim Dora had made about him. 'I can assure you that cake will be every bit as good as it looks, so tuck in. Dora baked it this morning in honour of your visit.'

'Can we get you something, sir?' Bould asked, slicing up the sponge, watching the knife stain with strawberry jam and cream, and thinking how much this was going to meet with Cobb's approval.

'You most certainly can. Dora's cakes are another of my ever dwindling pleasures in life . . . come to think of it, I don't do so badly. I've got my pipe, my view and a first class cook. There's not much else a chap needs in life at my age.' The doctor's tone had been wry, but now he became more serious. 'Well, Inspector, you haven't come all this way to marvel at the English Channel, so what can I do for you? You said it concerned a patient of mine from two decades ago . . . thank you.' The last remark was directed at Bould who had just handed the doctor a small plate containing a large wedge of cake.

Just as Cobb opened his mouth to reply Dora reappeared, bursting through the door with another tray, this time loaded with mugs of instant coffee, a pot of tea and an old-fashioned tea strainer suspended in its own little cup.

'Here we are,' she said completely unnecessarily, but they had realised by now that she was a woman for whom silence was a fearful thing, to be held at bay with words of any sort.

A great show was made of pouring the doctor's tea and the sugar was added in a way they couldn't fail to miss. As each spoon's cargo was tipped in there was a great deal of tutting and sorrowful head shaking. Finally she dipped the dainty little spoon into the cup and gave it the briefest of stirs before handing the cup and saucer over to Dr Mathers. The spoon was kept back. Only after all this did she hand Cobb and Bould their coffees. Dora was a woman who understood the importance of precedence.

'Do either of you take sugar?' she enquired, her equanimity restored. It appeared it was only the doctor's intake of sugar that disturbed her, although when they replied in the negative she couldn't resist shooting Mathers a look and, satisfied that she'd made her point, she once more bustled away.

As the door shut behind her Cobb was finally able to discuss the reason for their visit.

'I know it was a long time ago, but you had some patients in London called the Davenports. There were two children, a girl called

172

Diana and a boy called David. Do you recall them?'

'How could I not? They've been in my mind a lot these past few days. Poor Diana's death has been in all the papers, and her stepmother's too, of course. That family has had more than it's fair share of tragedy over the years. But that's often the way, I expect you've noticed it too in your job.' The old man's voice became reflective as the years rolled back in his mind. 'Diana was a very pretty child, I remember, but I always thought she had a rather detached personality. Her brother David was quite traumatised by their mother's death, but Diana seemed to take it better. It may be the case that she simply buried her feelings. Children tend to do that more than adults.'

'What can you tell us about David?' Cobb asked. 'He died very young, so did he have a congenital health problem?'

'No, it was very sudden. Today they call it sudden arrhythmia death syndrome — SADS for short. It'd due to an electrical problem in the heart. You might perhaps liken it to a fuse blowing, although that would not be a good analogy at all. Something — and we don't understand what or why — interferes with the electrical rhythm of the heart and it just stops.'

'And healthy children can die of it?' Of

course Cobb had heard of this happening but he wanted to be quite clear on the facts.

'Healthy people of any age can. It is more common in males than females, and presents itself earlier as well. As it happens, eight is the average age for males. Usually, the patient has had one or two non-fatal attacks where they lose consciousness before the last, fatal attack, but this doesn't always happen, and hadn't occurred in David's case.'

'But you were quite happy that his was a natural death?'

The doctor gazed steadily at Cobb for a long moment, and the answer, when it came, was oblique. 'I'm assuming you do not believe that to be the case or you wouldn't be here.'

'We honestly don't know the answer to that one. At the moment we're exploring all possibilities.'

'There was never any doubt at the time, if that's of any help to you.'

Bould said, 'Was Diana very upset by her brother's death?'

'She was hysterical, and ran away from home at least once during this time.'

Ears pricking up at this news, both policemen unconsciously moved closer.

'Is that a normal reaction in a child?' Cobb wondered.

'You have to remember that this was the second death in her family in two years. Imagine what that must have done to her. First her mother dies, then her brother. Who could be surprised that she thought she would be the next.'

'Is that why she ran away — because she thought she was going to die?' Bould asked.

'That's what she told her father. He consulted me several times to explore possible treatments. She had had to be sedated on the day her brother died. I remember she was completely incoherent . . . and angry. That always surprised me, how angry she was. It's common knowledge that grief goes through stages and anger is one of them, but it's not the first.'

'What was she angry about?' Cobb said.

'Just about her brother's death. She kept saying 'it's not fair, he couldn't help it'.'

'Couldn't help what?'

'Dying, I suppose. I couldn't get any sense out of her then and as the days went by she became more and more withdrawn and sullen. Then came the running away.'

'What about Susan Davenport — how did she react to the boy's death?'

'Ah, now she was very upset, and seemed to think it was her fault. She consulted me several times, presenting with anxiety. I remember I prescribed her valium and nitrazepam for a time.'

'Why did she feel guilty?' Bould asked. The pages of his notebook were turning at speed as he struggled to keep up with Mathers recollections.

The doctor sighed heavily and scratched his neck. 'It's another common reaction to grief, and as the child's stepmother she felt it had been her responsibility to keep the children safe. I don't know if you've ever seen anyone die suddenly of cardiac failure, Sergeant Bould, but if not let me assure you it induces the most terrible feeling of helplessness, and to witness the death of a child is simply the worst thing.

'Cecil Davenport was devastated, needless to say. First his wife and then his only son, and on top of everything else Susan had gone to pieces — she was barely more than a child herself — and his daughter had withdrawn into a terror-filled world of her own. I have to say I did think we might have had to get a psychiatrist to look at Diana at one point.'

'So what happened to make you change your mind?'

'She managed to make sense of events and pulled herself together. Children are remarkably resilient in this way. But then Cecil suddenly decided to move to Wales, and try as I might, I couldn't dissuade him. He seemed to think they needed to get away from the past, start afresh, you know how it goes.' Mathers shifted uncomfortably in his chair, stretching out one leg and twisting it from side to side. A spasm of pain distorted his features.

'Are you all right, sir?' Cobb asked.

'Yes, yes. I'm fine. It's just old age. It'll come to you too one day.' Although he was trying to make light of it, the harsh edge to his voice gave the game away.

'Should we fetch Dora?' Bould asked.

Mathers gave him an old-fashioned look. 'I'm afraid that despite Dora's many admirable traits, there is no help she can give me on this. I need a new knee. I've had my hips done already. Not sure I'll have the knee done. Do you think it's right for an old codger like me to take up valuable NHS resources, especially when I smoke like a chimney, eh. What do you think?' His gaze bounced from one to the other. Through the pain in them they could see the delight he took in being provocative. He obviously wasn't expecting an answer, because he immediately returned to the subject in hand. 'I've seen people react in this way many, many times and it's a mistake. After they've been bereaved, a lot of people want to move house. They can't bear to stay in a property that contains so many memories, you see. You go into a room and out of the corner of your eye you see a loved one sitting in their favourite chair. For a truly wonderful moment you think it really is them and then it hits you — they aren't there and never will be again and the pain is unbearable. This is what they tell me, and this is what eventually I experienced myself. It comes to us all, you know, in the end.

'Do you want to know why I stayed put after my dear wife died? Because I've listened to too many of my patients telling me how much they regretted moving. A house of memories might be painful, but a house with no memories is even worse. I suggested to Cecil that he wait awhile. The pain stops you thinking straight, you see. Don't do anything hasty, I told him. In London David will always be with you, but in Wales . . . ? They had no connection with the place whatsoever. It's my opinion he just wanted to move as far away as possible. I wouldn't be surprised to find he stuck a pin in a map and that's how they ended up there.'

'Do you think you could talk us through the day David died? Everything you can remember from the moment you were called? I realise it was a long time ago but it might assist us,' Cobb asked.

'Let me see now,' the old man's brows drew together in concentration. He picked up his empty pipe and fiddled with it, turning it round and round in his hands. 'It must have been quite early in the morning. It was the winter, I clearly remember that: a bitterly cold day, with snow on the ground, quite a lot of it too. It was Susan Davenport who telephoned the surgery. She was hysterical and just kept repeating 'he's gone blue'. I had to ask her who she meant several times before I got the reply. I told her to call an ambulance but went round there myself as I thought there was a good chance I'd be there before the ambulance because my surgery was at the end of the street and, as I'm sure you know, every second is vital at such times.

'When I got there — I think it would have been around 8.30 — I found David lying on the sofa in the lounge in his pyjamas. He had stopped breathing and although I started resuscitation it was hopeless.'

'Looking back, was there anything that struck you as odd, or out of place, at the time?'

The doctor nodded. 'Yes, he was extremely cold. But as I say it was a cold day and Susan told me he'd been playing outside in the snow when it happened.'

'In his pyjamas?' Bould interjected, sounding surprised.

'Oh come now, Sergeant. You must have been a child once. Didn't you get so excited when snow fell that you couldn't wait to get outside?' Dr Mathers chided gently. 'He appeared to have gone out in his pyjamas and barefooted, so Susan told me. I always felt that was what triggered the fatal attack. It was the shock of the cold to his system, if you like.'

'Would you know if he went out alone, or was Diana with him?'

'I don't know. I didn't ask, but as all my attention was concentrated on David I didn't give the matter any thought at the time.'

'So you think David might have gone outside alone? What did Susan say?'

'She didn't say anything if I recollect right. We just didn't talk about it. I'm a doctor. I was there to try to save the boy, not interrogate the stepmother, and it wouldn't have done me any good if I had tried. She was traumatised, which was hardly surprising.'

'And there's nothing else that struck you as odd about David's death? Please take your time, but think very carefully. Was there anything — anything at all — that surprised you about the state of the body?'

A silence developed. The old man lay back in his chair, eyes shut, pipe now still in his hands. Finally he spoke. 'His hair was wet; it was completely soaked and he didn't have any shoes on.'

10

Light footsteps could be heard, practically dancing down the corridor.

Cobb and Bould looked at each other. 'Jenny,' they said in unison, and sure enough, a few seconds later, the small, dumpy figure of the pathologist appeared in the doorway, waving a slim manila folder.

'Toxicology,' she announced and handed the file to Cobb.

'Any surprises?'

'Yes and no,' she turned to Bould. 'Those packets of white powder in her drawer — it was cocaine, but it was sleeping tablets she was full of, and a certain amount of alcohol. The quantity of sleeping tablets was excessive.'

'Would that explain the absence of a struggle as she died?'

'Definitely. I'd say she was barely conscious to begin with.'

'Thanks, Jenny. That, at least, clears up one problem.' Cobb took the folder and speed read it.

'Does it? I'd have thought it led to more than it solved,' she replied.

'If she was drugged, then a woman could have strangled her,' Bould said.

'Yes, definitely.' A vigorous nodding of the head accompanied her words.

'And it means her death must have been planned.' Cobb closed the file and pushed it to one side. 'It knocks on the head any notion that the killing was a spur of the moment thing. I don't suppose you've any thoughts on how the sedatives were administered?'

'There were no needle marks on her so she must have ingested them in food or drink. She'd eaten not long before she died.'

'So, someone lures her to their house, or calls on her in London. Presumably it was someone she knew if she was happy to sit down to eat and drink with them. When the drug takes effect they strangle her, strip her and take the body to the gravel pits. What the hell is the significance of that place?'

'I can't help you there, but if you ask me, as neither woman came from round here, it's more to do with linking their deaths together than anything.' Jenny turned to go, then remembering something, turned back. 'I'm having a bit of a retirement do next month. You're both invited and I hope you can make it. It's upstairs in the Golden Eagle pub. I'll let you know the exact date later, but this is advance warning — I won't accept any excuses for absence.'

'You can count on it,' Cobb said.

And Bould added, 'I wouldn't miss it for the world. You're going to be sadly missed.'

'Rubbish. You'll have forgotten all about me come Christmas.' But as she darted out of the room they both saw her cheeks had pinked with pleasure.

Cobb drew the toxicology file back and tapped it absently. He was thinking, but when he eventually spoke it was on another matter completely. 'I think my blood sugar is on the low side,' he grumbled and fished in his pocket for some change. 'Fancy a doughnut?'

When Bould returned with a plate of the sugary snacks he found the DI lying back in his chair staring at the ceiling, legs stretched out, deep in thought. He sat up at the sight of the food and fired a question at his sergeant. 'Does this mean we need to discount the possibility she was killed in the Maida Vale flat?'

'She could have been given the drugs anywhere.'

'True, but if she wasn't at the flat, then where was she? Lady Lucas says Diana told her she was going to Wales to sort our Susan's house, but that has to be a lie.'

'Could she have been meeting another man? Lady Lucas said she was never without one, and also that Grogan was the jealous type.'

Cobb raised his eyes heavenward. 'God forbid if there's another unknown figure in all of this. We still haven't found the father of Susan's child, and considering no man has come forward, I'm beginning to wonder if you're right about the IVF. The only other possibility is that he's our killer. The last thing we want to do right now is chase our tails looking for yet another mystery character. This case is more unfathomable than a game of *Cluedo*.' Cobb gloomily studied the doughnuts on the plate, eventually picking out the one with white icing and hundreds and thousands, but Bould knew his mind was on anything but the cakes, and he wasn't looking forward to imparting his next bit of news.

'Then this isn't going to cheer you up any, sir. Rose has spoken to James Grogan's friend, Patrick Belfield, and he confirms their whereabouts on the Saturday. They went to the cinema and then for a meal, to an Italian restaurant in Oxford. Rose has spoken to the manager and he confirms they were there. The table was pre-booked in Belfield's name. He knows Belfield well as he's a regular there and his dinner companion matches Grogan's description. Belfield says they returned to his flat about 10.30. They had a nightcap and retired to bed about 11.00.'

Cobb took a bite of the doughnut. At times like this, food was a distraction; chewing helped him concentrate. He also believed the sugar helped him keep alert, sharpened his mind. Strangely, he never ate cakes of any description at home. It was purely a work thing, and the more complex the case, the more he ate. 'That's an hour earlier than Grogan said, leaving enough time to drive from Oxford to either Slipslade or Maida Vale, depending on where Diana was when she died, and kill her within the time limits. He'd then have all night to dispose of the body and return to Oxford.'

'She might have been killed in another place altogether,' Bould pointed out and helped himself to a chocolate doughnut.

'Yes, agreed but let's not complicate matters more than we need to. What have we got? Lady Lucas said Diana left the flat at around lunchtime on the Friday. We need to find out where she was between then and when she died sometime later that evening.'

'If she went to Lampeter there is no way the boyfriend could have got there from Oxford in the time.'

'Can we think of any reason why she would go to Wales? The family house had been sold the previous autumn.'

'Parry? Does he come into this? Could she have gone to see him? He could have killed her. She made that remark about him bleeding Susan dry. Perhaps she threatened to expose him and he killed her in a fit of fury.'

Cobb considered this briefly and then blew out his cheeks in frustration. 'No, that doesn't hold up. We'd already found him out. He knew we were going to report him to the Law Society — by the way, we must get on to that next — so he knew exposure was coming. Killing Diana wouldn't stop that.'

'I've got on to it,' Bould said, pleased to be one step ahead of the boss. 'Filed the complaint last night after we got back from Torquay.'

'Well done. Let's hope they strike him off. He must be in breach of several regulations.' The slender threads keeping that man on his pillar of respectability had been snapped, and Cobb was glad of it. It was funny how chance played such a big part in life. Take this instance. If he hadn't gone to the buffet at the exact moment he had, would he ever have spoken to Mair Evans? It was unlikely, for he had had no reason to think the sale of the Lampeter house had any bearing on Susan's death. Ruminating on the random nature of events was a weakness of his.

Now Bould was looking at him quizzically, wondering where his thoughts had taken him.

He picked up a second doughnut. 'Do we know of anyone else in Lampeter she might have gone to see? At present, the answer to that is no. So then, is it reasonable to assume she came to the Slipslade area?'

'She could have returned to the Maida vale flat without Lady Lucas noticing.'

'But why would she do that? She gave her neighbour the key, remember, so she must have been planning on going away.'

'Yes, but she lied about where she was going.' Bould paced over to the window, put his hands flat on the sill and peered out as if longing to escape. Whenever he was baffled, the call of the outdoors was stronger than ever. 'So she might have lied about other things. She lied about living alone.'

His suggestion gave Cobb food for thought. 'You think she was a pathological liar. It's a thought. She struck me as a woman who amused herself by fooling other people. It's a form of arrogance, thinking you're that smart. So we're now looking at this for a scenario: had she planned on bringing a new lover to the flat that night? She gives Lady Lucas the key, partly to lend some veracity to the story, and partly because secretly it amused her.'

Sometimes it was necessary to play the Devil's advocate in their line of work, and Bould did just that. Although he had originally suggested Diana might have gone back to the flat, now he said: 'Bit of a risk though, wasn't it, sir? Suppose Lady Lucas had come in and caught them in flagrante delicto?'

'She's an old woman and probably goes to bed quite early. If Diana was planning on sneaking back late, very late, she'd probably be safe, and I think she was the sort of woman who would have relished the risk anyway.' Cobb rubbed the side of his head, as if washing away his thoughts. 'No,' he said firmly. 'I can't quite believe in this as a likely case. Scrub it. I don't think she went back to London. She was killed elsewhere. Slipslade is the most likely place, if you ask me.

'We'll start house-to-house enquiries in the area, see if anyone saw her there on Friday. One thing's in our favour. She was such a striking-looking woman she'll be remembered if anyone did see her.'

'But what would she be doing there: was she trying to get into Susan's house. Do you think there might have been something there she wanted?'

'God knows, and we're only assuming she

went there at all, or if she did, that it was of her own volition. She could have died anywhere, but there has to be some significance to the killer in putting her body in the water. If only we knew what. This family is the most secretive I've ever come across. We can't find friends, family, enemies.' The strangeness of the case disconcerted him. Motives for murder were few and universal — betrayal, jealously, money, revenge — and in most cases the motive became clear almost immediately. With this case it was like wading waist high through treacle in the teeth of a force twelve gale: impossible to get anywhere.

Bould's thoughts returned to his first trip to Slipslade, and the reason they were able to identify Susan so quickly. 'If Diana did go to Susan's house, I bet I know who'll have spotted her. They don't come any nosier than that Eleri Griffiths woman.'

'In that case, take yourself round there straight away and see if she's got anything helpful to tell us.' All that remained of the second doughnut was a few strands of sugar on the desk. Cobb swiped them onto the floor. The sugar had failed to buck him up; instead he felt intensely irritated with the lack of progress. 'She told Lady Lucas she was going to Wales. If that's not true, why did she lie? It suggests that she was up to something, something she wasn't prepared to talk to her neighbour about even though they must have known each other very well. You don't usually discuss your drug habit with someone unless you're on intimate terms with them, so why not tell her where she was going?'

'It's a pity the car hasn't turned up.'

'Yes, but what's the betting when it does it'll tell us nothing useful. There's something here we're just not getting.'

11

Hopalong wove his unsteady way down Wharf Road, until he came to the bridge across the Birmingham and Worcester canal, known as Parsons Hill. It was possible to get down to the water from here and he descended the steps very carefully, taking his time, holding on to the rail with one hand and counting each step under his breath as if the number might have changed overnight.

Having safely reached the bottom of the flight he turned south, onto a narrow, muddy towpath that was all over the place; because of this very few people used it, and that was its real appeal to Hopalong. He'd be all alone down here.

At this time of the year, the path was so wet it would have been downright treacherous had there not been a hard frost overnight that had made iron of the ground, and bringing different hazards as frozen ridges snagged his shuffling feet. Progress was inevitably slow as he needed to stop every now and then to take a swig of cider from the open bottle in his hand; at the same time he took the opportunity to check that the other bottle was still safely tucked away in his coat pocket. The coat had been respectable when Social Services had first given it to him, but that was years ago and now it was tattered, full of holes and with seams frayed beyond repair. Not that Hopalong had any intention of getting it repaired. He couldn't afford it for one thing and for another had far better things to spend his money on. When it got really bad he'd ask the Sosh for another. That was about all they were good for, he thought bitterly.

His view of Social Security was necessarily ambiguous. Suspicious of their motives, he usually spurned any help they offered on the rare occasions he hoisted himself into their orbit. The difficulty was what they viewed as help he viewed as interference. Take his drinking, for example: he didn't have a problem with it, so why should they? Interfering, bossy bitches, and most of them young enough to be his granddaughters. No slip of a girl was going to tell Hopalong what to do! Instead of trying to force him to go into rehab they should be doing something more useful with the taxpayers' money. Not that Hopalong paid tax as such. He hadn't worked since he was twenty-five. Still, there was tax on cider, wasn't there, so that counted. Over the years he must have paid a small fortune to the Chancellor, who ought to be grateful to him. In fact, the government ought to encourage more drinking, not less. It was the likes of him that kept the economy going.

A little way along the towpath there was a bench, very rudimentary, just a plank on two uprights without a back. Hopalong misjudged the width and plonked his backside heavily down on nothing stronger than air. The front of the bench caught him behind the knees, his heels shot skywards and he somersaulted backwards, rolling down the bank, cursing until he fetched up against a tangle of last year's brambles and scrubby overgrowth.

Any pain the fall might have given him was as nothing compared to the mental anguish of watching his precious bottle of cider roll away, leaving a fizzy amber wake streaming out. He made a desperate lunge to catch it and missed. The bottle disappeared under the brambles. He dove in without a second thought, groping blindly for what he called his 'medication'. The bottle had come to rest against something black, with two vertical red stripes, and his fingers touched leather. He hadn't a clue what it was, indeed wasn't sure whether it did have two red stripes or whether it was the drink already making him see double. He dragged the find out along with the almost empty bottle. Experience and poverty had taught him everything was worth investigating and in the daylight, squinting to focus, he could see it was a handbag. The clasp took him a full minute to open. The shakes were getting really bad these days, regardless of whether he had a drink or not, but finally he could see what was inside.

He couldn't believe his luck. Most of what was in there was junk and he threw various items out but, hallelujah, what had he found here: a ladies purse and wallet heavy and bulging with what had to be money. Oh, Hain, who's laughing now? He went for the wallet first, that was where the serious money would be, and counted out fifty pounds in notes. Fifty pounds! He counted them again, rolled them up and kissed them, then spent a few terrified moments wondering where to put them that would be safe. His coat was falling to bits. The pockets weren't safe, but where else could be put them? His trousers were even worse. He'd put them in a pocket but keep hold of them at the same time, just to be sure.

In a little flap in the wallet there was a bank card and a credit card in the name of D Davenport. He threw the bank card away but kept the credit card. The signature was a simple one and he'd been good at forgery in the days when he had a still hand. With a bit of practice he might manage to copy that signature. After all, D could stand for anything. David, for instance. He might manage to get some decent booze with it.

For the past fifteen years Hopalong had lived in his own little world whose boundaries were set by the amount of cider he had to drink. He'd never heard of PIN numbers. He pocketed the credit card with the fifty pounds and slung the handbag back into the bushes.

★   ★   ★

A torn newspaper page drifted down the street, its random progress decided by a capricious breeze. It gave a peculiar air of desolation to Meadow Rise. The long, winding street was deserted. The drives of most properties empty. Most of its good citizens were at work and the silence was overwhelming.

'I don't think I'd like to live here,' Aaron Walker remarked, looking around him. He'd spent the entire journey — which was mercifully short — tapping on the dashboard with a biro. Despite Bould twice requesting him to stop it (the second time very sharply) he had both times recommenced the tapping within seconds. At one point Bould had nearly stopped the car and made him get out and walk.

'I know what you mean,' agreed Bould. 'There's something of *The Stepford Wives* about the place. It's because it's transitional living,' Bould told him. 'It's where young couples live before they have children and move somewhere bigger and better and old people who are downsizing — probably not through choice — end up. It's the sort of place where you would expect everyone to know their neighbours and nobody does.'

'There's someone in, look.'

Behind an upstairs window a net curtain moved ever so slightly and a hand swiftly withdrew.

'Just as I said,' Bould remarked sagely. 'I knew that woman was just the sort to spend her days checking up on the neighbours.'

Although they knew she had seen them in the road, Eleri still kept them waiting a good few minutes before she came tripping down the stairs to answer the bell.

'Goodness me, what a surprise. I wasn't expecting visitors,' she said in falsely bright tones, rather over-egging the cake.

'May we come in? We just want to ask you some questions,' Bould said and was bemused by the reaction his words were met with. It was only fleeting, but in her eyes he saw fear.

'What about?' She didn't budge an inch but stood blocking the doorway, one hand on the latch as if ready to repel borders.

'If we could just come in,' Bould repeated before realising he could strike a chord with this woman easily. 'We don't want the neighbours seeing you talking to two policemen on your doorstep. They might get the wrong idea.'

'You are so right there. People are very nosy these days, don't you think? Of course, I have no interest whatsoever in anything my neighbours do, for I'm far too busy with my own life.' she was self-righteous once more, and stood aside to let them pass.

Once in the lounge, she hovered behind the settee, her fingers plucking at the fine tasselled fringe running along its back, looking worried.

On his last visit, when Cobb had accompanied him, she had been soundly told off for misleading them on the gardening issue. Did she think he had come here again to berate her further? So uncomfortable did she appear, so fearful, that Bould began to feel sorry for her and decided to put her out of her misery as fast as he could.

'It's all right, Miss Griffiths, please relax. I'm not here to arrest you.' It was supposed to be a joke, and he thought she'd have realised it from the way he said it, but her eyes flew open and she whitened, her fingers digging into the plush velour sofa. Like a rabbit caught in the headlights, she stared at him wordlessly.

Good lord, these old spinsters! Bould had no doubt she was a woman of complete rectitude, so he began to feel a twinge of impatience at this behaviour. 'Miss Griffiths, we are here in the hopes that you can help us. I know you said before that Susan Davenport never had any visitors, but I want to make quite sure that it really was the case. Are you certain no one ever came to her house?'

She swallowed hard, as if trying to clear a blockage from her throat, before replying. Then she lifted her head high and let go of the sofa. Her hands resumed their normal position of being clasped together under her bosom. 'I never saw anyone go to her house, apart from the postman that is. But why should I? I do have better things to do with my time and I would like you to know I am not one of those people who watch what their neighbours are up to from behind my curtains.' She spoke with gravity and without any apparent irony.

'No one is suggesting for a moment that you would do a thing like that, Miss Griffiths.' Two could play at this game. 'We just need to know if you might ever have seen anyone. It's extremely important. In particular, has this woman ever been here, to your knowledge.' Across the sofa Bould handed her a photograph of Diana.

'What a very beautiful woman,' she said, running her fingers over the glossy print, almost as if caressing the face.

'But do you recognise her?'

'No.' Her arm shot out and she thrust the photograph back at Bould.

It had been too much to hope for, and if she said she hadn't seen Diana he was prepared to believe it. That didn't mean she hadn't been here — even Eleri had to sleep sometimes.

★ ★ ★

The station's reception area was crowded. It always was, whatever the hour. It was done up to pass as a little waiting room with rows of plastic bucket seats. Bould thought it a singularly depressing place. The walls were a colour that was neither blue nor grey and the carpet was the same. The overall effect seemed like the perfect set design for a staging of Jean-Paul Sartre's play *No Exit*, but then he had always subscribed to the view that Hell very often was other people.

At the counter, the desk Sergeant was deep in conversation with Rose Cadoxton who looked up as Bould and Walker passed.

'I've got some good news for you,' Rose said, looking at Bould. 'We've found the car.'

'Does the boss know?'

'Not yet. I only heard a minute ago and he's nowhere to be found.'

'Where is it?' Just let it be somewhere that makes some sense.

'Dorridge.'

'Where the hell's Dorridge?' Bould asked when they were on the other side.

'It's in the West Midlands. The good news is it's not too far from here.'

'And the bad news . . . '

Rose looked bemused. 'There isn't any. I just thought you'd like some good news.'

'The bad news is that we don't have any reason to place Diana or Susan in Dorridge,' Bould pointed out.

*　*　*

On his way back from the staff canteen, where he'd eaten an overcooked roast beef lunch and discovered there were no cakes of any description left, Cobb met Bould marching purposefully towards him.

'We've found the car, sir,' his sergeant

201

announced. 'In a place called Dorridge. It's in the West Midlands, about fifteen miles south of Birmingham. I've arranged to recover it — should be back here in a couple of hours and then Forensics can have a go at it.'

'Whereabouts in this Dorridge was it found? Do we need to see the scene for ourselves?' Cobb said shouldering open his office door.

Bould followed him in. 'It was in a car park behind a shopping precinct, locked up. One of the shopkeepers got worried when she noticed it hadn't moved for several days and called the police.'

Cobb scratched the side of his head. 'Get me a map. I want to see where Dorridge is.'

The atlas was spread out on Cobb's desk and the two men studied it closely.

'It's very close to both the M42 and the M40,' the DI said, stabbing at the page, 'and it's very central. It's not more than an hour's drive from either Oxford or Slipslade. The question is: why did she go there? Who do we know of in this case with links to Dorridge? Don't bother answering, Sergeant; that was a rhetorical question. I'd have been happier if the car had turned up in Lampeter.'

Just then, Ian Constable put his head round the door. Any hopes his colleagues might have entertained that he was the bearer of good news were dashed the moment they saw his face.

'I've been going through Susan Davenport's bank statements, looking for that £50,000.'

Cobb perked up instantly. 'And?'

'It came in as a cheque drawn on Ioan Parry's personal account in June two years ago, but she drew it out in cash in amounts of £10,000 over the next five months.'

'In other words, we've no idea what she did with the money.' Cobb slammed the atlas shut as the only safe way to vent his frustration. 'Let me know when Diana's car arrives, Sergeant.' He dismissed both his officers brusquely, wanting some time alone to think the case through.

The next two and a half hours passed with Cobb making notes, trying to form some order out of the known facts. It wasn't a productive task and it was quite a relief when Bould rang through to say the car had arrived.

★ ★ ★

'In the 1930s, Henry Ford said you can have any colour as long as it's black; today he'd have said silver,' Cobb observed as they studied the Audi A4 Cabriolet. It was sitting in the middle of a cavernous shed at the back of the main police station in Gloucester where Forensics had already started to take it apart. 'I don't suppose you remember a time when all police cars were black.'

Bould shook his head and walked round the car, inspecting it closely. His footsteps rang out in the hollow space. ''Fraid not, sir. I remember the jam sandwiches, though, and Panda cars.' A snort of derision reached his ears.

'Panda cars! No wonder we lost the respect of the crims. They were like tin cans on wheels.' He peered in through the windows, taking in the mahogany dashboard and white leather seats. 'My old man was an accountant, but I can't imagine him ever driving around in a car like this.'

'She must have been on a damn good salary to afford this,' Bould agreed, trying to keep the envy at bay.

One of the Forensic team appeared at their side, an anonymous figure in blue plastic overalls and face mask. 'We haven't found anything, I'm afraid. No fingerprints. It's been wiped clean, every last bit of it.'

It would have been too much to hope for anything else, and although he had expected this, Cobb's mood became even more depressed. 'When can you get me an analysis of these fibres?'

The blue figure shrugged. 'Could be a week or more. The lab's overstretched at the moment. A lot of people are off with seasonal flu.'

Cobb sighed and turned away. 'Try and get it to me sooner than that. We need to catch a killer.'

12

They could hear the strident protests as they approached the interview room, and when they opened the door the stench of stale sweat, filthy clothes and cider fumes took their breath away.

'How the hell did they manage to get a solicitor to take this case?' Cobb muttered under his breath to his sergeant.

It had to be said: the solicitor did look rather unhappy and had drawn her chair as far away from her client as she could.

Cobb and Bould sat down opposite the miscreant, and the DI switched on the tape, glancing at his watch as he did so. He stated the time and his name then turned to the others present, inviting them with a look to announce themselves. After Bould had given his name, the solicitor declared herself to be Mary Rogers. All heads turned towards the suspect who squirmed in his seat before eventually declaring his name to be Hopal-ong.

Cobb was scornful. 'That's an adjective, not a name,' he said sternly. 'I need your full given name.'

'I'll tell you something then,' the vagrant leant forward woozily over the table, treating the officers to a blast of his halitosis. 'Hopalong is the name I've been given by my friends, an' that's good enough for me.'

'Pity you're not among friends right now, because it won't do for us. I need your first name and surname as given to you by your parents.' Firm and slow, that was the way to get through.

'Can't remember,' the reply was quick as a flash and a cunning look came over Hopalong's face. 'Course, if you were to see your way to slipping me a fiver, just for medicinal purposes, I might remember.'

Cobb got to his feet, leant heavily on the table and put his face as close as he could, given the stinking odours emanating from Hopalong, and snarled, 'If it's drink you're after you'd better start getting used to the idea of having none for a very long time if you carry on like this, matey. I could have you locked up for obstructing the police, and I'm sure you know there's no alcohol in jail. Now, I'll ask you again, what's your name?'

The thought of being without his daily bottles of cider seemed to speedily sober up Hopalong and he became contrite. 'Arfer Preston.'

'Arthur Preston, good, of no known

address, I presume.' Although it wasn't a question, he still looked to Hopalong for confirmation. 'A nod isn't sufficient. We need to hear your reply for the record.'

'OK, OK. Keep your hair on. I haven't had an address in . . . wot . . . ten years.'

'Now we're getting somewhere. So, Arthur, you're not much cop when it comes to petty thievery, are you? You can't sign for a credit card in person any more. Didn't you know that? It's all high tech these days, luckily for us. Where did you find this card?' Between his fingers, like a magician plucking playing cards out of the air, Cobb produced Diana's credit card.

'Found it. I didn't steal it or nothing like that.' Preston was looking anxious and had started sweating profusely, and the air became even more unpleasant to breathe. Whilst the solicitor edged further away, the tramp seemed mesmerised by the card, unable to take his eyes off it.

'Where did you find it?' Cobb asked.

'Dunno, just somewhere.'

Looking at the state of the man, it was very probable he couldn't remember where he found it, but this was no use to them. Cobb decided to persevere with the softly, softly approach for the time being. 'Thirsty, are you, Arthur? Fancy a cup of tea?'

'I'd rather have something else.'

'You know that's not going to happen. You can have tea or coffee — that's your lot. Take it or leave it, although we might be able to throw in a sandwich too.' He had no illusions that a hot drink would sober the man up, not after all the years of alcohol abuse his body had taken. Preston's brain would be mashed by now, but he knew his sort. All coppers did. The Prestons of this world had a problem with authority and enjoyed being bolshie. A combination of bribery and threats were what was usually required to get any sense out of them.

'I'll have a ham and cheese sandwich, and I don't want no salad on it neither, and three sugars in my tea.' Preston seemed revitalised and gave his order in a surprisingly snappy voice.

'Oh, Arthur, don't you know fruit and vegetables are very good for you? Don't tell me you're not having your five a day,' Cobb said, finding sarcasm becoming more and more naturally suited to him.

'Five a day!' The tramp seemed scandalised at the very idea. Then a cunning look stole over his gaunt face. 'Cider's made from apples — that's fruit; so what with the amount I drink I must be all right there then.'

Both officers allowed themselves the luxury

of a thin laugh at this, and Preston grinned happily without realising they took it as a joke.

'I don't think it works quite like that, but my nice sergeant here will go and get you some tea and whatever sandwich he can find in the canteen.'

Bould took his cue and left them to it, thankful to get out into some clean air.

He returned shortly with a mug of strong tea and a plate containing a sandwich that aroused wrath.

'Here, this is egg an' cress!'

'It's all that was left. Pity you didn't get yourself arrested in Gloucestershire. The canteen's better there.'

'How's a man to nourish himself with egg an' cress. That's a woman's sandwich, that is.' Grumbling, Preston lifted one corner of the sandwich with a filthy hand and inspected the filling as if it was radioactive.

'I shouldn't let the female officers hear you say that,' Cobb responded dryly. 'Right. Now, let's have it. Where did you find this card?'

As this was met with a blank stare, Bould tried to help things along. 'Was it in the street?'

'Naw.' Despite his contempt for the type of food on offer, Preston had fallen on the sandwich as if he hadn't eaten for a week

— which may well have been the case — and even one word was difficult enough for him to pronounce through his bulging cheeks.

It was time to get tough. Cobb leant forward and made his words as menacing as he could. 'I don't think you realise just how much trouble you're in, Arthur. That card belonged to a woman who's been murdered.'

Startled, Preston dropped the bread. It hit the table and egg, mayonnaise and cress splattered out. A dollop landed on the solicitor's lap, and stung with annoyance, she leapt into the silence. 'My client was arrested on suspicion of fraud and theft. He denies any involvement in murder.'

'That's right, missus. I didn't kill no one. You tell 'em.' In extreme agitation Preston, jabbing the air with his finger, turned face on to her. The extreme discomfort she felt at his nearness was obvious to everyone but her client as she made a magnificent effort not to recoil from the combined onslaught of bad breath and body odour.

'No one is accusing Mr Preston of murder. However, the facts of the matter are that this credit card belonged to a woman who has recently been killed and we are very keen to trace her handbag and its contents. I have reason to believe that your client can help us with our enquiries.' Having got the formal part of his speech over, Cobb leant forward on the desk and addressed Preston slowly and carefully, reasoning the man's addled brain was no longer capable of processing information at normal speed. 'I want that handbag, Arthur, and if you've got it you could find yourself in very serious trouble indeed.'

The tactic worked and Preston shrank back in his seat. 'I haven't got it. I swear to you on my mother's life I haven't.'

'Then how did you come by this card?'

'I found it. I found the handbag. Yes, that's right. I found the bag and I took the card. Well, she didn't want it or she wouldn't have thrown it away, would she now? Finders keepers, that's what they say.'

'They say wrong, in that case. Theft is theft and you tried to use the card.'

Preston wiped a filthy hand across a filthy nose. 'Yeah, well it was only to buy a little bottle of something medicinal. I mean, what rich cow throws away a nice bag like that with all that money in — ' he stopped dead, realising what he had just said.

'All that money,' Cobb repeated, slowly and softly and full of menace. This was news to him. 'How much money?'

Backpeddling, Preston started lying frantically, 'I don't know. I didn't count it. I didn't touch it, I swear on my mother's life I didn't.'

'Your mother must be feeling quite dizzy from all the spinning in her grave she's doing, so let's leave her out of it. Just tell me what you did with the bag.' Cobb wasn't interested in the money. He didn't need to ask what had happened to it. Preston had used it to buy his bottles of 'medicine', although no pharmacy would have benefitted from the exchange. 'Listen to me, Arthur. You could be in more trouble now than you've ever been in before, or ever will be again. But I'm a decent bloke and I'm prepared to give you one last chance to help us out. You show me where that bag is and we might just be persuaded to forget about your little attempt at trying to obtain goods by deception. How does that sound to you?'

'You'll let me go?'

Cobb nodded and switched off the tape.

Preston's eyes were filled with slyness. He shifted in his seat, looked at the solicitor, then at the two officers, unable to change the habits of a lifetime. 'Course, it's all very well you saying that, but it's cold out there and I've gotta eat. If you could just see your way to helping me out, gentlemen — '

'Let's have this bag first; then we'll see what we can do.'

'I ain't got it, you know. I left it where it was.'

'Good. Then it will still be there, so you can take us to it.' Always supposing the man could remember where he had found it, and that was not a foregone conclusion by any means, and always supposing no one else had found it since.

When Preston remained seated and looked downcast, Cobb thought his fears were realised. 'Can you recall where it is?'

'It was along the canal. I know 'cos I went there to get away from Hain.'

'There's a lot of canal in Birmingham, you're going to have to be a bit more precise than that, Arthur.'

'It was somewhere in Selly Oak, 'cos that's where I usually go.'

'Good, then let's go there now.'

Selly Oak wasn't far as the crow flies, or as the canal boat travels, but it took them more than twenty minutes to negotiate their way through the city traffic. Birmingham had always been notorious for its one-way system, as Cobb remembered only too well. Shortly after completing his training at Hendon, he'd been posted here for several years. It had been bad then and, despite the massive redevelopment, it wasn't much better now. He was glad Bould was driving.

They drove south-west from the Central Police Station in Steelhouse Lane to Selly

Oak, past Muntz Park and onto Wharf Road; there were very few roads Cobb recognised and Wharf Road was no different. It had been widened, straightened, homogenised. Where was the essential spirit of place that he remembered? This might be Birmingham, but it could just as easily be anywhere else in the country. He found the whole thing profoundly depressing.

'Down there, that's where I go,' Preston came to life from an apparent stupor and started gesticulating excitedly as they passed over Parsons Hill bridge.

The traffic moved too fast to make parking on Wharf Road safe and so Bould turned the car into Chapel Walk and parked up.

Both policemen leapt out of the car the minute the engine stopped. It hadn't been a pleasant journey. Even with the windows rolled right down the smell had been overpowering; the only person who seemed to be unaffected was Preston. He didn't seem keen to leave the comfort of the car for the raw air outside and had to be practically dragged out.

And then, one on either side of him, because they couldn't be certain he wouldn't do a runner, Cobb and Bould escorted him along Wharf Road to where they could get down to the canal, but he stood uncertainly, half turning first one way and then the other, peering around as if the scene was new to him.

'Well?' said Bould encouragingly.

'I dunno. It's down there somewhere, but I can't remember which side.'

'Think back: where had you been before you came down here? You mentioned someone called Hain and said you wanted to avoid him.' Bould urged.

'Yeah, that's right. I remember.' Face screwed up in concentration, Preston gestured vaguely with a shaky hand to their right. 'I'd been to the shop to get . . . something.'

No need to ask what, Cobb thought. How strange we humans are that even when it doesn't matter we still want the world to think better of us. 'So if you came from that direction, you'd have gone down the steps to the canal here,' Cobb indicated the gap that led down to the water.

'Yeah, suppose so.'

'Good. Now we're getting somewhere.' Disinclined towards any more talking, Cobb took Preston by the arm and strode towards the steps.

At the bottom, two different worlds met. To his left, a wide, paved path with a brick-lined edge made it very clear they were in an urban setting where nature was kept well at bay, but to the right the towpath was just a narrow beaten path that in the summer would have been quite passable but was now black mud churned into a mess of rucks and icy troughs. The edge of the canal was frayed and at points the path dipped into the water before veering away. At other times it disappeared where last year's vegetation, spent and lifeless, had collapsed across it in tall clumps, and very quickly the trousers of all three men became spangled with little spits of frost as they brushed past. The surface of the canal was turgid and thickened with ice. There were no boats to be seen and the emptiness felt unnatural.

They walked in silence until the roughly made bench hove into view, and then Preston became animated.

'It's here. This is it. This is where I found it,' he cried, relieved at last to have recognised the spot.

'You're sure?' Cobb asked.

'Yeah. I wouldn't forget this place. I went arse over tit because of that stupid bench. Whoever built it should be shot. It ain't big enough to park your bum on. I rolled right down the bank; hurt myself rotten, I did — not that you care. That's how I found it hidden in the bushes. I was looking for . . . ' a crafty expression crossed his face, 'something.'

Cobb found himself getting irritated with this endless pretence. What was going through the man's mind? Did he really think they couldn't work out what it was his euphemisms meant? He was a plain speaker, that was his trouble, or so Sarah said. In order to get through life without upsetting everyone, she'd told him very sternly one day, you're going to have to be a little more circumspect. He couldn't put a high enough price on her judgement and so he'd tried to follow her advice, oh how he'd tried. If he'd been a more patient man, or one who didn't see things so black and white, maybe success, however modest, would have come. In the end, he'd decided he preferred to speak his mind. That way everyone knew where they stood. Even so, he hadn't the heart to remonstrate with the sad wreck at his side whose body was already becoming wracked with tremors as it tried to cope without its regular fix of alcohol.

Bould was already hunkered down in front of the bench, trying to see through the dense mesh of bramble shoots. With a warning glance at Preston to stay put, Cobb squatted down as well. They worked slowly, hampered by the long-dead but still sharply thorned stems that snagged at their sleeves and pricked their bare hands.

It was the red leather stripes they saw first. It if wasn't for them the bag would have been nigh on invisible.

Cobb donned a pair of gloves and carefully retrieved his long-sought prize. The bag was open and water had got in. A diary and a cheque book were visible, both soggy. A diary — his pulse picked up. With any luck there would be information in it that might help them nab a killer.

'Is this it?' he asked Preston, allowing him a clear view of the handbag.

'Yeah, that's it, right enough.'

'You're absolutely positive this is the bag you took the credit card from?' It was vital there was no doubt; he hoped Preston, despite his befuddled state, understood that.

'Yeah, yeah. I told you. That's definitely it. Can I go now?'

Bould held open a large plastic sack and Cobb dropped the bag into it, saying as he did: 'Hardly. We need to go back to the station and get your dabs.'

Something akin to naked panic showed in Preston's face. 'You told me I could go.' He sounded like a tiny child who had just had a prize toy snatched off him by the school bully.

'You can, once we've got your prints.' Cobb

could see he'd have to spell it out. 'It's for elimination purposes only.'

'Oh, that's all right then. Mr Cobb,' the tone became wheedling. 'I've been very helpful to you, haven't I? I've helped you catch a murderer.'

'Not yet, you haven't.' There was no need to ask what the old soak was after.

'Well, I've helped you, so how about you show your gratitude in the proper way.' A hand, ingrained with dirt, with blackened, splintered fingernails was thrust under the DI's nose.

Cobb pulled out his wallet, extracted a fiver and waved it about. Preston was like a rabbit mesmerised by a snake. 'See this? It may be yours, but if you think I'm daft enough to let you have it now, the drink's done your brain more damage than I realised. We're all going to go back to the station; I'm going to take your fingerprints and then we'll have to see if that nice Sergeant Watson will be prepared to drop charges against you. It's up to him, of course. This isn't my patch. I can't tell the Birmingham police what to do, but if you behave yourself I'm sure he'll be reasonable.'

During this conversation, Bould had walked a short distance off and was radioing in to the Central Birmingham Station. 'We've got a crime scene here and need a SOCO team out ASAP.'

There was a wait of twenty minutes before the team arrived. The sky was mutinous; the cold penetrated to the very marrow of their bones and Preston wasn't the stoic type. His complaints got louder and more pathetic as the minutes ticked by: Why couldn't he wait in a cafe up on the road? That request was greeted with sardonic laughter from his companions who knew that would be the last anyone saw of him if they allowed him out of their sight. So he stamped his feet, blew on his hands and generally moaned in a dramatic way until they were all very glad indeed to see the team of three forensic officers picking their way along the towpath.

Cobb filled them in on the situation, adding, 'We're still missing the victim's clothes: white shirt, black trousers, black and white checked jacket. They don't appear to be where the handbag was found and they may not be here at all. We think the area was simply used to dispose of the bag. The clothes might be somewhere else altogether as we have no reason to connect Selly Oak directly to the victim.'

He watched them don their white protective suits and set to work quietly and efficiently. It always surprised him how

SOCO teams acted as a collective whole, almost as if they operated on telepathy. They never seemed to need to communicate verbally in order to perform their tasks. He was reminded of a colony of ants as they began swarming over the bank, bent double, almost on hands and knees. 'I'll stay and supervise here. You take laughing boy back to the station; I'll meet you there when we're done,' he told Bould.

'Right, sir. What line do you want me to take regarding the credit card charges?' These last words were spoken quietly, so that Preston wouldn't hear.

'At the end of the day, it's up to them whether they charge him or not. He committed the crime on their patch. We can't interfere, but you might point out to Sergeant Watson that nothing much will be achieved by bringing it to court. He was never going to get away with it, and there are far more serious criminals to go after. Tell them not to waste resources in such an inefficient way.' How proud of him the CS would be if he could hear these words.

13

They left central Birmingham Police Station in Steelhouse Lane, turning onto the Queensway, Birmingham's inner ring road system. The weather was causing chaos, as snow was falling once more. Offices and shops were being shut down; staff frightened by forecasts of blizzards and drifts of up to six feet deep later that evening had no desire to be stranded in the city overnight and were heading home early. Traffic was nose to tail; speed could be measured by the pedestrians who were overtaking the cars.

Cobb looked at his watch with irritation. 'I had hoped for an early finish tonight. Sarah wants to go to a concert in Cheltenham.'

'You'll make it, sir. Once we get clear of the city and pick up the motorway it'll only take an hour.'

Two and a half hours later they arrived back at the station. By now, although it was well after six, there was still time to get to the concert and Cobb wasn't sure whether to be pleased or not. The programme featured music by Stockhausen, not his favourite composer by a very long way, and he wouldn't be even remotely upset to give it a miss. Sarah would, though, and he hated disappointing her, so he would suffer it. There would be a bar, and knowing his dislike of the composer (although she preferred to say lack of understanding), she had offered to drive, enabling him to take the reward and consolation of a drink or two to dull the pain of what she called music and he called a bloody row.

'Get Forensics to go over the handbag first thing in the morning. I suppose it's asking too much to hope for any prints other than Preston's and the victim's. It would be nice to think we might get a break in this case at some point, but I doubt this is it. It's a pity we haven't found her clothes,' he grumbled to his sergeant. The thought of an evening in the company of Stockhausen was enough to make anyone miserable.

'The car was in Dorridge, the bag in Selly Oak and the two are only about eleven miles apart. Is our killer based in that area?' Bould asked, adding to the DI's misery.

'God knows, but I sincerely hope not. We might not have got very far as yet, but we'd have to start from scratch if the West Midlands decides to become the star attraction. I'm trusting to it having no more than a walk-on part. Muster the troops for nine tomorrow morning. We'll talk it through some more then. Now, I've got to go — I've a social engagement I don't want to miss.'

★ ★ ★

Even a good night's sleep hadn't been enough to eradiate the cacophony still reverberating in his head, and so the team found their boss in an unusually bad mood the next day.

Cobb entered the CID open-plan office clutching a black coffee and chewing on the last of a chocolate doughnut. He was wondering how many people had been driven to suicide after an evening of Stockhausen.

'Any news from Forensics?' he asked Bould.

'Not yet, sir.'

'OK. Well chase them if we've nothing by the end of the day. We need to get a useable lead ASAP. The trail's colder than a deep freezer in an igloo as it is.' He then proceeded to bring the team up to date with yesterday's events, finishing with: 'Any questions or thoughts, please.'

'You know, it could have been suicide,' PC Aaron Walker said, jingling the coins in his pocket. 'She was pregnant and forty-two, with no man that we can trace, so he's obviously done a runner. Maybe it was all too much for her. And her hormones would have been running wild — pregnant women can be very unpredictable.'

'What!' The look Rose Cadoxton shot him would have felled a sensitive man on the spot. 'Lots of women bring up children by themselves — and I don't blame them,' but she muttered the last five words under her breath.

'I could check the stats out,' Ian Constable said. 'It might be interesting to see what percentage of suicides are pregnant women.'

'That wouldn't prove anything one way or the other,' Cobb said. 'It wouldn't tell us Susan killed herself, and if she did, why she removed her clothing. That suggests to me that our killer wanted us to know it was murder and not an accident or suicide.'

'Then why not kill her in a more obvious way? Strangulation, like the second victim, or stabbing?' asked Rose.

'It's a surer way to avoid detection,' answered Cobb. 'A close-quarters killing means the victim might fight back; they might scratch their killer and we could recover skin cells from under their fingernails, or the killer's clothing could be blood-spattered, or harbour fibres from the victim's clothing. Remember Locard's Exchange Principle: 'every contact leaves a trace'. But I think there is another reason: Susan Davenport's murder was very deliberate and cold blooded, so it was pre-planned. It strikes me it was revenge for something, but the method used for killing Diana was very different, so do we have two killers on the loose or was Diana killed in the heat of the moment?'

'Perhaps she found out who killed her stepmother, confronted the killer who panicked and killed her to prevent her going to the police,' Rose said.

'But she hated her stepmother,' Cobb reminded everyone. 'She seemed pleased she was dead, so it seems unlikely even if she had discovered who killed Susan that she would do anything about it.'

'Perhaps she tried to blackmail the killer,' Bould suggested.

'Yes, that's good. Hold on to that idea; that could make a lot of sense,' Cobb responded quickly. 'Ian, take a look at her finances, see if she was living beyond her means. If she was in need of money it might explain why she died. It still doesn't bring us any nearer to finding out who killed her, though. I think that's all for now. Ian, I want some quick results on Diana's finances.'

'I'm on it to now, sir,' Constable said, heading happily towards his beloved IT equipment.

Later that day, Bould called into his superior's office. 'Forensics say they've got problems and it's going to cause a delay in things.'

Stockhausen, earlier successfully banished from his brain, returned with a vengeance. Cobb felt his head pulsate with the clashing chords. 'Why?'

'Snow got inside and soaked everything. They need to dry the diary and chequebook out carefully; the ink's run. They won't have anything just yet.'

'I would say everything seems to be conspiring against us, if only I didn't realise how fortunate we were to get that bag. OK, Sergeant Bould, it's your lucky day — you can go home before the 10 o'clock news.'

* * *

'Forensics found two mobile phones in her bag. One's an account phone, the other's pay-as-you-go,' Bould informed his boss a day later. 'And you'll never guess whose number was in the pay-as-you-go memory.'

'Surprise me,' Cobb spoke dryly. He felt dry too, and poured himself the first of the day's many coffees. He held the pot out and when Bould shook his head, replaced it on the little metal hot plate.

'Susan Davenport's.'

Cobb didn't speak until he had settled himself behind his desk. 'So, she lied to us when she said they didn't have anything to do with each other. What a pity she'll never be able to tell us why. What about the diary?'

'That's a mess at the moment. The water's reduced the pages to pulp, and the entries are all but illegible. They want to dry it out slowly and carefully,' Bould said. He didn't sit down but remained standing. He seemed restless.

'How slowly? We're getting nowhere fast on this case. The CS has gone back to complaining that we're spending too much of our time traipsing around half the UK, and to date I can't give him any answers as to what benefits our journeys have brought other than an improvement in our knowledge of geography. Have Birmingham Forensics come up with anything on their crime scene?'

'They've drawn a complete blank. There was nothing else to be found on the canal bank.'

'No. That would be too much to ask. As her clothes weren't there and her car was some miles away, can we assume the killer went to Selly Oak simply in order to dump her bag there?'

'Why didn't he or she throw it in the canal? That way it would never have been found?'

Cobb groaned. 'The obvious answer to that one is we're dealing with the type of psychotic maniac who likes to taunt the police with their own cleverness.' They both knew that sort of killer was every policeman's worst nightmare. 'And if that's the case, we've got to nab them PDQ before the bodies pile up. The other possibility is that the killer didn't go down to the water at all but threw the bag over the bridge. If it was dark it would be unlikely they'd be noticed as there are no houses nearby. You can see there's a lot of trees and scrub from the road, so they must have thought once it was down there it would never be found again. And I doubt even the most meticulous murderer would allow for the antics of a drunken vagrant when calculating the odds.'

At that moment there was a rap on the door, and Ian Constable poked his head round. He looked pleased with himself. 'I've been looking into Diana's finances. There is nothing unusual in her bank accounts, *but* I decided to take a look at her car because most people buy their car on credit, but Diana seemed to have no debt at all so I got on to the dealer where she bought her car from a couple of years ago. It's a top-of-the-range Audi convertible as you know, sir, and guess what?'

'Surprise me.'

'She paid cash for it.'

Constable had succeeded in surprising him after all, and Bould too, from the looks of him. 'Cash — is that a fact. Well, well. I take it you're going to tell me exactly how much she paid for it?'

'Thirty-five thousand pounds.'

'And I take it that, like the diligent copper you are, you've gone through her bank accounts and salary details and I hope you're going to tell me you can't figure out where that money came from.'

Constable gave a smile that acknowledged his boss's insight. 'That's right. *Also*, you'll be interested to learn that the car was purchased during the fourth month that Susan was withdrawing her monthly £10,000.'

'We must be careful not to jump to conclusions,' Cobb cautioned. 'It would be easy to assume that Diana was blackmailing her stepmother, and it may well turn out to be the case, but even if it is, we still don't know what she was blackmailing her over, and without that information we're no further on. If anything, it muddies the water.'

'How so?' Ian asked, moving further into the room in his curiosity.

'We're agreed both deaths are connected, right? So if we say Diana was blackmailing

Susan over something from their past, we shouldn't necessarily assume it's relevant to their deaths. It could be coincidental. All right, I know it's not likely, but we can't overlook that possibility, and if it is relevant, then we have to assume their murderer also knew about it and yet we can't find anyone alive who knew the family when they were living in Lampeter or London.'

'Apart from Dr Mathers,' Bould said unexpectedly.

Cobb stared. 'You're not serious, Sergeant? You saw the state of the man. He could barely stand. The idea of him being able to strangle Diana is preposterous.'

'I know that, sir. But he is from their past. He was the family GP; he was first on the scene when David died. He'd be well placed to notice anything suspicious about the boy's death. He could have been blackmailing Susan.'

Cobb couldn't fail to hear the acerbity in his sergeant's voice and realised he had been a little sharp with him. Bould wasn't a fool and he valued their relationship; the last thing he'd meant to do was show him up in front of a junior officer. 'No, you're right there. However, he couldn't have killed Diana, so are you thinking that he might have had an accomplice?' Good heavens, the only person who sprang to mind was his mad house-keeper, Dora. Surely not — didn't she fall into the completely dotty but harmless category?

'It wouldn't be beyond the realms of possibility; a great many murderers have operated as a partnership.' It wasn't Bould but Constable who replied. He seemed quite taken up with the idea. 'Perhaps he's got a son somewhere we don't know about. Shall I do some digging; see what I can find in terms of family for him?'

'Not yet. I don't want us to get sidetracked, and I really don't see how or why the doctor should figure in this. You see, even if he was blackmailing Susan, it doesn't bring us any closer to our murderer because it doesn't explain *why* either woman was killed.'

Bould was still smarting from his earlier put-down and now seemed impatient to restate the facts. 'Look sir, Diana had her stepmother's phone number programmed into her mobile despite telling us they hadn't seen each other or spoken for years. Then she buys an expensive car for cash shortly after a great deal of money goes out of Susan's bank account. Money Susan clearly thought of as hush money. It has to be the case that Diana was blackmailing Susan.'

'Then we need to find some proof. Ian,

keep going with Diana's finances. If cash was being handed over, they had to meet somewhere. If we could pinpoint a meeting place we'd be laughing, but it could have been anywhere.'

'It wouldn't have been Lampeter,' Bould said. 'It's too small a place; people would have noticed.'

'Yes, and if it was London, it's so big no one would have noticed. We'd have a better chance of seeing Lord Lucan ride Shergar to victory in this year's Derby than discovering where they met.' He felt unusually pessimistic and it wasn't only due to the direction this case was taking. Another cup of coffee seemed like a very good idea at this point, and something sweet to eat wouldn't go amiss, but his watch said it was only half past ten and that was wherein the problem lay. The routine annual medical had earned him a strict telling off because his cholesterol was far too high. Much less fat and more exercise was the gist of it. The big mistake had been to tell Sarah because now all that was on offer at suppertime were salads and bits of steamed chicken, when what he really wanted was roast beef and Yorkshire pudding served with potatoes roasted in dripping. The intention not to have anything sweet to eat before lunch had seemed like a good one at the time (just

234

before he went to bed), but now, at mid morning when the case wasn't going well, it seemed like a very bad one.

* * *

'Get yourself in here; we've got something.' Cobb put the phone down and returned to his study of the dozen or so photocopies Forensics had recently delivered. He shuffled them through his hands like a conjuror practicing a card trick.

It was amazing what a day could do. Yesterday his thoughts around the case were shrouded in disappointment and frustration, but the results Forensics had come up with revitalised him. Impatient now they had a positive lead, pacing around the office, tapping the sheaf of papers against his hand, he sketched out their next moves in his head whilst waiting for his sergeant to arrive.

When Bould tapped on his door a few minutes later he called, 'Come in,' without taking his gaze off the sheets. 'I want you to take a look at these and tell me what you think.' He fanned them out on the desk, standing by as his sergeant picked them up one by one and scrutinised them intensely.

'These are Diana's diary entries, I take it.'

235

'They are. Some of them have been enhanced. Where the ink has run badly Forensics have filled in what they think the words are from the indentations left behind on the page. Look at the one for the day Susan died.'

'Two p.m. — Millwheel,' Bould read out loud and looked at Cobb, the thrill of the chase already showing in the glint in his eyes. 'But what is Millwheel — a restaurant?'

'If it is, it must be a very old-fashioned one. Sounds more like a tearoom to me, but I don't see Diana as a frequenter of tearooms. It could even be a private house. It's a pity she couldn't have been more obliging in the way of an address. Whatever this place is it could be anywhere. Get Ian to see if he can come up with anything on the Internet. If it's a pub or restaurant, with a bit of luck they'll have a website.'

'What about the date Diana died?'

'Now that would be too much to ask. There's nothing at all after the Thursday, and that just appears to be work related, although I've got Aaron checking it out, just to — ' he was cut short by the telephone ringing. He answered it with his name, listened briefly and hung up. 'This'll have to wait. There's been a robbery at a subpostoffice just outside Cheltenham. Grab your jacket.' He was already halfway through the door, shrugging himself into his coat as he went.

★ ★ ★

In an ink-black sky, a cold moon glistered, and a hard frost was already coating everything. On his way home at last, impulse made Bould detour past Cathy's house, hopeful that on the off chance she'd be in. He was too tired to go home and cook. He could just grab a takeaway pizza, but that was hardly appealing either. If Cathy was in he'd treat her to a meal out, for however tired he might have been the thought of seeing her revitalised him.

Luck was on his side, and by the way she threw her arms around his neck and kissed him, she was more than pleased to see him as well. Taking his hand, she led Bould into her small and eccentrically decorated lounge, fetched cold beers from the fridge and listened as he briefly told her about his day, finishing with: 'How do you fancy dinner at La Traviata?'

'Do I?' Her face lit up. It was the best restaurant in town. Then she remembered something and looked doubting. 'But you'll never get a table at this time. You know how popular it is.'

'It's got to be worth a try,' he protested.

She indicated the phone. 'OK, then. I won't try to stop you. I've wanted to go to La Trav for ages but it's totally out of my price range.'

Three minutes later and Bould was triumphant. 'They've had a late cancellation, so get your glad rags on, Cinderella, and you shall go to the ball — or at any rate a decent restaurant. We've got to be there in fifteen minutes.'

'Fifteen minutes! You are joking. I've got to get ready.' Her last words were lost as she shot up the stairs, leaving Bould to finish his beer alone.

★   ★   ★

'That really was something special,' she said, pushing her empty dessert dish away. Resting her chin in her hand she gazed at Bould. 'I don't know how you managed to pull a table at La Trav just like that. Most people have to book weeks in advance. My mother's going to be livid when she hears. She had to make do with the Millwheel for lunch today.'

Bould had been about to take the last sip of his wine, but his hand arrested in mid air. 'The Millwheel — what's that?' His tone was sharper than he meant and the look on his face reminded Cathy of a dog that had just scented a rabbit.

'It's the old roadhouse on the Tewkesbury Road. It used to be called the Weston Arms but the landlord changed the name in the hope of picking up new business. Sounds a pretty desperate idea to me: the place has been dying a death for years. I've been there once or twice and thought it was rubbish but his wife is a very good friend of my mum, so she's doing her bit to try and help out. Have you ever been there?'

Bould shook his head. 'No, but I've heard of the Weston Arms. When was the name changed?'

Cathy frowned and twiddled her spoon between her fingers, giving the matter some thought. 'Not sure, but it must have been quite recently from what mum said. Now it's your turn.'

Her lover feigned ignorance. 'Turn to do what. Oh, you mean pay the bill.' With an exaggerated movement, his hand went to his inside pocket.

'Don't you dare give me that!' The words flashed out, but her laughter betrayed the sentiment. 'Come on; let's have a *quid pro quo* here; I've told you what you wanted to know; now you owe me. What's your interest in the place?'

'Do you think it's the place you're looking for?' she asked after he had filled her in on events. 'I don't want to play Jonah, but there must be lots of Millwheels around. Sounds like the sort of name you'd give a teashop in a cute little country village.'

'That's what Cobb said. Do you actually know of any teashops called that?'

She shook her head. 'No, but then I'm hardly what you'd call the teashop type.'

⋆　⋆　⋆

Bould strolled into his superior's office feeling more pleased than perhaps he had a right to.

Cobb, looking up, could scarcely fail to notice the satisfaction in his sergeant's face. As Tuesday's Post Office raiders were still on the loose and they had very little in the way of clues or information to go on, he was immediately irritated. 'Unless you've some good news for me you can stop looking so damn cheerful.'

'Actually, sir, I have got some good news for you. I've discovered where the Millwheel is. It's the old Weston Arms roadhouse on the Tewkesbury Road. The name changed a few weeks ago.'

'The Weston Arms; that's about three miles

from here. I don't recall Diana telling us she'd been visiting the area the day her stepmother died.' Cobb was on his feet and pulling on his jacket. 'Right: let's get out there straight away.'

Their progress was contained when they found Bould's car blocked in by one of the squad vehicles. Fuming, Cobb marched back into the station, leaving no doubt in any bystander's mind that someone was going to get a rollicking. Sure enough, two minutes later a young, red-faced uniformed constable shot out, apologising profusely and moved the offending car.

Somewhat appeased, Cobb climbed into the passenger seat and they set off.

The Millwheel was set in open countryside on the Tewkesbury Road. The name was pure whimsy, for the nearest mill was miles away and it had been built in the 1930s as a roadhouse. The single bar room was huge, with a floral carpet and small tables set around the edge, leaving a yawning space in the centre big enough to stage a West End musical. The walls were cream coloured and set along it at regular intervals were pairs of bracket lamps with cream and crimson parchment shades. At the opposite end to the bar a great fire blazed in a stone hearth with a large basket of logs on one side. The effect was charmingly olde worlde, which was quite clearly the intention.

'Place will be shut for good in a year according to Cathy,' Bould said, taking in the three well-preserved elderly women sitting by the fire. There were two bottles of wine on their table, both empty, and they were having a high old time, judging by the uproarious laughter convulsing them.

'Gentlemen, what can I get you?' Beaming in happy anticipation at the prospect of new business, the landlord had stepped out from behind his bar and come forward to greet them. Middle-aged, tall and gaunt with lank, overlong hair fringing his head in a horseshoe, he looked like a lugubrious circus clown. But looks belie and he exuded the type of bon hommie that could appear both false and genuine at the same time to different people, possibly depending on how cynical they were.

Both officers produced their warrant cards and watched the smile on their host's face dissolve into disappointment. 'How can I help you gentlemen? I'm Stephen Hargreaves. I'm the tenant here.'

Cobb produced a photograph. 'Have you ever seen this woman in here?' he asked, thankful once again that Diana was such a striking woman. Any man seeing her once would not be likely to forget the encounter.

The landlord only needed to give the picture the briefest of glances. 'I'll say I've seen her. You wouldn't forget a face like that in a hurry. What a corker.'

That was an expression Cobb hadn't heard in years. He revised his assessment of the landlord's age. 'When was this?'

'Oh, I can tell you that straight away. First Saturday of the month.'

'Are you sure about that?' Cobb asked.

'Yeah. I'll tell you how I remember. Wales were playing England at The Millennium Stadium and I wanted to watch it on the box, but the wife had to go to Birmingham because her mother wasn't well. I was pretty annoyed, I can tell you, but then *she* came into the pub and well, it sort of made amends.'

'What time would this have been?'

'Just after two, I'd say. The trade goes a bit quiet then and I thought that would be it until the evening, then she arrived.'

'Was she alone?'

'She was when she arrived, but then another woman turned up shortly after.'

Cobb produced another photograph. 'Would it have been this woman?' It was Susan Davenport.

Now Hargreaves seemed less certain. He

243

took the picture and squinted at it. 'I think it might have been. Sorry, gentleman you'll understand why I didn't look too closely at her. She's rather ordinary.'

'Then think harder,' Cobb snapped. 'We need to know for certain.'

'OK — I'm pretty certain it was.'

Unsatisfied with this response, Cobb pushed him further. 'What was she wearing?'

The landlord made a great show of concentrating his thoughts. The brow furrowed and the eyes screwed up tight. 'Trousers and a jumper,' he said finally.

'Colour?'

A shrug of the shoulders. 'Something dark; I dunno . . . black, brown. It didn't stand out; she didn't stand out.'

It matched near enough. The clothes they had found by the pool were black. 'What did these women do?'

'Do?' The question was repeated as if he thought Cobb was an imbecile.

'Yes, do. It's not a difficult question. Did they have a drink, a meal, what?' Cobb's temper was beginning to fray at the seams. Was the man being deliberately obstructive? No wonder the place was near enough to empty. The dramatic decline of the traditional pubs was a constant source of sorrow, but with half-baked landlords like this around,

244

was it any wonder? You needed flair and vision to survive in these straitened times, and this man seemed to lack both.

'Oh, I see what you mean. Yes, they had a drink. The looker had a large glass of red wine, the other one had mineral water. They had some food; just sandwiches as that's all we offer. It's not worth doing anything else. We have tried, but the interest isn't there.' The heartiness had gone from his voice and leaden defeat dulled his words.

'How long were they here?' Bould asked, but his words were drowned out by a loud burst of raucous laughter from the corner.

'Those old girls certainly know how to enjoy themselves,' the landlord said approvingly, ignoring Bould's question. 'In here every week they are. Widows, all of them.' There was envy in his voice, and wistfulness too, as if the thought of being without a spouse had great appeal.

'Never mind about them, I asked you how long the two women were in here the other Saturday.'

'Oh, I'd say probably for the best part of an hour.'

'I don't suppose you noticed the cars they arrived in?'

The landlord brightened. 'I saw the looker's car. It had real style. Audi coupe;

must have cost a bomb.'

'What about the other one?'

Another shrug of the shoulders. 'There was another car out there, some little silver thing. You know the type women drive. I didn't look closely at it.'

'And I don't suppose you noticed the direction they left in,' Bould asked wearily. Men like this depressed him beyond words. He had no doubt Hargreaves had not taken his eyes of Diana until she was literally over the horizon. Susan might as well not have been here.

The landlord became indignant, stung by the unspoken assessment of his character. 'As it happens, I did. I had to take some rubbish out to the bins and the Audi turned in the Tewkesbury direction.'

'What about the silver car?'

'No, that went the opposite way.'

Cobb and Bould exchanged glances. What had seemed a promising lead had taken a frustrating turn. Both of them had been hoping the meeting in the Millwheel was just a rendezvous point.

'You're quite sure about that?' Cobb asked.

'Absolutely.'

'They went their ways separately?' Although it was vital to be certain on this, Cobb wondered why he trusted the landlord so little he felt it necessary to labour the point.

'Yes. Look what is this all about?' Hargreaves eyes kept sliding over to his only customers. One of them must have seen the warrant cards; either that or the sight of two reasonably presentable men was cause for excitement in itself, for the women had gone quiet and were casting speculative glances at them. The conversation, which had been so very loud only minutes before, now consisted of urgent whispers behind hands.

'We're just conducting some routine enquiries,' Cobb said blandly, wondering whether Hargreaves ever bothered to read the papers.

'When they were lunching, how did they seem?' Bould enquired.

'In what way?'

'Did their conversation seem amicable or did they row?'

'It's funny you should ask. They knew each other, I could see that, but they weren't what you'd call overfriendly. It was more like two people at a wedding — you know the sort of thing. People who don't know each other very well, or don't like each other, but have to be polite and make small talk, but as soon as they can they clear off.'

'All right, that's very helpful. We'll need you to come down to the station and make a statement as soon as possible.' Cobb handed his card over. 'And whilst we're here, we might as well have a drink.'

'Of course, gentlemen. What's it to be?' Hargreaves brightened up once more at the prospect of getting something out of the situation.

'I'll have a pint of bitter and my sergeant here will have something non alcoholic as he's driving.'

They took their drinks over to a table as far away as possible from the trio of merry widows who, as soon as Hargreaves had gone behind the bar, had taken the opportunity to order a third bottle of Chardonnay. It seemed necessary for all three of them to go up to the bar and as they sauntered past Cobb and Bould they brazenly gave the officers the once over. Then they hovered, looking for an opportunity to open a conversation, becoming quite coquettish amongst themselves and sending girlish glances around the room.

'God in Heaven, let's get these down and get out of here double quick before we end up betrothed,' Cobb said, turning his chair round with a thump so his back was very pointedly to the room.

Keeping his head low so there was no chance of eye contact, Bould watched the women return to their table, deflated. 'It's all right, sir, you're safe — for now.'

Cobb rolled his eyes. 'This job gets more dangerous by the day. So Diana lied to us about not seeing her stepmother since Cecil's funeral,' Cobb stated flatly, taking a long pull on his beer.

Bould took a frankly less enjoyable sip of his mineral water. 'They arrived separately and left separately, travelling in opposite directions if Hargreaves is to be believed. What was their meeting all about? Do you think Diana was trying to extract money from Susan again?'

'That would depend on who instigated the meeting, and if it was Diana, how had she managed to trace Susan? The really important piece of information we need is this: was that the last they saw of each other, or did they meet up again later that night?' Cobb blew out his cheeks in frustration. 'You see, if Diana was blackmailing Susan she wouldn't have killed her, and even if she did, who then killed Diana? Which ever way you look at it we still have a killer on the loose and not the slightest sniff of a motive. Neither do we have the slightest idea who fathered Susan's child; the fact that he hasn't come forward is more than suspicious in my book.'

'You think he may be the killer? What if she had visited a fertility clinic and plumped for an anonymous donor? That would explain the absence of a man in her life.'

'She'd have some paperwork at home. However shady the clinic, there would have to be some sort of paperwork. Anyway, where would she have found the money? I'd like to know how she's been living all this time, as it is.'

'So, are we thinking that the father of Susan's baby killed her?' Bould asked.

His boss considered the matter and answered the unasked question. 'I know, even if we go down that road, it wouldn't explain why that same man would kill Diana, especially as it's a racing cert the two couldn't have met each other.' The day would come when Bould would go for promotion and that day wasn't one he was looking forward to. They worked so well together; each seemed to know instinctively what the other was thinking, and there was a mutual respect between them, which was a massive improvement on the relationship he'd had with his previous sergeant. Farrows had been a truculent bugger and they had nearly come to physical blows on more than one occasion. He'd eventually been thrown off the Force for misconduct and it hadn't come a day too soon for Cobb. He finished his pint and stood up. 'Right. Let's get back and pull the team in. They need to know what's going on.'

14

There was a surprise waiting for them on their return. As they passed through the reception area, a portly figure rose to accost them.

'Inspector Cobb, can I have a word please?' Gone was the bluff, hail-fellow-well-met manner and in its place was a pale-faced nervous wreck.

Cobb felt almost sorry for the man. 'Mr Parry, what can we do for you?'

'Can you spare me a few minutes. I know you're a very busy man but I really would like to speak with you.' The solicitor's manner was pleading and there was a hunted look about him.

Cobb hesitated. 'What's it about?'

'Susan Davenport.'

'In that case, come with us.'

Punching the code in the security lock, Cobb led the way through to the private part of the station. Parry trailed behind the two officers like a dingy in the wake of an ocean liner.

They didn't speak again until Cobb opened his office door. 'Now then, Mr Parry, take a seat and tell me what it is that was so important it has brought you all the way from Wales to see me.'

'It's the Law Society, you see. They'll strike me off unless you can put in a good word.' Parry sat forward on the edge of his seat, visibly distressed.

'For God's sake, man, we've got a murder investigation on our hands and you come here with a problem of your own making. Why should I put in a good word for you?'

'I'm not a bad man, Inspector.' Parry spoke so quietly that Cobb had to lean forward to catch his words. 'It's my wife, see. She likes the expensive life, she does. I do my best, but there's only so much money to be made on wills and conveyancing.'

'You're making my heart bleed. I've never met a poor solicitor yet; have you, Sergeant?'

'Can't say I have,' Bould replied, equally sardonic.

'So, let's get this straight. You're pinning your gross misbehaviour on your wife, are you?' Cobb was furious. The man was beyond a joke.

Sensing that he wasn't going about things the right way, Parry hastened to deny the suggestion. 'No, no. It's not her fault, not really. She thinks I make a lot more than I do, see. She likes to boast about it to all her friends and . . . well, what can a man do?' He spread his hands wide in a helpless gesture.

'You'd be surprised how many times we hear a similar tale,' Cobb said in the same tone as before. 'Apparently, there wouldn't be any crime at all if it wasn't for these dreadful wives forcing their honest and morally upright husbands into breaking the law. Isn't that so, Sergeant?'

'It's touching to see what love can do to a man,' Bould replied. He had taken up a stance behind Parry, which only served to make the sweating solicitor even more uncomfortable because he couldn't look at both officers at the same time and had to keep twisting in his seat.

'What's love got to do with it?' Parry squeaked, his voice rising several octaves in horror. 'I can't stand the bloody woman, but she'd take me to the cleaners in a divorce, as she's not slow to remind me. So there you have it, see. I can't stand her and I don't think she likes me very much either, but she likes the lifestyle and the standing she has in the community as my wife, and I can't afford to divorce her.'

'Sounds as though she's got just as much to lose,' Bould observed. 'Perhaps you should put it to the test.'

'No, no,' Parry shook his head vehemently.

'I don't want to put it to the test. A man in my position, he needs a wife to take to social functions, and in our circle people just don't get divorced. It wouldn't do, see. It would reflect badly on me.'

The dislike Cobb felt towards the man was almost physical. He decided it was time to end this interview and pushed back his chair. 'Well, Mr Parry. I don't think we're going to be able to help you — '

'No, but if you could just tell the Law Society I was pushed into it. After all, I owned up to everything immediately and it must have helped your investigation. If you could just say I was weak. I am a weak man, I know.'

'Do you seriously think it would make any difference?' Now Cobb was incredulous. 'I'm an extremely busy man and only agreed to see you because you said it was in connection with Susan Davenport — '

'It was.'

'Not in the way I took you to mean. So unless you have some new information concerning her death — actually, maybe you can throw some light on a matter concerning the Davenport women. Did you know that Diana and Susan were in contact with each other and met the day Susan died?'

'No, I didn't.' And judging from the

expression on his face, it would seem he didn't.

'Do you think it likely that Susan would have instigated a meeting with her stepdaughter; and by the way, let's drop any of this pretence that they liked each other. We know they didn't.'

'How could I possibly know if Susan wanted to see Diana? I hadn't seen Susan since she moved away and until Susan's funeral I hadn't seen Diana since her father's interment.'

'Did the two women speak much on that occasion?' Cobb asked.

'Let me think.' Deep lines appeared on his forehead as he concentrated on past memories. 'No, I don't think they did. They just sort of nodded to each other across the room at the wake afterwards. It was held in Brynteg and I remember the weather was very fine that day. But funnily enough, I do remember Susan and Diana's boyfriend seemed to spend a lot of time together.'

If an electrical charge of 50,000 volts had been passed through the room, the atmosphere couldn't have become more charged.

'Diana's boyfriend — would that be James Grogan?' Bould asked, moving round in front of Parry.

'It might be. I'm not sure I can remember his name.'

'Well, was it the same man she took to Susan's funeral?' Cobb demanded to know.

'Oh yes, it was definitely the same one. Couldn't stand the flash bastard. Typical Londoner. The sort we get all the time buying up our country cottages and pricing the locals out of the market.' For a minute Parry forgot his own woes and became quite animated.

'Let's be quite clear on this, Mr Parry,' Cobb said, pinning Parry into his seat with a black stare. 'You're saying that Diana went to her father's funeral in the company of James Grogan — for that's the name of the man who accompanied her to Susan's funeral — and whilst there James met Susan and spent time with her. You're absolutely certain on this, are you?'

'Yes, yes, that's right. You've got it,' Parry nodded eagerly, glad to have finally got in the officers' good books.

'Thank you very much, Mr Parry. I'm going to ask you to stay behind for a while so that we can take a statement from you to this effect. I'll arrange for someone to attend to you as soon as possible, but if you'll excuse us, we've got work to do.' It was as Bould started to usher Parry out, ignoring his repeated requests for a good word to the Law Society, that a distant memory flashed into Cobb's mind. At the time something had never seemed quite right and now he knew what it was. 'Mr Parry, I don't suppose you'd know the answer to this one, but did Diana and Susan ever abbreviate their names.'

Ioan turned round, still pathetically keen to oblige in any way that might benefit him. 'In what way? If you mean did Susan get called Sue, yes she did, but Diana was very particular about her name, and you'd get a real telling off if you didn't call her Diana in full. She hated being called Di, which happened a lot because of the Princess of Wales. You know how the papers always referred to her as Lady Di; so of course people started calling Diana Di and she was not amused, oh dear me, no. She was not amused.'

'Is that so? Thanks, you've been very helpful, very helpful indeed.' Betraying no sense of the excitement he was feeling, Cobb was bland as he dismissed the solicitor. It didn't matter how much hard work and diligent effort was put into an investigation, so often what it came down to was luck.

They left the solicitor in the care of Rose Cadoxton and hurried outside, their breath freezing in the thin winter air. As usual, Bould drove, cursing the traffic as they turned onto the main road and immediately got snarled up in the mid-morning scrum as Cobb radioed the Met, asking them to pull James Grogan in. He also made a further call to Aaron, asking him to get on to the Magistrates Court as a matter of urgency.

There had been a bad accident on the M4 and it took them three hours to reach London. A cold, frosty darkness had fallen as they pulled into the car park for the ugly 1960s concrete box that was Paddington Green Police Station.

They were expected. The duty sergeant led them straight to an interview room where an angry James Grogan was pacing up and down in the company of his overfed, Armani-suited solicitor. They looked two of a kind, Cobb thought, with ill concealed disgust.

As soon as they entered, Grogan was on them. 'What the hell do you think you're playing at?' he yelled. 'Sending a couple of woodentops to my place of work, dragging me out like a common criminal. What do you think that's going to do to my reputation? I'll be slapping a writ on you so bloody quick you won't know what's hit you.'

'Is that a fact, sir?' Cobb enquired blandly. 'I'll look forward to receiving it.'

His attitude served only to infuriate Grogan. 'I doubt very much that you will. Do you know how much this is going to cost your force? Do you have any idea how much money I earn in a day? More than you earn in a year,' he sneered, 'so just start thinking about how large my claim for damages is going to be. They'll have you back on the beat for this.'

'Perhaps you'd like to sit down, sir, and then we can get this over with as soon as possible,' Cobb said, still keeping his equanimity. He and Bould took their seats across from the solicitor and, after a second's hesitation, Grogan placed himself beside his solicitor.

'I want to ask you about a key ring Lady Lucas showed Sergeant Bould and myself,' Cobb began and was pleased to see the baffled look on Grogan's face. Whatever he had been expecting, it wasn't this, and it was always helpful to wrong-foot a suspect from the very beginning. 'It was the one Diana Davenport kept her spare key on. I'm sure you must know it — it has a big silver jewel-encrusted D on it. I thought that D stood for Diana but it didn't, did it?' He waited encouragingly.

'I take it you haven't dragged me all the way here from the City for this?' Grogan knuckled the table, face crimson with rage.

Cobb half-lifted his hand and motioned his quarry to be still. 'Now I'm not very good with fancy jewellery and that sort of stuff, as my wife would tell you. I can't tell one designer make from another, but there was a little cartouche on that key ring and I noticed that it was stamped 'Dior'. That was what the D stood for wasn't it? Dior, not Diana.'

The solicitor, who had announced himself as Mark Heaton, stirred. 'Is this of any relevance, Inspector?'

'Indeed it is, as will become apparent shortly. Well, Mr Grogan, can you confirm what I've just said.'

Grogan's breath escaped with an audible sigh. He didn't fear this question. His colour returned to normal and when he answered he adopted a mocking, ironic tone. 'Well done, Inspector. You're smarter than I realised. What an asset you must be to the good citizens of Gloucestershire. No doubt they feel able to sleep easy in their beds at night with you around.'

Cobb ignored the bait. 'Just answer the question, Mr Grogan.'

'Yes, the D stands for Dior and not Diana. For your information, Diana hated her name being abbreviated in any form. There's no way she'd be known as D.'

'So she'd never have given you, say, a book by Clive Cussler for Christmas and signed it D?'

And then, suddenly, Grogan saw the trap

too late. He became wary, blustering. 'I don't know. I can't really say. Diana could be very intransigent; she used drugs prodigiously, as you may or may not know, and could became wholly unpredictable.'

'Oh, intransigent. That's a good word. Make a note of it, Sergeant. I might want to use it myself some day.'

And Bould made a big pretence of writing something in his notebook, much to Grogan's increasing agitation.

Cobb's voice became steely. 'We found just such a book in the back of your wardrobe. Hidden away, you might say. We wondered why at the time, didn't we, Sergeant?'

'Yes,' Bould concurred.

'So now I'm wondering who gave it to you if it wasn't your official girlfriend.'

'My client can't prevent people giving him presents, and there is most certainly no crime against it,' Heaton said smoothly.

'No, and I quite understand how embarrassing it must have been for him, which, no doubt, is why he chose to hide it. On the other hand, he could have thrown it away.' Turning from the solicitor to his client, Cobb raised his voice, 'But you didn't, did you? You kept it because it meant something to you. We have a witness who has just come forward and he informs us that you and Susan

Davenport met at her husband's funeral and, furthermore, that you got on very well together. Yet you told us not so very long ago that you had never met. In the light of this new information, I'm inviting you to reconsider your earlier statement.'

Grogan pressed his palm into his forehead, playing for time. 'Good God, I can't be expected to remember every single person I've met in the course of my life.'

'But I'm not asking you to. However, I would have thought you might have remembered meeting your girlfriend's stepmother at her father's funeral. You can't go to too many of those, surely? In which case, I'd have thought that would have been quite a momentous occasion and one that would stick in your mind. Wouldn't you agree, Sergeant?'

'Absolutely,' said Bould.

'And our witness informs us that you and Susan Davenport were getting on like a house on fire. Funny you can't remember.'

'All right. Yes, yes, I remember now. We did meet at the funeral, but I spoke to a lot of people then and it just slipped my mind.'

Cobb continued to look sceptical. He raised an eyebrow and sounded weary. 'Even though you got on so well together?'

'No, that's not true. I was just being

friendly towards her, towards everyone. I mean, at a funeral you can't go round being unpleasant to people, can you? As you say, she was my girlfriend's stepmother, I had to show a bit of interest.' He was clutching at straws now, his composure completely rattled.

'It seems very strange to me that you should feel that way, considering Diana hated Susan and didn't speak to her. I can't imagine she was over the moon to see you dancing attendance on her.'

'I wasn't dancing attendance on her. I was merely being civil. Whatever quarrel Diana had with Susan was nothing to do with me. I was brought up to have some manners, you know.' It seemed the man couldn't help himself. Natural smugness seemed an inherent part of his make-up and the last sentence was delivered with such complacency that Cobb was enraged.

'I'm so pleased to hear it. I was only saying to my sergeant on the way down here that good manners seem a thing of the past. How reassuring to know that someone is still hell-bent on keeping up standards.' Despite his sarcasm and upbeat front, Cobb was unhappy. He knew a guilty man when he saw one and he wasn't seeing one right now. The case was going up in smoke.

At that moment, there was a knock on the

door and a uniformed constable slipped into the room.

'Excuse me, sir. I understand you are waiting for this.' A single sheet of paper was handed over.

'Thank you,' Cobb said, glanced at it and put the paper in his pocket as the PC left the room.

'Where were we? Oh yes, at the funeral. You were just being pleasant to Susan. You seem to have gone out of your way to be pleasant to her. That can't have gone down well with Diana though, surely, considering she made no bones about hating her stepmother, so she can't have been thrilled to see you dancing attendance on Susan.'

'I've told you once, I didn't dance attendance on her!' Grogan was on his feet, yelling and banging the table, his face red. Sweat trickled down his cheeks.

'Please sit down, Mr Grogan,' Cobb intoned and waited until the man had done just that before continuing. 'Let's start again from the beginning, only calmer this time. You do admit that you met Susan Davenport at her husband's funeral.'

'Yes.'

'Thank you. Good. Now we're getting somewhere. How often did you meet after this occasion?'

'We didn't. I never met her again.'

'In that case I assume you will have no objection to giving us a DNA swab.' Was he clutching at straws here? It was an almighty leap into the dark and one he could scarcely give credence to himself. But if there was one thing all his years in the Force had taught him it was never to jump to the sort of conclusions sane men jumped to.

Mark Heaton, who had been quiet throughout this exchange, sprang into life as abruptly as if he had been poked with a cattle prod. 'My client most certainly does object. What would be the purpose of this test, pray?'

'Susan Davenport was three months' pregnant when she died,' Cobb explained. 'We have been unable so far to find any man in her life who might be the father of this child. Now, you can say I've a suspicious mind, but your client has lied to us about knowing Susan Davenport and I have to ask myself why he would do this. So, I ask myself, could his relationship with Susan have gone beyond 'merely being civil', to quote his words. If your client has never slept with Susan, then he can't have fathered her child and surely he will have no objection to proving it.'

Grogan had become very quiet during this time but Heaton had summoned up enough anger for the pair of them. 'Unless and until you charge my client, I shall strongly advise him not to agree to such a procedure.'

'Very well then, I'll do just that.' Cobb reached into his pocket. 'I have here a warrant for the arrest of your client, Mr James Grogan, for the murders of Susan Davenport and Diana Davenport.'

There was uproar from both Grogan and his solicitor, but through their storm of protests Cobb calmly read their suspect his statutory rights.

'I didn't kill Susan, I swear to God I didn't.' Fear had ruined the arrested man, and his denial was cracked and hoarse. He slumped forward, head bowed, forearms on the table, with his wrists together as if waiting for the handcuffs to be snapped on.

'Do I take it, then, that you admit you killed Diana?' Cobb said.

'You don't have to answer any more questions,' the solicitor said, scribbling furiously in his own notebook.

'But I want to. I've nothing to hide. You're putting words into my mouth,' Grogan accused the DI. He swallowed hard and ran his finger round his collar, pulling it away from his throat as though it was choking him.

'We can now, of course, take our DNA swab,' Cobb reminded all concerned. 'As we will know the answer for definite one way or the other, you might as well save time by telling us now, Mr Grogan. Were you the father of Susan's child?' Whilst his words hung in the air Cobb watched in fascination as a succession of emotions passed across Grogan's face. Fear, for sure, was there but also something akin to cockiness.

Grogan's eyes slid sideways towards his solicitor who was scribbling furiously in his notebook and didn't make eye contact. Uncertainty as to what to say made Grogan's reply slow. 'Yes, it's my child. Susan was in love with me.'

'Were you in love with her?'

A silence developed and it was obvious to all that the arrested man was trying to find a way of expressing himself that wouldn't make him look a complete bastard. 'Love isn't the word for it,' he said eventually.

'What is the word then, Mr Grogan? I ask purely out of interest, but I really do not like prevarication, and neither will the jury.' Cobb kept his voice light and as pleasant as he could make it. He'd seen dozens of Grogans in his time. Vainglorious, amoral predators who thought any woman was fair game.

Grogan decided to play the all-men-together trick. It was probably the only one he knew. 'Look, Inspector. What would you have done in my shoes? No man ever turns down the offer of sex. She wasn't a bad-looking woman, you know — she was only six years older than me. It wasn't like I was sleeping with my grandmother, and she had a nice personality. She was very different from the women I meet usually, in London I mean. They are all high flyers, career women, go-getters. It was just a refreshing change to meet somebody ordinary.' He stopped and looked around to see how his little speech was going down. Only his solicitor seemed to find some understanding in the words, as he nodded in agreement, but then he was of an age and type, so it was hardly surprising. The hard stares he met with from the police officers told a different story. He changed tack. 'Look, all you've heard is what Diana told you and she wasn't able to see her stepmother objectively.'

'And why was that?' Cobb asked, almost conversationally.

'Because Susan killed Diana's brother, David.'

His words caused a sensation; the other three men sat up, galvanised. Even Heaton looked mildly surprised.

'Let me be quite clear about this, for the sake of the recording,' Cobb said. 'You are telling us now that Susan Davenport *killed*

David Davenport, her stepson.'

'Yes.'

'How do you know this? It was long before you met Diana.'

'Susan told me. I could never understand why Diana was so hostile towards her, and even though I asked her more than once she refused to talk about it. She came out with some rubbish about how I wouldn't understand. You know the usual stuff women trot out. It was after Susan and I became . . . well got to know each other that *she* told me.'

'And why would she do that?' It was hard to believe any woman would confide in this man, but then how many seemingly well-balanced, intelligent women had lost their senses over some total heel? And he'd never met Susan. You couldn't assess someone's personality from a photograph and a few impressions passed on from third parties.

'She was keen to tell someone her side of the story. You know how women like to talk; they make such a big deal of it and she'd had to keep this all to herself for a very long time, and it was quite an astonishing story she had to tell.'

'Then perhaps you'll tell us what Susan told you,' Cobb said.

'I know for a fact that the first part of what she said is true because I'd heard some of it from Diana. Susan was only nineteen when she married Cecil Davenport. Well, to be honest, that's all Diana ever told me apart from the fact that they used to live in London and moved to Wales when she was ten. She hated it, as any normal child would have. Imagine being dragged away from the capital to that godforsaken hole.' He paused for a moment, dwelling on this act of madness, before continuing. 'Susan told me that she'd had an unhappy childhood. Her mother had wanted a son, but got Susan instead and then found herself unable to conceive again. Apparently she blamed Susan for this, and was just nasty to her when she wasn't ignoring her. Susan's father's job took him away from home a lot: an awful lot, if you know what I mean.'

From the meaningful look that accompanied this, it was obvious some inference was meant to be drawn, but for the life of him, Cobb couldn't think what. 'Explain that remark,' he ordered, immensely tired of this man.

'When Susan was young she had no idea what was going on, but later on she wondered if he didn't have a second family somewhere in the Midlands.'

'Is this relevant?' Bould asked.

'I doubt it,' his boss replied. 'Just stick to

what you know, Mr Grogan. Pointless speculation won't help.'

Piqued, Grogan seemed disinclined to accept the DI's word and looked at his solicitor for some help. Heaton simply nodded, and returned to his note-taking.

Clearing his throat as if he was about to make an important announcement, Grogan continued: 'Well, whatever the truth there, Cecil Davenport's wife died and, being no fool, he set about looking for a mother for his two young children pronto and what do you know — enter Susan.'

'Did she tell you how they met?'

'He had a clothing factory and she worked in the office as a typist or secretary or some such. Of course, Susan jumped at marrying him. She must have been the envy of the place: little office worker marrying the boss. You can't do better than that. But if she thought it was going to be a life of luxury and glittering social occasions, she soon learnt better. The truth was, he found it cheaper to take a wife than employ a housekeeper and nanny.'

'It wasn't a happy marriage, then?' said Bould.

'I think Cecil was very happy indeed with his side of the deal. It was Susan who drew the short straw. It's the way of business,

Inspector, and Susan was no businesswoman. You need to read the small print before you sign the contract, but she did all right out of it. A nice house in Swiss Cottage and a better social life than she'd have had if she hadn't married him.'

'It's funny how some women think there might be more to marriage than a nice house and a few evenings out.' Bould's tone was acerbic, and distaste was written all over his face.

'You must forgive my sergeant. He's not a businessman either and has these quaint notions about marriage being a union of two people who hopefully love each other, but at least have a relationship based on honesty and respect.' Cobb left time for his words to have their desired effect before continuing, although he doubted the likes of Grogan fully appreciated irony. 'Please continue, Mr Grogan.'

'Susan found Diana and David really tough going. They resented her and she didn't know how to make them behave properly. David was particularly difficult. He was nasty and spiteful to her and doing her head in; and he was still wetting the bed despite being eight years old. Susan spent all her time running around after these little brats and one day, she just snapped. David had wet the bed again and she lost it. She only meant to teach him a lesson. That's what she told me and I believed her.'

'And what was this lesson she decided to teach him?' Cobb prompted, as it appeared Grogan had come to a full stop.

'There was a big stone trough in the garden. In the summer there were plants in it, but this was February and it was empty. She filled it with water from the outside tap, stripped David and dunked him in it.'

'Outside? She put the boy, naked, into a bath of cold water outside in February?' It was impossible for Cobb to prevent his revulsion from showing. Jesus, up until then his sympathy had been with Susan. Poor, naive, little Susan, not realising what she was letting herself in for. Dreaming of a marriage made in Hollywood and then discovering it was less Grace Kelly and more Mary Poppins but without the fun or the magic.

Grogan was keen to tell his tale and hurried on: 'She didn't think it would do him any harm; it was only meant to teach the little brat a lesson. It was only cold water, for God's sake. It wasn't her fault his heart packed up, there was obviously something wrong with him. The mother had died of cancer, so I wouldn't be surprised if there was some genetic abnormality in her children. He could have died at any time, the doctors said.'

'She may not have intended to kill him but her actions led directly to his death,' Bould said. 'Not only that, but she then lied about what happened, telling the family doctor that he had been playing outside.' It wasn't just the penny that suddenly dropped, but a whole pound coin, as the doctor's words came flooding back to the sergeant. 'She had the presence of mind to dry him off and put him into a pair of pyjamas — pity she forgot to dry his hair.'

'What?' A look of confusion crossed Grogan's face. Then he seemed to dismiss it as unimportant, and slumped back, his tale told.

'What about Diana? Did she witness this?' Cobb asked.

'Of course she did. That was part of the objective. Susan was trying to get the pair of them to behave. It wasn't her fault their precious mother had died, why should they take it out on her?'

Cobb tried to imagine what witnessing her brother's death would do to a vulnerable young girl who had just lost her mother. No wonder Diana had thought she was next on the list and had run away. No wonder Dr Mathers had found it necessary to sedate her. No wonder she was filled with hatred for

Susan. And what was her father doing all this time? Was he so wrapped up in his own grief he didn't realise his child bride was out of her depth, or was he simply pleased he had solved his housekeeping arrangements so easily? An image of a mischievous little boy in a faded photograph washed into his mind and the sour taste of anger filled his throat. What a stupid, pointless waste of a life. 'But why didn't Diana ever say anything to anyone?'

'Susan told her not to ever tell anyone because no one would believe her and she'd would be taken away by Social Services and put in a home and never see her father again.' Grogan seemed unsatisfied with the impression he was making, and cast around for something to say that would improve the officers' understanding. 'Susan was very upset by it all, you know.'

If he thought that would do the trick, he was sadly mistaken. Cobb snorted in disgust and Bould looked disbelieving, but both managed to hold their tongues.

'Is that why the family moved to Lampeter?' Cobb asked.

'Yes. They wanted to get away, put the past behind them. Cecil, poor fool, always believed David's death was nothing more than a terrible natural tragedy.'

'Did Diana blackmail her stepmother later

in life?' Bould threw this unexpected question quietly into the ring and was rewarded with a knowing smile.

'Yes, she did. How clever of you to find that out. Not that Diana told me any of this. It all came from Susan. Do you know, I think she found it a relief to finally talk about it after all those years of having to keep stum. She was getting desperate about things because Diana didn't need the money. She just did it to punish Susan.'

'Perhaps she felt some justification there,' the words had slipped out before Bould could stop himself. Policemen weren't supposed to be judgemental.

'There was nothing wrong with Susan,' Grogan responded hotly. 'Haven't you ever made a mistake when you were young?'

'You're calling what at the best is the manslaughter of a child a mistake? A child that Susan Davenport had care of; a child she should have protected?' Cobb spoke carefully. He thought he'd seen it all before, but this was a rum match by anyone's standards. Even allowing for Grogan's assertion that no man passed up the opportunity for sex when it was freely offered — and he would dispute that — it was still almost impossible to get to grips with the idea that such a self-serving, shallow narcissist would have bothered with Susan

Davenport. But then, what did he really know of Susan's character? Perhaps they were two of a kind.

'She — didn't — mean — to — kill — him!' Hoarse and sweating, Grogan was on his feet, leaning on the table, breathing heavily and staring almost wild-eyed at Cobb. He had reached the end of his tether and was on the point of losing it completely.

'I think we should have a break for a few minutes. My client is clearly upset by your line of questions.' Mark Heaton stirred and came to life, shooting his cuffs in a way that seemed to declare his self-importance. About the same age as Grogan, he was of a type, cast from the same money-loving mould. There was something unmissable about these city types, an aura of wealth that clung to them and their top designer clothes. And not just money. There was a smugness about them, an invincibility; they wore their financial success like a shield, believing it would protect them from anything.

'Very well,' Cobb switched the tape off. It never hurt to let suspects stew for a bit. Far from having a calming effect, it usually just panicked them a bit more. He had a shrewd idea that this solicitor, for all he might know of financial scams, probably had never before had to represent a client accused of murder.

'I suggest you use the time to get your client to cooperate fully with us.'

'I would have thought that was just what he had been doing,' Heaton riposted as the officers left the room.

Outside in the corridor, Cobb glanced at his watch. 'We'll give them fifteen minutes.'

'Do you think he's telling the truth, sir? I mean, about Susan being in love with him?' Bould asked, staring at the door as if he could still see the man on the other side.

'It seems scarcely credible, I know. We need to retrieve that book from Diana's flat.'

'The Cussler novel?'

'Yes. A comparison of the handwriting should be a simple matter, and a DNA test will certainly prove Grogan's paternity, or otherwise. The question is, do we believe his story? There's a lot of inconsistencies, even accepting the idea that a man like Grogan would have an affair with Susan. He's the sort who needs a trophy girlfriend to parade around town, and he had it with Diana. Are we to assume he used to drive over to Lampeter and Slipslade to meet her? All we seem to have is more unanswered questions than before.' Impatient and frustrated, Cobb swung away and set off briskly down the echoing corridor. 'I need a coffee and something to eat.'

'What about those two in there?' Bould indicated with a nod of his head the interview room.

'Leave them be. They might be more cooperative if they're hungry and thirsty.'

The officers headed for the canteen. Bould had briefly been posted to Paddington Green straight after Hendon, and knew his way around the mazelike building. It had once been described as a concrete bunker and that still summed it up.

As they pushed through the canteen doors, Bould said, 'Does this mean that Grogan killed Diana?'

The canteen was packed and very noisy. As they took their places in a long queue, Cobb said. 'He's our only suspect, and it might make some sort of sense if he killed Diana. Proving it is going to be another matter altogether.'

'But why would he kill her?'

'Because she killed his pregnant lover,' Cobb replied. 'Before you say anything, I know it's about as weak as it gets and I don't believe it either. He's not the type. That sort never is. They don't have it in them for all their bluster. But if he didn't kill Diana — who did? You realise we're back to square one.'

'Cheer up, sir, we might have solved Susan's death.'

'Except we've only Grogan's word for any of this. As Diana's dead, we can't prove anything. If she was still alive we wouldn't have enough to make a case on circumstantial evidence. It would never get to court.'

The queue shuffled slowly forward. Cobb viewed what was on offer with a sinking feeling. He hadn't eaten since breakfast and the large metal tins under hot lights contained unidentifiable congealed food.

'Yes?' A stout woman with greasy skin and wisps of grey hair escaping from under the hairnet rammed on in the name of hygiene curtly addressed them, brandishing a stainless steel ladle like an offensive weapon.

'What's on offer?' Cobb indicated the tins with an unhappy glance.

'Beef stew and dumplings; fish in a white wine and cream sauce; chicken stir fry and noodles.'

'What type of fish is it?' Bould asked.

'God knows,' was the gloomy reply. 'Do you want me to try and find out?' she said in a voice that dared him to say yes.

'No, it's fine. I'll have the stir fry.'

'And I'll try the stew,' Cobb said.

The food was dolloped out onto cold plates. 'Do you want chips with the stew?'

Remembering his cholesterol, Cobb hurried to refuse. 'Broccoli and new potatoes, please.' As if the day wasn't bad enough as it was.

It was a further twenty minutes before they returned to the interview room and recommenced the interview. In that time the room, little bigger than a cell, seemed to have closed in on Grogan, who now sat like a man heavily defeated.

His solicitor seemed as self-assured as ever.

Cobb and Bould took their place across the table and tried but failed to make eye contact with their suspect.

'Now you were telling us that Diana Davenport killed her stepmother,' Cobb began. 'Before you tell us exactly what happened on the night in question perhaps you would let us know how Diana found out where Susan was living. After all, I assume the reason Susan changed her name and moved to Slipslade was to prevent Diana tracing her.'

Grogan nodded. 'Yes. She was frightened Diana would just keep on fleecing her. It was my idea for her to move there.' The familiar boasting tinged his words once more. 'The Cotswolds was where we used to go for holidays when I was young. I remembered Slipslade as a quiet place, but not too difficult to get to from London. Diana was already suspicious that I was seeing someone else when she found that book you were on about. She wanted to know who 'D' was. I tried to make out I was given it before we met, but Diana wasn't a woman to take your word for anything. So she checked it out and discovered the novel had only been published the previous autumn, and that blew my story out of the water. We had a row, and then some. She wasn't easy to live with, you know. In fact, she was bloody demanding.' Grogan's voice had risen in indignation at the thought of just how long-suffering he'd been, but then his tone softened as he talked of her stepmother. 'Susan was the complete opposite. She just wanted to be with me and asked for nothing else.'

Of course she asked for nothing. Despite the terrible thing she had done, Cobb felt some stirring of sympathy for the lonely middle-aged woman with neither friends nor money, who suddenly found a successful young man showering attention on her. It must have been such a poisoned relationship. What was the real motivation behind the relationship for both of them? Did Susan enjoy quietly taking her revenge on her blackmailer by sleeping with Grogan? And what about Grogan. Was the attraction down to the fact that Susan made him the centre of her life, whereas Diana would never have done that? 'How did Diana find out it was her stepmother you were seeing?'

A humourless smile touched Grogan's lips. 'She followed me there one night. How careless is that?'

'Really? That's very interesting. Susan's neighbour said that she never had visitors.'

'No, she wouldn't have seen me. I never went to the house. I used to pick Susan up from the end of the road in the evenings and we'd go to local hotels.'

'If you had such strong feelings towards her, why the secrecy?' Although he posed the question, Cobb thought he could guess. Human nature was depressingly familiar.

His guess turned out to be right. Grogan began to bluster, eager to present himself in the best possible light. 'You have to remember it wasn't that easy for me. There was Diana to consider, you see.'

'Ah, you were thinking of her, were you? I expect you didn't want to hurt her feelings.'

His quarry narrowed his eyes, recognising the sarcasm. 'Actually, you're right. I didn't. I wouldn't expect you to understand.'

The two stared at each other, hostility on both their faces. Grogan was the first to drop his eyes and look away.

Satisfied, Cobb continued: 'So Diana followed you one night, and saw you pick up

Susan, is that right?'

'Yes.'

'How did she find out Susan's address? She could have lived anywhere in the area.'

'Really, Inspector, for a detective you're not up to much,' Grogan chided.

As he seemed to swing alarmingly between abject self-pity and arrogance, Cobb wondered how mentally stable the man was, but then if he had a serious drug habit — and Cobb didn't believe for a single moment that it was only Diana who indulged, whatever Grogan said — then he could well be suffering from some form of mental health problem by now. Refusing to rise to Grogan's bait, Cobb sat back in his chair, arms folded.

It didn't take long for the silence to be broken. It never did. The likes of Grogan were all too keen to let everyone know how clever they were. 'You do it on line; I'm guessing even rural policemen know what the Internet is. There are lots of websites that show you what properties have sold in the area. Then you check with the Land Registry. Susan had bought the house in her real name as it was all done very quickly, but it was her intention to change her name by Statutory Declaration as soon as she could. She'd made plans long ago about what she was going to do when Cecil died. Go abroad, that was plan

A. Then, obviously, once she'd met me she wanted to stay in the UK.'

'But the Slipslade house cost a lot more than the one she sold in Wales. Where did she get the money from?' Bould asked, although he thought he could guess what the answer would be.

'I gave her the money to make up the difference. It was nothing to me. I gave her money to live on as well.' Boasting again, smirking almost, Grogan seemed to grow in his chair.

'You must have been very fond of her to do all that,' Cobb observed, trying to keep his tone neutral and failing dismally.

The sarcasm didn't go unnoticed for the second time. He had riled Grogan, whose face darkened as he half-rose from his seat as he leaned across the table, thrusting his face as close to Cobb's as he could get. 'You people just can't get it, can you? You love to sneer at people like me, who make money, and lots of it. You think that makes us heartless but we do have feelings too, you know. I was very fond of Susan.'

The two men eyeballed each other with mutual loathing.

'Sit down, Mr Grogan,' Cobb said levelly, and after a heartbeat he did.

'So what were you going to do about the

child? Where you planning on marrying her, or was she always going to be your bit on the side.' Bould enquired.

That seemed to sober their suspect up. 'It was all very tricky. Susan didn't want a baby. Perhaps you might understand now why that would be.'

'But you did?'

A shrug of the shoulders. 'Not particularly. We were making arrangements to get rid of it.'

Cobb, keen to get the discussion back on track, interrupted. 'So Diana found out where Susan was living and went round to confront her. She must have been furious. Here was the woman who had killed her brother and had now stolen her boyfriend. Did she know Susan was pregnant?'

'Yes. Susan told her.'

'That must have been too much for Diana to bear. Is that why she killed her?'

Grogan's eyes slid sideways to his solicitor, who took up his cue with the old familiar words: 'You don't have to answer that.'

'Look, if it gets me off the hook, I'm going to tell them everything they want to know. I didn't kill Diana and I'm not being put in the frame for it.'

'Then I'll ask you again, did Diana kill Susan?'

'Yes. Finding out about me and Susan was the final straw.'

Abruptly changing direction, Cobb asked: 'Why did Diana meet Susan in the Millwheel pub at lunchtime on the day she died?'

Grogan couldn't help a humourless smile thinning his lips. 'Diana was nothing if not determined to have her kilo of flesh. She wanted to see if she could squeeze one last dollop of money out of Susan, but of course there was none left to be had.'

Cobb nodded to indicate this line of questioning was closed. 'So let's move on to the evening of Susan's death: how did Diana manage to get her out to Cotton Country Park?'

'She had a starting pistol — if you don't know anything about guns they look like the real thing. Most people do as they're told if they've got a gun pointed at their head.'

'And how do you know all this?'

'Diana told me a few days later. The awful thing is, she wanted to gloat over it. We had a terrible row.'

'I presume that's why and when you killed Diana.'

The solicitor jumped as if the table had just been wired to the mains. 'My client has no comment to make,' he started, but his client had a great number of comments to make.

'I didn't kill Diana. Why would I do that?' Grogan shouted wildly, leaping to his feet and storming around the room.

'Please sit down, sir,' Bould said automatically.

'I didn't kill her.' Now Grogan was bearing down on Cobb and Bould was on his feet, intervening.

'I didn't kill her, I swear I didn't. Why would I?' Grogan collapsed in his seat. He searched the others' faces, his brow creased with bafflement.

'Why? I'd have thought it was obvious why,' Cobb said. 'In revenge for her killing Susan. You may even get off with manslaughter if you get a very good barrister.'

'But I didn't kill her.' Here was a man, stripped down to his soul, desperate to be believed. 'That's why I went away for the week. I didn't know what to do. I always knew Diana was a cold fish. She was empty inside; only deep, deep down was a black hole. You know about black holes? They eat everything up in their path. The only energy they have is for destruction, and that was Diana. I didn't know what to do when she told me what she'd done, so I went away to think things over. Then when I returned, it was to discover you in the flat telling me she'd been killed.'

288

'You could have told us what you knew, for a start. It would have saved a lot of time,' Cobb was very angry.

'How could I? When Diana was alive it would have been my word against hers, and once she was dead I thought I was right in the shit — as I am now. At best you think I killed Diana and you still might try to pin Susan's murder on me as well, for all I know.'

Cobb and Bould had interviewed many suspects, some innocent and many guilty. They knew when they were being lied to and they knew this wasn't one of those times.

'Inspector, unless you have some proof, you are going to have to let my client go.' The solicitor had sensed the uncertainty in the air and was taking full advantage, deciding to do something for his money at last.

'No. I think you'll find I'm going to charge him,' Cobb said.

'With what?'

'Obstructing the course of our investigation.' He sat back with folded arms and watched their reaction.

Relief, obviously, but not that surreptitious cockiness that the guilty just couldn't help but show when they thought they'd got away with it.

'In what way has my client obstructed your enquiries?'

'He never told us about his relationship with Mrs Susan Davenport. If he had, it would have saved us a lot of time and trouble and who knows . . . ' now Cobb's voice was fierce and he stabbed at the table to make his point, 'it might even have saved Diana Davenport's life.'

Grogan looked bewildered. 'Diana's death can't have anything to do with Susan's. There's no one alive who cared enough about Susan to want to avenge her death.'

Those were some of the saddest words Cobb thought he'd ever heard, and some of the most callous. This was, after all, her lover — the father of her unborn child — talking. Talking as if her death meant nothing to him. Which it probably didn't. At times like this he really did think it was time to throw in the job. Far from getting hardbitten, the older he got the more people like Grogan got to him. 'And here was me thinking you felt some sort of affection towards Susan. If you didn't want a child, I can't understand why you didn't take steps to prevent Susan becoming pregnant in the first place. Do you ever think of anyone apart from yourself?'

Stung by the criticism, Grogan responded fiercely. 'You've no right to speak to me like this. Who do you think you are? I took care of

Susan in other ways. How do you think she's been living all this time? She hadn't got any money at all. I've been keeping her. She had a better time with me in the last eight months than she'd ever had before.'

'I see, and because of that you didn't think there was any harm in sleeping with her when you were living with her stepdaughter. Did it never occur to you that you were playing with fire?' Cobb was incredulous.

'I didn't expect you to understand. Why not? It could have worked. It *would* have worked if Diana hadn't found out. It's not exactly a unique situation.'

'But it didn't and now both the women are dead.' Cobb pushed back his chair, disgusted with the man's attitude. 'Charge him, Sergeant Bould,' he said and left the room with its claustrophobic, fetid atmosphere.

The corridor was another world. The air felt cooler and fresher. In the distance, a police siren wailed. An office door opened and the sound of muted voices drifted towards him. Two WPCs walked smartly past, one carrying a thick sheaf of papers. He took a deep breath, as if to rid himself of the contagion within.

A few minutes later, Bould joined him. They watched as Grogan was led away, followed by his solicitor.

'Do you think he's telling the truth?' Bould asked.

'Over which particular bit? Susan's death? Diana's death? We've only his word for any of it. He could have killed them both.'

'But why would he kill Susan if she was happy to have an abortion, as he wanted.'

'Suppose he's lying. Suppose Susan wanted to have the child.'

'Is that likely, given what we've heard about her? She hardly sounds the maternal type.'

'She's certainly not a candidate to replace Mother Teresa, but I say again, we can't corroborate his story. It could all be pure bollocks.'

'But if it isn't and the story about how David died is true, finding out about her boyfriend sleeping with her stepmother might have tipped Diana over the edge,' Bould argued.

'Yes, and depending on how he felt really about Susan it could then have given him a motive for killing Diana. If Jenny's right about the time, he could just about have managed it.' They began to walk towards the exit. 'All we've been able to charge him with is obstruction. He'll get bail for that.'

'He came across as genuine to me,' Bould said, hitting the security release button that allowed them out into the world.

'Yes,' Cobb sighed, knowing his sergeant had got to the nub of their problem. 'I don't see him as our man. He's vain and arrogant and everything I dislike in a man, but he's not a killer, and in that case we're back to square one. So who else is there in this case? Have we been barking up the wrong tree all along? We've assumed Diana's death is directly connected to her stepmother's, but perhaps it isn't. It could be a copy-cat killing. We'll get the team together first thing in the morning; see what we can't come up with.' He glanced at his watch, and was unsurprised to notice it was nearly seven. 'Let's go home. I've had enough for one day.'

15

The CID room was even colder than Cobb's own office, and that was saying something. The central heating had broken down again. This had become as traditional a part of winter as Christmas.

Ian Constable sat peering intensely at his computer screen, sipping from a mug of coffee, his right hand hovering lovingly over the mouse.

Cobb made his way over. 'I want you to find out all you can about the people who lived here.' He scribbled some names and an address down before pushing the paper towards Ian, who shuffled it round so that it was the right way up for him to read.

'You haven't got any dates for when they were living there, have you?' Ian asked, expertly reclaiming his pen that Cobb had used and looked as if he was about to pocket.

'There shouldn't be any need for you to go back more than twenty years, probably less. I want to know everything about these people — what colour pyjamas they wore, what toothpaste they used, everything — and I need this information yesterday.'

Unseen by the DI, Ian rolled his eyes at Rose who gave him a sympathetic grin. The boss was in a foul mood. The investigation was going badly, and didn't they know it.

A gust of warm air streamed into the office as Bould walked in.

'Where have you been?' Cobb snapped.

'Sorry, sir, traffic problems.' No point arguing with the boss when a case was going wrong. The signs were always the same.

'Right. Let's get started then,' Cobb raised his voice and the room fell silent. He then spent five minutes bringing the team up to speed, finishing with the work he had asked Ian to undertake. 'It's a long shot, but it's all we've got to go on at present. Now I know how busy we all are, so that's it for now. Neil, you come with me; we're going to see a man about a dog.'

On the way out, the DI outlined his thoughts to his sergeant. 'It's the one avenue we haven't explored,' he offered in explanation.

'But what's the connection and what would it prove if it turned out she was lying? We know she lies.'

Cobb scratched his ear. 'I'm not sure what it would prove, other than to provide a psychological insight into her character. If someone is a pathological liar does it mean they are unbalanced in general? Are they more likely to be driven to murder for the sort of trivial reason another person would simply shrug off? Come on, you spent three ill-gotten years studying the subject, so see if you can put it to good use now.'

'Sir, I don't think I'm qualified to give psychological assessments of anyone. Shouldn't you call the experts in if that's what you want?'

'If it comes to it, then yes: as a last resort we'll get a psychological profiler in, but I don't think it's going to come to that. I spent half the bloody night thinking about this case and I've just got a feeling about it. I don't have to tell you what I mean, so come on, let's get on with it.'

★ ★ ★

The hotel was little more than an overgrown pub. The outside had been painted white with the coping stones and window surrounds picked out in black. Some of the black paint was already flaking off, and in a couple of years it would revert to being a run-down wreck. The hotel was right at the back of Overingham, down a narrow lane. Out of sight was out of mind as far as most of the population were concerned, so its days were surely numbered.

'They'll tear it down and build another lot of retirement properties, mark my words,' Cobb said, making a shrewd assessment of the hotel's destiny, as they pushed through revolving doors into a wide entrance lobby. A small reception area occupied one corner. A large bar led off to their left, and a smaller room, set up for the lunchtime trade, led off to their right. The bar room was empty apart from two elderly men sitting in silence at a table under the window with half pints of bitter. The men were in their shirt sleeves because the temperature in the room was tropical. A large log fire was roaring away in a huge hearth, boosting the central heating to new heights.

The sweat started to break out on Cobb's brow. 'Let's get this over as fast as possible, before I pass out. This amount of heat's good for nobody.'

Passing into the restaurant, they found it deserted. For a moment they were unable to see where the manager might be, until they noticed a discrete opening behind a screen leading back into the kitchens.

As they made their way towards it, a tall, well-built man strode through. 'What's it to be, gentlemen — table for two?' he enquired, gathering up menus from the service area as he advanced.

They produced their warrant cards again, which seemed to bewilder him. He looked from one to the other waiting for an explanation.

'Are you the manager here?' Cobb asked and received a reply in the affirmative.

'And your name, sir?'

'Henry Bebb. Look, what's this about?'

Bould produced a photograph. 'Do you recognise this person?'

Bebb took the picture and studied it closely. 'No,' he said finally, with a shake of his head. 'I've never seen her before.'

'Not one of your regulars, then?'

'Definitely not. I know everyone who comes in here regularly by name.'

'How many days of the week are you on duty?' Cobb said.

'Every day we're open. We're closed for meals Mondays and Tuesdays but otherwise we're open for lunches and dinner the rest of the week.'

'And you're certain you're never seen this woman before?'

'I've told you that already. Excuse me a moment.' Bebb broke away as a middle-aged woman in a formidable hat accompanied by a short, scrawny man entered.

Cobb and Bould waited whilst he showed them to a table and settled them with menus.

'Is there anything else you want to ask me?' The manager's voice had sunk to a whisper, and he kept glancing over to the couple, anxious that they shouldn't discover the presence of policemen in case it put them off their lunch.

'Yes, we'd like to see your reservation book,' Cobb said, running his finger round his collar and loosening his tie slightly. His neck felt swollen to twice it normal size with the heat.

For a minute it looked as if they were going to have a fight on their hands.

'Can I ask why?'

'No,' Cobb replied tersely.

Shrugging his shoulders, Bebb tried to look indifferent. 'Bear with me then, gentlemen.' There was an ever so slightly sarcastic stress on the last word, as he made his way back to the service area. Returning, he wordlessly handed over a dog-eared hardbacked book.

It didn't take long for Cobb and Bould to look through it, for they were only interested in one day of each week. Satisfied with what they saw, Cobb handed it back to Bebb who was hovering behind them, looking as if he'd like to shoo them out of the place if only he dared.

'We may need a statement from you,' Bould warned as they left.

His words had a baffling effect. 'Why? Look, I do feel that you might tell me what all this is about.' The manager was beginning to have the look and sound of an aggrieved man.

'We're investigating the murders of two women round here,' Cobb informed him, keeping it short and sweet.

Bebb nodded, more to himself than anyone else. 'The gravel pit bodies. I read about them in the press. But I really can't see how this hotel features . . . ' the unfinished sentence hung in the air, inviting elucidation. None was forthcoming.

With a polite smile, Cobb merely said, 'You've been very helpful, sir. If we need to contact you again I take it we can find you here — other than Mondays and Tuesdays, that is.'

'You can find me here most of the time. I live on the premises.'

'That's even better. Goodbye.'

The frozen air hit them in the face the instant they were through the revolving doors, and how they savoured it as they walked back to the car.

'What do we make of that then, Sergeant?' The DI asked eventually.

'She's told us a lot of lies and I think she's

a very lonely woman who seems to be living in a fantasy world, but does that make her a murderer? And she didn't know Diana, so I don't see how she could have killed her.'

Cobb sighed. 'That's the trouble. For all this, I don't know if we are any further forward. In fact, if you ask me, she's got the least reason to kill Susan of anyone we've come across so far. Still, let's go and see what she's got to say for herself.' The information they'd discovered certainly hadn't improved his mood. It simply tidied up a little matter, but whether it had any bearing on the case remained to be seen.

Bould turned the car onto the main road out of Overingham and they sped along a wide, straight road lined with black hawthorn hedges. After a couple of miles they came into Slipslade just as the sun finally broke through the cloud. Bright sunshine cascaded down on the village in sync with the car as it travelled down the street. They passed the shops, tearoom, pub and pretty little terraced cottages lining the road and at the far end turned left and then almost immediately right.

The street they were now on was very different to the mellow limestone charm of the old part of Slipslade. The houses that lined it were modern boxes squeezed tightly together, with miniscule, open-plan front gardens. Open plan because there wasn't enough room for fences, let alone hedges. Bright, shiny new cars filled every driveway on Meadow Rise.

Bould pulled up in front of number 23. A silver Renault Clio was parked in front of the garage.

'She's in, from the looks of it,' Bould commented.

'Good; we've had enough of our time wasted as it is. Let's see if we can get this over with quickly.'

She opened the door so swiftly they suspected she had been watching from the window. It wouldn't have surprised them; it was the sort of thing very lonely people did. Most people thought it was nosiness but it wasn't. It was the need to connect with the real world in some way, however remote and second hand.

'Miss Eleri Griffiths?' Cobb enquired, holding out his warrant card, and went on without waiting for a reply. 'May we come in.' It wasn't a question.

'Of course, Inspector, please do.' The door was opened wide and she ushered them in with a beaming smile. If she had any idea why they were there she wasn't showing it.

They followed her into the lounge but

declined her invitation to sit.

Cobb looked around the unloved room. Just how much of the day could you consume with housework. What did she do then to while away the hours? Was the TV the thread that connected her to the outside world? 'You live here alone; I am right in thinking that, aren't I?'

'You are quite correct,' she affirmed, standing before them like an attentive bird, hands clapped under her generous bosom.

'How long is it since your mother died?' Bould said.

She blinked — the question surprised her. 'Three years.'

'Do you not feel lonely here? Never thought of returning to Wales to . . . ' Cobb still couldn't pronounce it.

'Ty'n-y-Groes,' she helped him out. 'No, I haven't.'

'Why would that be? I'd have thought you would have friends there.'

Her lips tightened, and she seemed to withdraw into herself. 'I'm perfectly happy here.'

'Yes, of course you are, because you've got a male friend here; the one who takes you to lunch every Saturday. I remember you telling me and WPC Rose Cadoxton all about it the very first time we called round here. I expect you remember it too,' Bould spoke casually and wandered over to the window.

'What's his name?' Cobb said.

She must have guessed what was coming next, and took a small step towards them. 'Oh, now see, I'm not meeting with him any more. He was very keen to get married but I told him straight, I said, no I'm quite happy living here by myself, I am.'

'Is that so? But you used to go to the Red Lion in Overingham for lunch. How long ago did that stop?'

Some of her confidence disappeared. When she spoke her voice was diffident. 'Just last week, it was.'

'So up to last week you were still dining at the Red Lion?'

Unable to keep still, she walked behind the sofa and started fiddling with a cushion, plumping it up, replacing it and then moving it again, but she didn't speak.

Cobb watched her, giving her time to reply, and when she didn't he carried on: ''We've just been to the Red Lion and the restaurant manager says he's never seen you.'

Her head shot up. 'How would he know what I look like?' Relief bringing a quick response.

'Well now, my sergeant did something very naughty when we were here the other day. He took a picture of you on his mobile phone when you weren't aware of it. Shouldn't have done it, but there you are. I'll have to give him a strict telling off when we get back to the station. But the thing is, the restaurant manager didn't recognise you. Now I know the pictures you get on a phone leave a lot to be desired, but even so.' He paused, letting her become more discomforted, before delivering the *coup de grâce*. 'On top of which, we had a look at the table bookings list and there was no regular twosome booked at Saturday lunchtimes in any name.'

He let the silence grow, and her unhappiness with it. When it became clear she wasn't going to say anything, Cobb pushed the subject. 'There is no man friend, is there Miss Griffiths? You made him up, didn't you? There's no harm in that. Lots of people make up a partner or friend. It's not a crime.'

Still she didn't reply, but moved slowly around the furniture, touching every piece, her hands making pointless movements over the surfaces. 'It didn't do any damage, it was just for fun. I've never had a boyfriend, you see. I wasn't bad looking when I was young, I could have found someone. I know I could, but my da needed me on the farm. He was proper strict; I wasn't allowed to go out with my friends, not even to the cinema when I was young. Even when I was grown up and teaching I couldn't get away. There's no money in farming, not for the hill farmers anyway. He couldn't afford to pay for labour so I was needed at home. That was my life. Teaching and helping on the family farm. There was never any chance to meet a man and my da would never have allowed it.' Her fingers gripped the back of a chair, knuckles whitening. A sob became impossible to hold back and a tear trickled down her check.

Cobb ignored her tears. 'So there is no man who takes you to lunch every Saturday?'

'No.'

'But surely you have some women friends here?'

He watched her hesitate, deliberating how to answer. 'Eliza Hobbis was my friend,' she said eventually.

'And Eliza is dead. You must have been very upset,' Bould said.

'I was.' Spoken softly, her words seemed to be addressed to the chair she was still holding on to. 'It was lovely to have a friend after all this time on my own. When mam was alive I had her, but after she died . . . well, those here don't mix much, and they're mostly young couples with children, so they don't want me.' She moved round to the front of the chair, all the time keeping her hand on its back as if to let go would plunge her world into chaos. Almost gingerly she seated herself. 'I was so happy when Eliza moved in. You see, she was on her own too. We both needed each other.'

'And then what happened?' Cobb asked gently.

It was as if a spell had been broken. One minute she had been lost in introspection but now her head came up sharply and a crimson tide flooded her cheeks. 'Someone killed her and took my friend from me. I thought you'd come here to tell me you'd found out who it was.'

Cobb studied the huddled, unhappy figure before him and wondered if he was going to get anything useful from her. 'Miss Griffiths, you've already admitted lying to us twice. You might think such lies are unimportant, but they waste our time, so I want you to think very carefully now and when you answer I want no more lies. Is that understood? I'm asking you directly: is there anything else you want to tell us — anything that might help us find the person who murdered your friend? I'm thinking in particular about the fact that you told my sergeant that the last time you saw Susan Davenport was on the Saturday morning when she was going shopping and that she returned whilst you were out having lunch with the man friend who you now admit doesn't exist. So, what we need to establish is whether you did see Susan return from her shopping trip.'

With a shake of her head, Eleri replied, 'No, I didn't. You see, I thought she'd be back by midday, but she wasn't. It was too bad because I was waiting for her to come back. I'd made some soup, you see, and I was going to ask her round for lunch, but she hadn't returned by two and I was so upset I couldn't settle, so I got in my car and went for a drive. I like driving; it's nice to get out and I find it soothing.'

'What time did you come back from your drive?' Bould said.

Bit by bit, Eleri was regaining some of her composure. 'Let me see, it would have been about four. I know that because it was still light.'

'Was Mrs Davenport back by then?'

'Yes, she was. I went round and rang the bell.'

'How did she seem?' Bould asked. 'Was she upset or did she seem the same as usual?'

'Well, do you know, she was quite short with me. She said she was busy, but I think it was more than that. She seemed put out, even a bit cross. And that wasn't like her at all.'

'And that was the last time you saw her?' Cobb added.

'Yes.'

'Did you see anyone else visit her after that time?'

'No.'

Deciding that this was about all they were going to get out of her, Cobb brought the interview to a close.

'Won't you gentlemen stay for some tea?' Eleri was on her feet, practically barring their exit. 'I've made a cherry Madeira cake just this morning. I'm sure you must be in need of some refreshment.'

The one thing Cobb hated about the job was how his work exposed the sadness and emptiness at the heart of so many lives. There were thousands of Eleri Griffiths in this world but what the hell did you do about them? He decided to let her down gently. 'Sorry, Miss Griffiths. Your offer is most tempting but unfortunately we haven't the time to spare right now.' He couldn't bring himself to look her in the eye. It was like shooting Bambi.

16

The CID room was empty apart from Ian Constable who was glued, as always, to his computer. His jacket hung over the back of his chair and his sleeves were rolled up because overnight a minor miracle had happened and the central heating had been fixed.

'Any luck with that check I asked you to run?' Cobb asked, looking in on his way to his office.

'Yeah, boss, and I think you're going to be pleasantly surprised with what it's thrown up.' Constable pushed a printout across the desk to his boss. 'You'll see it was negative. No property with that name exists in the area. So I decided to widen my search and I did manage to trace the names of the family to a house with the same name somewhere else.'

Cobb took the sheet and perused it. The information it contained made him raise his eyebrows. 'Well done, Ian. It looks like we might finally be getting somewhere. He strode off in a hurry, the printout rolled up in his hand, then turned back. 'No, wait, I want you to run a further check.' Returning to the desk he scribbled down some information. 'See if she was ever on the staff there.'

In the corridor he ran into his sergeant. 'Take a look at this,' he said without preamble, thrusting the paper into Bould's grasp.

There wasn't a lot of information on the page, and Bould scanned it quickly. 'Is this enough to make an arrest?' he wondered.

'As far as I'm concerned it is. There can be no innocent explanation for this.'

And Bould had to agree.

★ ★ ★

'Good morning, Miss Griffiths, may we come in?' Without waiting for an answer, Cobb stepped inside.

Not that she seemed displeased to see them. Far from it, and Cobb had a sad feeling that she was now viewing him and Bould as her new friends.

She followed them silently into the lounge and stood waiting, her eyes yo-yoing from one to the other in watchful expectation.

Cobb's words, when they came, were stern. 'Miss Griffiths, you've not been exactly truthful with us up 'til now, I'm sorry to say. In fact, you've lied repeatedly and you've lied

311

about why you lied, so now I'm going to ask you some questions that you will answer truthfully. Do you understand: I want the absolute truth. There's no point in lying any further to us. I've got a member of my staff checking out Ceredigion Council employment records even as we speak.'

Eleri looked away. Her hands were trembling, but she stood proudly.

Bould took out his notebook and positioned himself by the door as his boss continued.

'So, Miss Griffiths, you told us once that you came from a village in North Wales. Now, I remember very well the name of the farm you said you lived in because you told us a rather Gothic story about how it acquired its name, and you can call me a suspicious fellow if you like, but bearing in mind all the lies you've told us so far, I had your story checked out, and what do you think I found?' He paused, giving her the opportunity to at last redeem herself, but not a sound came from her tightly drawn lips. The silence lasted only as long as Cobb let it. 'There was no such property anywhere near Ty'n-y-Groes, but we did find a Ty Coch Farm in Betws Bledrws. Do you want to tell me where Betws Bledrws is?'

She raised her eyes, giving Cobb the

opportunity to see the great depths of misery they contained. 'It's in Ceredigion, Inspector, as you seem to know already.'

'Indeed it is.' He nodded in confirmation. 'But Ceredigion's a big county, so in itself that wouldn't necessarily be significant, but Betws Bledrws isn't just anywhere in Ceredigion. It's very close to Lampeter, it is. In fact, you could say it's just a stone's throw away.'

Her eyes never left his face but she said nothing, remaining very still apart from her hands, which were working tensely as she clasped them under her bosom.

Cobb went on: 'Now, Miss Griffiths, you also said you'd been a PE teacher and swimming instructor, and although I'm not normally a betting man, I've got a wager with my sergeant here that we're going to find you taught swimming at the very school Diana Davenport attended. Am I right?'

It was all too much, and with an abrupt movement Eleri turned to face away from him. A convulsive step was taken as if flight was intended, then she stopped and the officers could see her back stiffen. One hand went to her head and began obsessively tightening an already tight curl. 'Yes, you are right.' She addressed the corner. 'As you say, you'll find out from the school records. Diana was my star pupil. She could have been a champion but her father wouldn't allow it. Wouldn't let her travel, see.' She swung round, suddenly alive once more, animation pinking her cheeks, and her gaze fell on Cobb with a kind of hunger. 'If only she'd have been allowed to take part in competitions she could have been a national champion. We could have gone to London, perhaps even abroad. I'd have had to go with her because she was only a child and it wouldn't have been proper for her to travel alone.'

'You'd have liked that, wouldn't you?' Bould said sympathetically.

She turned to him, nodding eagerly, sensing he understood, that he was on her side. 'I never got the chance to go anywhere. When I wasn't at the school I was needed on the farm. My da couldn't spare me, not ever. I never had what you'd call a holiday.' Self-pity tinged her words, as it so often did with her sort.

'Was Diana a popular child with her peers?' Cobb asked, wanting to focus her on the important matters, to turn her away from feeling sorry for herself.

Caught like a tennis ball in play between two experts, she was forced to swing round once more to face Cobb. 'No, that she was not. She didn't mix. She was lonely, see, like me. We were two of a kind.'

Dear God, had she thought she could make a friend of one of her pupils? 'So why did you kill her?'

Eleri stared blankly at him as if she found the question so obvious she couldn't believe he was asking it. 'She killed my friend, Eliza, my only friend, don't you understand? She deserved to die in turn. The Bible says 'an eye for an eye'.'

'And you interpret that to mean you can act as judge, jury and executioner?'

Although she couldn't see Bould now, as he was behind her, she could hear the incredulity in his voice and her brow creased into a deep frown, as if she resented his inference, and her tone became riddled with indignation. 'Why not? Diana shouldn't have done what she did.'

'That's why the law exists, Miss Griffiths. Only dictators and madmen take it upon themselves to deal out summary justice.'

She didn't take Bould's remarks kindly, and responded primly. 'As ye sow, so shall ye reap.' Her lips settled in a firm line and her head went back, daring him to contradict her. But a tic had set in under her left eye.

'How did you find out Diana killed her stepmother?' Cobb never took well to having the Bible quoted at the best of times and he spoke sharply.

Now suddenly her mood changed and she became disdainful; as if unable to believe they couldn't work it out for themselves. 'Oh, that was easy. I saw her arrive, that night she killed my friend.' The self-pity had been banished, its last traces smothered by the newer, overwhelming urge to crow about her cleverness. The tic stopped and her eyes became resolute once more. 'I see most things that go on here, even at night. The lighting's very good, you see, and I've got excellent vision. Like a young girl's, you know.

'Eliza used to go out on foot some evenings and not come back for a long time. I thought, now where's she going in these cold and dark winter nights? She couldn't be going far without a car and yet she didn't know anyone — so she said. So one time I followed her. She only went as far as the end of the road and then she was collected by a big flashy car. I'm not a fool; I could work it out for myself. I said to myself, she's got a gentleman friend, and I was right. Of course, I never saw his face, it wasn't possible. There are not many bushes or trees around here and it wouldn't have done for me to have been seen. I don't want people to think I'm nosy.'

'Is that why you made up the story about your gentleman friend?' Bould asked, comprehension dawning.

She beamed at him, as if pleased he'd cottoned on so quickly, and quite forgetting her earlier annoyance. 'I couldn't be outdone, now, could I? And I could get a man if only I could meet one, so what was the harm in it?'

It was impossible to give a serious answer to that remark, so Cobb said, 'Let's get back to the night Susan — Eliza — was killed. You saw Diana arrive and you recognised her, even though she was just a school girl when you last saw her?'

'Oh yes, I recognised her immediately. Well, that sort of tarty good looks you don't forget. I hadn't seen her in fourteen years or so, but as soon as I clapped eyes on her I knew who it was. It was quite a surprise, mind. I thought, what's she doing here and how does she know my friend.'

'What time was this?' Cobb asked. He knew now she'd started she wouldn't stop talking until she'd told them every little thing. Not that he was complaining; it made his job a lot easier, particularly as evidence in this case was going to be thin on the ground and a confession would speed things up nicely. That would help keep the budget down — CSI Black would be pleased if no one else at the outcome of this desperately sad case.

'About seven in the evening. It was dark, but Eliza had a security light over her front door which came on automatically when someone approached the house, so I was able to see, right enough.'

'Then what?'

'Eliza let her in. I don't think she wanted to because Diana seemed to be in rather a state but then Diana forced her way in. I watched for a bit, but nothing happened and there was a programme on television I wanted to see. The one where the stars dance. Beautiful to watch, it is. When I looked again her car was gone.'

'Diana's car?'

'No, Eliza's. I didn't see Diana's car at all. She must have parked somewhere else. Then, in the morning, Eliza's car was back. Of course, I thought that meant she was back, but when I went round I got no answer.'

'And you didn't see either of them leave on the Saturday night?' Cobb asked.

'No,' her lips quivered and she became tearful with regret at what might have been. 'If only I'd gone round there. I thought about it, soon as I saw Diana, I thought I could go round too. Eliza would have had to let me in, wouldn't she, seeing as how I knew Diana. I might have saved her life.' She started to weep quietly, with that hopeless despair of knowing nothing will be right ever again.

Bould was curious. Ignoring her crying, he said: 'How did you trace Diana? I take it she didn't come back on her own accord?'

Something of Eleri's personality re-emerged from the wreckage. The sobs died away and she straightened up a little, remembering that her tale, and cleverness, wasn't done. 'When she left school she went back to London, I remembered that because she was always telling people she couldn't wait to get out of Lampeter and go back to London. Not that she needed to tell people — it was obvious a girl like Diana was never going to be satisfied with what Lampeter had to offer.

'So when she was on Eliza's doorstep I could see how well dressed she was. She looked a real city girl; so after I read about Eliza's death I knew it had to be her who had done it, so I went to London, to a public library because I know they keep the telephone books there. Then I went through them and rang all the Davenports until I found Diana.'

'Davenport isn't a particularly unusual name. It must have taken you some time to do that,' Cobb observed.

The smile that touched her face suggested that she had some insight into her situation after all. Smoothing an imaginary stray hair back into place, getting comfort from order, she said: 'Time is one thing I'm not short of, Inspector. In fact, it gave me something to do and it didn't take all that long. There aren't as many Davenports as you might think.'

'So you rang her. Then what?'

'I told her I'd seen her at Eliza's. Of course I had no idea she was her stepmother because I'd never met her. It was always her father who came to the school.'

Cobb found this hard to believe. 'But Lampeter is such a small place. Surely you must have seen Susan at some point in all those years? She worked in the teashop there.'

A convulsive movement of hands, and impatience in the voice. 'Really, how many more times must I tell you that when I wasn't at the school I was helping my family on the farm? I never had time to go to a teashop in my life until I moved here.' She was cross, worked up at his lack of understanding of just how hard and dreary her life had been.

Holding up his hand to silence her, Cobb steered her back to the matter in hand. 'Tell me what you said when you rang Diana.'

'I told her who I was and said I'd seen her at Eliza's and now Eliza was dead, and I would like her to come and see me to discuss what happened.'

'Were you intending to blackmail her over this?' Bould asked.

He was rewarded with a look of astonishment. 'Of course not. I was going to make her pay for what she'd done. An eye for an eye. It's very simple and the Bible makes it very clear what you must do.'

'And how did you do it?' Cobb asked.

As if realising the end of her story was nigh, Eleri moved over to the sofa and settled herself neatly on the edge. She took her time. First, she carefully smoothed her skirt. Then she crossed her legs at the ankles and tucked them back. Only when she was happy with her position did she clear her throat and continue. 'It was easy. First thing when she came in, she wasn't happy. Oh no, not at all. But I persuaded her to sit down and have a drink. I thought she'd like a drink and I was right. I'd got a lot of my mother's sleeping tablets left. Chronic it was, how badly she slept. You've no idea what a martyr to insomnia she was. It was lucky really, wouldn't you say, that I kept all her tablets. Couldn't bear to throw them out, that was the thing. They were a part of her, see. All I had to do was crush them up in some wine. I've always got some wine in the house. I like a little glass at night when I'm watching television. A little celebration, it is.'

What of, Cobb wanted to ask — what on earth could this poor miserable woman have to celebrate? How many other people, even on the road she lived on, knew she existed, far less cared about her. In his job, Cobb often came upon the lonely; he knew that for some elderly people calling a police officer round to complain about some trivial or imagined offence was sometimes their only contact with another human being from one week's end to another, but Eleri Griffiths's life seemed particularly desperate.

She had stopped talking, seemed to be lost in unknowable memories, so Cobb pushed her tale forward. 'And then, when she was unconscious you strangled her.'

Eleri held out her hands, turned them over, holding them up for the officers to admire. 'I'm strong, see. It comes of being a farmer's daughter. Used to help out on the farm a lot, I did. Always humping bloody great bales of straw and hay around, I was.' There was bitterness as she ruminated on the memory, until she pushed it to the back of her mind. 'Anyhow, she was nearly unconscious from the sleeping tablets so it wasn't hard. Then I put her body into her own car — not mine, see, because I know you can find traces of DNA. I watch all the detective dramas on television and I know how it's done. So I put her in her own car and drove her to the gravel pits. It was only right, mind, that she was found there. That's where she killed poor Eliza. Then I drove her car to Warwickshire. I just needed to get it as far away from here as possible. I don't know the name of the place I left it, but there was a railway station so I caught a train to Birmingham, got on the first bus I found and when it went over a canal I thought 'there's a good place to dump her handbag. No one will ever find it there', so I got off the bus and threw the bag over the bridge. Then I got a train home.'

'What about her clothes?' Cobb asked. 'What did you do with them?'

'I put them in a black bin bag and took them to the tip.'

There was something that Bould had been itching to ask for some time, but didn't dare interrupt the flow. Now she was quiet he took the opportunity to say: 'Did Diana tell you why she killed Susan Davenport?'

Darkly ominous clouds were rolling across the sky, prematurely bringing darkness to the winter morning. Bould reached out and switched on the lights. The light filtering through the old cream parchment shade was warm and soft and fell on Eleri directly below, illuminating her like the central actor in a play.

'At first she denied it, so I said 'well then, perhaps I should contact the police and tell them what I saw that night'. That made her think, I can tell you. She had a whole glass of wine in one go. Between you and me I think she was an alcoholic.' This was delivered in a tone that suggested being an alcoholic was a far greater crime than being a murderer.

Over her head, Cobb and Bould exchanged a look.

Having had the time to gather her thoughts, Eleri now continued: 'I gave her another glass, and then another. Inspector, you've never seen a woman drink like that one. It was quite disgraceful! Of course, by now the wine was having an effect — the sleeping tablets take longer you know — and she started to get really unpleasant. I told her who I was, see. I told her I used to teach her PE at school, but she said she didn't remember. Didn't remember, how could that be possible, Inspector? She was my star pupil. She must have remembered me. I think she just said that to upset me. Oh, she deserved to die, take my word for it. She told me then all about her family's past and why they moved to Wales and what had happened to her brother and that Eliza's fancy man was really her boyfriend. So all in all, she thought the same as me. That some people deserve to die because of what they'd done to others. That's rather funny, don't you think? See, we both thought it was poetic justice. An eye for an eye.'

'But you still killed her anyway?' Bould asked.

'Whatever Eliza had done to her did not justify Diana's actions,' Eleri stated with such absolute certainty that both men could barely contain their incredulousness.

'And doesn't the same set of rules apply to you?' Cobb recovered first and got in whilst Bould's mouth was still half open.

Eleri raised her eyes and smiled at him. 'That's different,' she said.

Epilogue

It was late. Eleri had been arrested at 10.30 in the morning, but it took the rest of the day to deal with procedure and the accompanying paperwork.

Cobb felt bone tired. Definitely too old for the job, he told himself, fishing his car keys out as he stepped from the station into the cold night air. The union rep would have all the info on early retirement deals. Tomorrow, first thing, he'd speak to him. As far as tonight went, he was going home, having a shower and then, whatever Sarah said, he was taking her for a slap-up meal. Dorothy would be all right for a couple of hours. The thing was, she wasn't senile, and yet Sarah was beginning to treat her as if she was. It grieved him to acknowledge it; made him feel like a traitor when he knew how much Sarah loved her mother and wanted only to help her, but he thought she was killing her with kindness. All the way home he puzzled how to tell her this in a way that wouldn't bring his marriage to an end. He was no nearer an answer when he pulled into his drive. Christ, he was so tired it hurt to think. For a few moments he sat in the car, scrubbing his eyes with his fists. Then with a weary sigh, he came to a decision and dragged his exhausted body from the car.

As he walked into his hallway, the atmosphere was warm and full of love. As Sarah came towards him, arms outstretched and a great smile on her face, he forgot his earlier resolution.

He'd talk to her about Dorothy tomorrow — or the day after, or the day after that. Perhaps it wasn't important, or at least not as important as having someone who did what they did for you out of love.

We do hope that you have enjoyed reading this large print book.

Did you know that all of our titles are available for purchase?

We publish a wide range of high quality large print books including:
Romances, Mysteries, Classics
General Fiction
Non Fiction and Westerns

Special interest titles available in large print are:
The Little Oxford Dictionary
Music Book
Song Book
Hymn Book
Service Book

Also available from us courtesy of Oxford University Press:
Young Readers' Dictionary
(large print edition)
Young Readers' Thesaurus
(large print edition)

For further information or a free brochure, please contact us at:
Ulverscroft Large Print Books Ltd.,
The Green, Bradgate Road, Anstey,
Leicester, LE7 7FU, England.
Tel: (00 44) 0116 236 4325
Fax: (00 44) 0116 234 0205